"If I can help with anything, I want to. Research or tracking down people. I seem to be pretty good at that." Peter didn't want her to leave. That was becoming a habit.

"I may take you up on that," Lauren said as she shifted her bag to the opposite shoulder.

"I hope you will. Or if you need a distraction. Concord Court has a pool. There are zero fish in the water there." Peter reached for her fingers and smoothed his thumb over her knuckles.

"What's your strategy now, Peter?" Lauren asked. Her confusion was easy to read. "I've agreed to help. You don't have to try to win me over anymore." She lifted their tangled hands.

The urge to pretend he had no idea what she meant came and went.

This was the real problem he kept circling. "No strategy. No plan. I wanted to do it, so I did. Are you familiar with the concept?"

Lauren inhaled slowly. "Run it past me again. Draw a diagram. I need the basics."

Dear Reader,

"Friendly rivalry" seems like a contradiction in terms, doesn't it? If you've been blessed with a competitive spirit (like me), the phrase immediately brings a rival to mind—someone who also wanted the only spot left on the team or the top score on a test or the award for selling the most figurines in the sixth-grade fundraiser. Not that I would know anything about these very specific examples!

In *Winning the Veteran's Heart*, Peter and Lauren pushed each other to excel in every college class they shared. She was serious, determined; he was charming but no less determined. Now he needs her help. She's the best defense attorney in Miami, and his nephew deserves the best. Lauren wants the distraction that Peter Kim has always provided, but this time, there's more at stake than bragging rights. I hope you enjoy reading how this friendly rivalry turns to love.

To meet my dog, Jack, and find out more about my books, please visit me at cherylharperbooks.com. I'm also on Facebook (cherylharperromance) and Twitter, @cherylharperbks.

Cheryl Harper

HEARTWARMING

Winning the
Veteran's Heart

———

Cheryl Harper

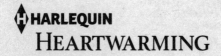

HARLEQUIN
HEARTWARMING

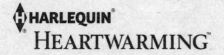

HARLEQUIN®
HEARTWARMING™

Recycling programs for this product may not exist in your area.

ISBN-13: 978-1-335-58461-8

Winning the Veteran's Heart

Harlequin Enterprises ULC
22 Adelaide St. West, 41st Floor
Toronto, Ontario M5H 4E3, Canada
www.Harlequin.com

Printed in U.S.A.

Cheryl Harper discovered her love for books and words as a little girl, thanks to a mother who made countless library trips and an introduction to Laura Ingalls Wilder's Little House books. Whether the stories she reads are set in the prairie, the American West, Regency England or Earth a hundred years in the future, Cheryl enjoys strong characters who make her laugh. Now Cheryl spends her days searching for the right words while she stares out the window, and her dog, Jack, snoozes beside her. And she considers herself very lucky to do so.

For more information about Cheryl's books, visit her online at cherylharperbooks.com or follow her on Twitter, @cherylharperbks.

Books by Cheryl Harper

Harlequin Heartwarming

Veterans' Road

Second Chance Love
Her Holiday Reunion
The Doctor and the Matchmaker
The Dalmatian Dilemma
A Soldier Saved

Otter Lake Ranger Station

Her Unexpected Hero
Her Heart's Bargain
Saving the Single Dad
Smoky Mountain Sweethearts

Visit the Author Profile page
at Harlequin.com for more titles.

Every book I write should be dedicated to you, the reader. I like to tell stories. Thank you for giving me the chance to tell you this one.

CHAPTER ONE

ON LAUREN DUNCAN'S third full day of unemployment, she decided to put on an old bikini, drive to the beach and read a book under an umbrella. A day at the beach had been a daydream for too long, and there was nothing holding her back anymore. The spur-of-the-moment plan required two stops to find the book, the umbrella, a folding chair and a cold bottle of water. Beach-going had been crowded out of her life by her career, so she had none of the necessities in her condo.

"But I won't have to say that tomorrow," Lauren muttered as she stretched her legs out in the sand. Unexpected unemployment had rearranged her priorities in a heartbeat. Leaving the public defender's office with no plan in place was like speeding down the freeway and stopping on a dime, all screeching brakes and shaky recovery after the adrenaline faded.

One minute, she had been outlining a mediocre plea deal offered by the prosecuting attorney. Then her boss had advised her to take it and move to the next file in her caseload without once looking up from his computer.

As if that decision was trivial or less important than the glut of emails in his inbox.

The choice would sentence her client to jail time without a full, fair defense. His lack of concern pushed Lauren to do something she'd believed impossible.

She had quit without notice or a plan for her next paycheck. Her goal of becoming a criminal defense attorney had directed Lauren's choices ever since high school. In an instant, she'd taken that solid purpose and torn it in two.

Panic threatened to overwhelm her, but Lauren was fighting it.

It wasn't time to worry about work or money or the meaning of her life yet. She had years of missed vacation to cram into a couple of weeks of rest and relaxation.

Even if it killed her.

Of course it wouldn't *kill* her, but finding a hobby soon was critical. She needed a good reason to get out of bed.

"I can use my new umbrella and chair again

whenever I want. Tomorrow, I'll go shopping for a new one-piece in case I want to do this again." Lauren tugged the top edge of her bikini bottom higher on her stomach and tried to remember the last time she'd worn this suit.

For three full days, she'd had nothing but her thoughts to occupy her time. It wasn't easy. What would happen to the defendants who were awaiting trial? How quickly could she find a new job? When would her savings run out? Once the concern started to spiral, Lauren grew desperate for a distraction.

An actual vacation that involved plane tickets and reservations would have been better than her staycation half an hour away from home, but that required planning and a budget, and both things had been scrambled by her justified work meltdown.

Which she absolutely did not regret. At all. Yet.

Since exactly no one was paying attention to her on the hot, beautiful day, the old swimsuit was fine. Her umbrella and chair were comfortable. Lauren read two more pages of her new book before her eyelids grew heavy.

"Are you kidding me?" Sleeping again? She put the book facedown to hold her place and rested her head against the chair. The sound of waves was soothing. Conversations and happy kids laughing created buzzy background noise, but no way was she snoozing through this beach day.

Lauren had spent the last two days in her dark, cool bedroom, waking up slowly, dropping back to sleep quickly and eating everything in her refrigerator in between. That had been the best way to stave off unemployment worry and recuperate from a high-stress, too-many-hours-for-too-long job. It was tempting to stay there, with the blankets pulled over her head to keep the real world out.

That had been her mother's coping mechanism, so Lauren knew how depression could sneak in and derail a life if she let it. Getting up and getting out of her apartment had been the answer.

So far, not even the mystery she'd grabbed off the shelf on the way back to the beach umbrellas in the big-box store was holding her attention.

Was it time to give up for the day? Napping in her beach chair could be dangerous, even with 100 SPF sunscreen. Her skin hadn't seen anything harsher than fluorescent light in too long.

"Not yet. I'm no quitter."

The little voice in her head said, "Oh, really? You *quit* your job a few days ago. Isn't that the definition of quitter? Let's check the dictionary."

Lauren shook her head as if to chase the voice away. At least her spot in the sand could be counted on for a supreme people-watching post. Little family groups were scattered up and down the beach as far as Lauren could see, some parents coaxing kids into the waves while others tried to prevent their daredevils from going too far.

"That has to be exhausting," Lauren muttered. It was more fun to watch the bigger group of teenage boys and girls to her right execute some weird mating dance that was made up of teasing, laughing, flexing muscles and tossing hair. Had she ever been that carefree? Her goals had always ruled every minute of every day, even in college. Having a father who'd bounced in and out of jail and in and out of her life had meant everything she accomplished was up to her, so there weren't too many beach days then, either.

Lauren shoved stray pieces of hair back in the braids she'd hurriedly done as she tried to decide if there were any couples among the group or if the pairs were still to be determined. Then her phone rang.

Lauren sipped her water as she grabbed her cell. The sun was too bright to read the display, so she was forced to answer. "Hello?"

"Are you ready to come back to work?" her boss asked without greeting or identification.

Her *ex*-boss.

"You have the wrong number," Lauren said, tempted to hang up immediately.

"Don't hang up," Blake Bennings said quickly. "I understand your frustration, and you deserve to take some time off, but I can't lose you. You're the best we have, Lauren. Think of all the people who need public defenders like you."

That last bit had been the part that kept her at her desk trying to uphold the promise of a top-quality defense for everyone when others had faltered and moved on to easier careers. The system had used Lauren's own commitment to justice for all against her. Too many cases and not enough defenders led to time-saving decisions, and she couldn't keep up the fight alone. Her service had lasted longer than most, but there had to be a limit. Otherwise, she'd grind herself to dust.

"I know you get tired of taking deals," Blake said, "but the caseload doesn't get any smaller. You want to argue until the last breath for everyone. There are definitely defendants we can help, but we have to be able to get to them." Common sense. Logic. What he said was true, but it didn't help her sleep at night.

Lauren sighed. "What I can't handle anymore is weighing these cases to see who deserves a real defense and who gets the advice to settle for the easiest way out, Blake. That's my problem." Every one of her clients and their family members and friends who loved them deserved to be treated equally. Accepting those pleas had been failing them.

Blake was quiet for a minute. Lauren wondered if she'd gotten through to him, but then she realized it didn't matter. Not anymore. If he'd had a solution five years ago, changed the trajectory of the office when he'd taken the lead, they might be in a different spot. If he'd shown care and concern four days ago, Lauren would have returned to her desk, taken the deal, struggled with the decision and opened up the file for her next case.

He didn't have the passion for the job.

That meant he didn't inspire it in others, either. Lawyers weren't applying for jobs in the public defender's office and everyone who got a better offer took it as soon as they could.

Except for Lauren, who had slept for two days straight at her first opportunity. It was too much.

"I appreciate the offer, but I'm content with my decision. I apologize for not giving you more notice, but leaving was necessary to protect my mental health." She'd written something like that in her resignation letter and it was still true. What she hadn't said was that having a dedicated boss and committed coworkers would also be necessary for her to stay, and she didn't ever see either happening under Blake Bennings.

"Have you already accepted another position? Is it with Miller and Rainey?" Blake asked. "I knew they'd snap you up."

Some of the tension in Lauren's shoulders bled out at the suggestion that the busiest criminal defense firm in Miami would be making her an offer and quickly. Having no job? That didn't work for Lauren. She had only herself to rely on.

His certainty that Lauren would find her way soon made it easier to answer. "I don't have another job yet because I was telling you the truth. Fifteen years as a public defender, Blake. That's like a century in normal lawyer years."

His reluctant laugh strengthened her resolve. She had made the right choice.

"You know, if you take a position with Miller and Rainey, you'll only be in the same spot, Lauren. Except this time, instead of reviewing the facts of the case to see if you can fight and win, you'll wait for the check to clear to build the defense. What will investing your talent and limited time on only the defendants lucky enough to afford you do to your conscience?"

Lauren closed her eyes as that truth settled in her stomach. "That was a direct hit. Good one."

She'd been the idealistic attorney who'd joined the public defender's office because she wanted to help people who needed her. Then she'd learned how much her hands were tied.

Now she wouldn't even be representing

people who had no other defense. Guilt and innocence might matter even less.

That was a problem with joining Miller and Rainey or a similar firm, but it changed nothing about the situation she'd left, either.

"Maybe you're onto something. It might be time for me to practice another kind of law, one with different stakes. Real estate law. Tax law." Saying those words made her want to yawn. "I need a break. I wish you the best. If I can help in some small way, please don't hesitate to reach out." Lauren hung up, blocked his number and leaned back in her chair, the guilt of offering help with no intention of giving it heavy, but she refused to blame herself.

He could blame her enough for both of them.

Lauren rubbed the knot in her stomach. Miller and Rainey might make her an offer, but it wasn't one she could accept. Where did that leave her? Looking for a third option.

Could she even practice a different kind of law? Lauren inhaled slowly as anxiety frayed her nerves.

"Of course you can, Lauren," she murmured in her most reasonable voice, and pushed away the image of herself drying up to dust as she hunched over tomes of tax code. "There's a whole world out there with options." She'd never considered them; her whole life had been dedicated to criminal defense. "Doesn't matter. People change directions all the time. You can, too."

Eventually. In two weeks. That was the deadline she'd given herself. At that point, she'd figure out a new job.

Today, she was going to read, listen to the ocean and relax. It took a minute to push back the budding panic attack that made it difficult to catch her breath. Especially since her heart was pounding loud enough to drown out everything around her. She focused on the waves and the kids and all the people who were living whole lives, no matter what their jobs might be. Slowly, her heart returned to a normal beat.

At the two-hour mark, Lauren could feel the prickles of sun on her skin that had to be the precursor to a sunburn. She'd managed to read three chapters of the book and nap for half an hour, neither one of those personal bests, but for her return to the unusual concept of a "vacation day," she'd proved her mettle.

The other thing Lauren had loved to do before work had taken over was to drive the scenic route home, so she headed north to Hollywood, where she'd grown up. When hunger pangs hit, she was convinced to turn back southwest to her condo in Coconut Grove. At some point, she'd have to visit her mother and tell her about her career change, but not yet.

On the way, she picked up a pizza. If she couldn't be outside in the sun and reading, that left catching up on movies, so many movies. Pizza, movies and air-conditioning for a free evening—it was a match made in heaven.

Her first clue that something was not quite right was the car parked in her usual spot. It was a sleek sedan, which could have belonged to any of her neighbors, but the fact that it was in her spot? Yeah, she and her neighbors had all marked their territory in the parking lot years ago.

Juggling the chair, the umbrella and the pizza box, Lauren hurried up to her door, determined to make it inside before any of those neighbors could ask why she was home during the day, why she was wearing a bikini top, had beach hair or smelled like coconut. All of those things were also out of the ordinary.

The man sitting on the top step in front of her door stopped her in her tracks. He was wearing khakis and a polo. Business casual didn't seem appropriate for a daytime robbery, so she waited for more information. Was he selling something?

When the man glanced up from his phone, Lauren nearly dropped the pizza box. "Peter Kim?"

His slow grin was confirmation enough. He didn't have to speak or nod because she'd seen that same grin a million times while they'd battled in their undergraduate classes at Sawgrass University. The fact that she hadn't seen the grin since they'd graduated and she'd gone on to law school while he'd joined the military didn't dim the memory, either.

Peter Kim had always been too smart and too handsome for her own good.

How long had it been? Fifteen years? Longer?

Time and distance had been kind to him. Faint lines around his eyes added a rugged touch, and his shoulders seemed broader, stronger. It was hard to picture this man standing across from her, arguing the dangers of environmental restrictions that protected Florida's native wildlife. He'd always chosen the hardest argument, the losing side, and half the time he'd pulled out the victory.

Debating with him had been infuriating. He'd liked to zig when she expected him to zag.

"I wondered if you'd remember me. I should have known better," Peter said as he stood and took the umbrella out of her hand. "You never forgot anything. Can I help you with any of this?"

Lauren gripped the pizza box tightly, unwilling to surrender her hold on her lunch-slash-dinner-slash-leftovers for the next day.

"It's too much to hope that you're lost and managed to park in my parking spot and find my step to sit on while you waited to ask for directions, isn't it?" Lauren asked as she unlocked the door. One quick glance around her living room reassured her she'd managed to put away all her laundry over the weekend. Folded clothes tended to pile up on her couch for entirely too long because she hated putting them away.

"Considering the work I put in to find you, I would have sat on your doorstep all night if that's what it took," Peter said as he paused in her doorway. "May I come in?"

Wishing she'd put her tank back on over her bikini top and too hungry to waste much more time with polite conversation, Lauren waved him in. "You're determined. Let's hear what brought you back into my life after all these years."

Lauren set the pizza box down on her kitchen island, grabbed two glasses and filled them with ice and water. She glanced longingly in the direction of her walk-in closet for a good old-fashioned T-shirt, before offering him one of the two filled glasses.

Peter sat in the same spot her folded towels usually occupied and put his glass carefully down on a coaster on the end table. Asking for permission to enter. Using coasters. He had better manners than she would have given him credit for when they'd battled through their college classes.

"Have you come to pledge your undying love to the girl you could never forget?" Lauren drawled, determined to show him she hadn't lost a step from their epic back-and-forth. Their rivalry had been intense.

He shook his head. "I wish. That would be less stressful."

That was a shock. It must have shown on her face.

"I'm here because I need your help," he said before grimacing as if the admission left a bad taste in his mouth.

Lauren would have said there was nothing Peter Kim could have said to get her attention, but he'd used the one phrase she couldn't resist.

"I've spent a week tracking down the best criminal defense lawyer in Miami." Peter braced his hands on his knees.

"That brought you to my front door?" Lauren wasn't sure how anyone would determine who the best was, but it didn't surprise her that her name was somewhere on the list. She had sacrificed so much to get it there.

He nodded. "I started with the phone book and a web search. I mean, the most expensive attorney in town has to be the best, right?" Lauren shook her head vigorously and he agreed. "Right. I got that impression, so then I contacted the public defender's office to see if the guy assigned to the arraignment would give me a suggestion. He named the same firm I'd been calling."

"Makes sense." Lauren had made that recommendation many times. Miller and Rainey. The firm was excellent and took all clients who could afford them. Blake had been right on that point. "I can give you another name. Not the most expensive, but someone who's great in court." Then she frowned. "But that still doesn't tell me why you're at my front door."

It didn't surprise her that he'd followed such a winding road. When something had been important to Peter, he'd been impossible to shake, even at twenty-two. Time and experience had obviously taken that trait and refined it. He was good at coming up with new leads on the information he wanted, even if he was still focused on the same goal: being the best.

Or in this case, *hiring* the best.

"I wanted another recommendation, so I went to the nearest police station to beg for help." Peter rubbed a finger over the line in the middle of his forehead. "The officer behind the front desk must have been having

an easy day because she took pity on me."
He was serious as he met her stare. "Officer
Estevez told me if she ever needed a defense
lawyer, she'd pray you were assigned to the
case. Then she told me it was too bad you'd
resigned."

He drew imaginary steps on a map. "Web
search. Address lookup. Add all that together,
and here I am, camped out on your doorstep
to beg for help."

Beg for help. Lauren committed that to
memory so she could return to it later.

Was she flattered that he'd pursued the recommendation so single-mindedly and continued all the way to the end, even after he
knew she was the one waiting there? A little.

She wasn't going to take his case, but she
was curious about the answers to the big
questions.

"Who needs a lawyer, Peter?" Lauren asked.
"Are you in trouble?"

His eyebrows shot up before he blinked.
"No. Not me. My nephew, Davey. He's
twenty. No previous arrests. He was stopped
a couple of blocks from his apartment at two
in the morning. He'd run a stop sign. The
cops searched his car and found drugs. The

prosecutor wants a felony charge. His public defender was fine for the arraignment, but he's going into the pretrial hearing in a couple of weeks and then a court trial facing a felony charge…" Peter exhaled slowly. "I want someone to fight for him."

Lauren fought the urge to pick up the notebook she always used to keep beside her to jot down notes as she worked. The itch to organize the facts in a bulleted list might never go away.

"Your public defender will recommend that you take the deal. The prosecutor will offer you lesser charges for agreeing to the guilty plea. You might be able to avoid significant jail time since he's a first-time offender." As soon as Lauren said it, she could hear her boss saying the same words. "But that's not what you want to hear. I get that."

Peter tangled his fingers together. "Kid's the apple of my parents' eyes, the only grandchild, smart. He's on a full scholarship to Sawgrass and works nights on the hospital's janitorial crew to pay for an apartment, car, life. If I can do anything to help him set this right, I will. Davey deserves that."

Peter Kim had been frozen in her mind

as an overconfident, know-it-all twenty-
two-year-old. He'd been easy to forget. The
man across from her was new. Hearing him
talk about his family, his nephew, made him
real. Instead of an obstacle, he became one of
those people she wanted to fight for.

"Are they his drugs?" Lauren asked. This
was where it always got sticky. It was so easy
to blaze with righteousness when defendants
were unjustly accused.

Parents, grandparents and uncles were almost always certain the charges were un-
founded. Sometimes convincing them of the
truth was the hardest part of the job.

Peter shook his head. "He says no. And
I know—" he held up both hands "—that's
what a guilty person would say, too. I've
heard that plenty of times in a whole series
of law classes, but not this kid. I believe him."

Lauren absorbed that while she reconsidered gently explaining how often family members were wrong in that faith. Then
she realized it wasn't important here. Davey
wasn't her client. Peter Kim would be moving on soon.

She leaned forward. "I don't get it. You're
a lawyer, so why aren't you defending him?"

Lauren wondered how she'd missed Peter Kim moving in Miami's legal circles. Had he changed personalities after all? Undergrad Peter would have strutted into the courtroom with his charm and know-it-all attitude turned up to high and might even have pulled out a win. She would have heard about it, seen it even.

Peter's lips curled. "You're going to make me say it, aren't you?"

She wasn't sure what he meant, but she definitely wanted to hear him say whatever it might be.

"I'm in law school. Final year." Peter sighed. "I'm not the best. Yet. So right now, I need you."

CHAPTER TWO

PETER FORCED HIMSELF to sit calmly as he watched Lauren Duncan evaluate everything he'd told her. It was a relief to be in the air-conditioning after an hour outside waiting and wondering if she'd even let him in. Ever since he'd heard her name and known he had to track her down, she'd been on his mind.

After serving nearly two decades in the air force, he'd retired and come home, ready to spend time with his family and figure out what he wanted to do next. He'd never expected it to be anything like this.

Kims didn't have arrest records.

His parents had tried scaring him straight when he'd gotten his first speeding ticket in high school by forcing him to volunteer on a road cleanup crew for a weekend. The lesson hadn't convinced him to slow down entirely, but he'd managed to stay out of trouble. Hearing his father tell him how much they depended on him to do the right thing had stuck with him through babysitting his little sister and high school and college and years away from home.

The threat of disappointing his parents kept Peter Kim on track.

When his nephew called from jail to ask Peter what to do next, Peter had immediately told David not to tell his mom over the phone. The kid needed support to break the news of something like a drug arrest to his mother and grandparents, and now that Peter was back in Miami, he was happy to be that support. Taking care of his baby sister, Nicole, had been his job since she'd wrapped tiny fingers around his pinkie the first time his parents let him hold her.

Calling the family together to tell David's story one time had made sense.

Then, after the kid's confession, everyone in his family had turned to him, as if he would have the solution to Davey's problems. Because he was in law school? Peter wasn't sure, but the guy Lauren used to know might have tried to bluff his way through. Finding and hiring the best representation was something he *could* do. So the plan was easy enough. He'd never doubted his success.

Here, in Lauren Duncan's modern, beigey-beige condo with windows that overlooked a small pond, he was experiencing his first qualms. Admitting her excellence, groveling for her assistance… What else was there? From what he remembered about her, she should have snapped up her opportunity to save the day and do a victory lap.

Instead, he was waiting. There wasn't much to stare at while she thought. The only real color in the room came from the bookcases that lined the wall across from the door. From here, he couldn't read the titles, but these books didn't appear to be for pleasure. They were large and covered in leather, not ratty paperbacks with broken spines like he stacked up on shelves at home.

"Did you hear me, Lauren? I need you," Peter said slowly. That should have been enough. He was at a disadvantage. How could she fail to capitalize on that?

She pursed her lips. "It loses some of the power when there's no one else to hear you say it."

Peter was amused by that. He understood

what she meant. They'd always performed better in front of an audience. What an exciting opponent she'd been.

"Peter, I can't." Lauren waved her hands to wipe away the humor between them. "I quit my job at the defender's office. It was a pretty spectacular way to go. I stormed into my boss's office, plopped down my case files and tossed my resignation letter at him. Everyone in the office was watching me go. I imagine the gossip has made it through the courthouse by now. The prosecutors and judges will be watching me closely, waiting for another meltdown, if I turn up again after all that. Let me recommend another attorney, someone who isn't known for emotional outbursts."

That did surprise him. He hadn't gotten all the details, but he would have said logical Lauren would have crossed all the t's and dotted the i's before leaving to be certain she didn't burn any bridges. It sounded like she'd set the bridge on fire before she was fully across it.

"I need to focus on a new direction and finding another job." She sighed as if the idea was exhausting.

"You aren't practicing criminal law any-more, either?" Peter asked as he quickly considered a few different arguments, searching for the most likely winner, his best shot to convince her to take on at least one more case.

She shrugged.

That confused him.

If she didn't know the answer... Who did?

"Well," he said slowly, "if criminal law is what you want to do, perhaps for one of those firms you'd recommend, a solid win in court could stabilize your reputation." Did he believe that? Didn't matter. It was a good argument and he *needed* to keep her talking instead of showing him the door. It was probably true.

He cleared his throat. "You already have people in town who will say you are the best defense lawyer around. Show them that nothing has changed when you're in front of a judge. Lauren Duncan doesn't give up. Do you remember the day you disagreed with our American history professor about one of the answers on an exam? In front of the whole class, you proved him wrong. We all got an extra ten points that day."

"What if..." Lauren bit her lip as she studied his face. The logic was working but there was something else worrying her. "Practicing criminal law for a private firm might be worse than serving people who couldn't afford a lawyer. Before, I was focused on fairness, justice. At a firm, those things have an actual price tag." Her grimace punctuated her point. "See? What if that's worse for me? What if I need something totally different?"

He could see the instant she realized she was talking out loud in front of an old rival and that it might not have been the wise choice. Lauren straightened in her chair. "That's why I need this time off. I have to think about what I want to do and determine which steps to take first."

"Sure. What was it Professor Shelton told us?" Peter smiled. "'Plan the work and work the plan.' We learned how to argue from one of the best." They'd shared one or two courses every semester at Sawgrass as they'd both been completing a history major. He'd competed with Lauren in a composition class, a knockdown, drag-out speech class where they'd faced off on almost every issue, several literature courses, one ill-fated creative writing elective and, oddly enough, a bowling class taken to meet a physical education requirement.

That had been an adventure.

The spark in her eye convinced him she was remembering the same battles. While others around them were fully enjoying a college experience and losing their scholarships because of it, he and Lauren had driven each other straight to the top of the class and then higher.

"I can't relax if I'm working on a case, Peter," she said softly. Her tone was sad. "When I'm working, there is only the work, see?"

She was about to tell him no and ask him to leave. He needed some delay, a deflection to buy himself time.

"You don't have an escape already planned, a trip to some exotic island?" Peter asked as he thought. He could set a date in the future, ask her to review the evidence of the case and meet Davey, too. If she'd gotten bored with too much time off, a solid possibility, she might be more open to getting back in the ring.

But while he was strengthening his case,

Lauren could also be firming her resolve to say no.

Some kind of distraction that also made it harder to refuse this case…

"Can't afford that now." Lauren shrugged. "Luckily, the beach is never far from home around here."

Peter held his hands out. "I'd also be happy to offer my services. I'm keeping things easy at law school, taking the simple route. That's why I've chosen estate law as a specialty."

"Wills? Things like that?" Lauren pursed her lips. "When you join a top firm in Miami, they're going to take a dim view of that opinion. For them, you'll rack up lots of billable hours or you'll…go." She frowned. "I'm surprised no adviser warned you about that or tried to get you an associate position at one of those firms this summer. It's the best way to get in."

She was right about the summer job. It would have been a huge boost to his résumé, but he wasn't interested in the stress and politics of it all.

"The old Peter Kim would be working downtown today. I was offered two different positions." It was satisfying to show her that he hadn't been without options. He was still good in school, even without her nipping at his heels.

"But you didn't take them?" she said doubtfully. He understood that, too. The urge to say yes to one or the other had been nearly overwhelming. Spots were limited. Landing one of them would have boosted his ego and his career prospects. He had a long record of saying yes to every opportunity or challenge. It was how he'd wound up here.

"I'll go into business on my own when it's time." He was happy he had an answer to this. "So, I can take my boat out tomorrow. Do you know how hard it is to worry about the future on a boat? Pretty much your only choice is to relax when you're on the ocean. No bills to pay. No phone calls or texts to answer. That is the number one rule on my boat—no cell phones. Just peace. Water. Sunshine." He smiled slowly. "You wouldn't even have to change your clothes, Lauren."

She immediately glanced down at her bikini top and closed her eyes. "I was trying to forget that I was wearing this when you reappeared in my life."

"If you do forget, don't worry. I've committed it to memory." Peter enjoyed the way color filled her cheeks. He hadn't come here to flirt, but for the first time in days, his own nerves had receded a bit.

Convincing her was completely within his skill set. He'd been winning people over for decades.

"That's all it will take? An hour or two on your boat?" she asked, uncertainty evident on her face. "I'll be relaxed and my future will be clear to me?"

"We can repeat the trip as many times as it takes." Peter leaned forward, certain he was half a second from victory. She was weakening. "How can you resist?"

Her phone rang and she pulled it out of the front pocket of her shorts to see the display. He thought she muttered "blocked" before she tossed the cell on the seat next to her. "Leave my phone at home, you say?"

Peter grinned. "Cutler Bay Club. Tomorrow. I can pick you up on the way."

She shook her head. "I'll meet you there."

CHAPTER THREE

PETER WAS RIDING high when his doorbell rang that afternoon. He'd successfully post-poned Lauren's final decision, earning time to strengthen his case and deliver exactly what his family needed. A first-rate defender. There was nothing to stand in his way of helping his nephew now.

And tonight he would celebrate on the town with a beautiful woman, one who might be interested in Peter as a man, not an old foe. He grabbed a tie out of his closet before trot-ting into his living room to answer the door.

Finding Brisa Montero on the threshold shouldn't have surprised him. Tonight was the blind date she'd arranged to "help" him find the woman of his dreams.

"Is this what you're wearing?" she asked as she brushed him aside in a breeze of fancy perfume and determined woman. "It's nice, but kind of…"

It was his date suit. Kind of what? "I don't need you here shaking my confidence, Montero." Peter draped the tie around his neck. "This suit has done well in previous testing."

Her head snapped up from where she'd been frowning at his shoes. They were polished. Black. Nothing was wrong with his shoes, either.

"Plain. That's what I was going to say, but that tie helps." She swatted his hands away and tied it in a complicated knot that surpassed his usual over-around-through-and-down choice. Had she learned it in finishing school or something? "There. We upgraded you to a trinity knot. Candace will notice. I like this color." She smoothed the dark red tie down. "Classic. That's what I meant, not boring."

"You said plain, not boring." Peter grunted. "So glad you're here to save me from *boring* knots."

Brisa shook her finger at him. "You can make or break my reputation as a matchmaker, Peter. I still contend Wade and Mira were a good gamble."

The group of friends he'd made at Concord Court had slowly but surely paired off, two by two, leaving Peter for Brisa's matchmaking endeavors. Funny, she hadn't set up any of the happy couples, either. "Even though Mira was already married and Wade was always going to fall for you?" Peter drawled. Mira Peters had been secretly married at the time of Brisa's supposed brilliant match of her sister with Wade McNally, the trauma surgeon now wrapped around Brisa's finger. Jason Ward had found his match in his creative writing professor, Angela Simmons. Sean Wakefield, the guy who oversaw the Court's buildings and grounds, had charmed Brisa's older sister, Reyna, into true love. Peter's best friend, Marcus Bryant, had finally realized how he really felt about the girl next door, Cassie Brooks. Brisa might want to be a matchmaker, but around Concord Court, the matches made themselves.

Her confidence could withstand some teasing. Everything was working out for Brisa Montero exactly as it should.

"I didn't know Mira was married, and Wade..." Brisa clasped her hands together. "Well, everything turned out right in the end, I guess. I won't let this night fail. I made reservations for you on the terrace at Las Estrellas for seven. Candace loves paella, so I know this is going to be a big win. The chef there…" She stopped as if words failed her.

"I've tried to get into that place for three months. How'd you do it?" Peter asked. Thanks to his current string of first dates, he had lots of opportunity to try out the most popular restaurants in Miami, and there were so many to choose from. Las Estrellas had been on the top of every best-of-the-best list ever since it opened.

Brisa pointed to herself. "Montero. That's my last name, remember? I never hesitate to use it for my friends."

Peter rolled his eyes. Brisa's wealthy father was one of Miami's celebrities, and the name definitely opened doors. It also drew attention that had made Brisa's life more difficult, but she was turning that all around and using it to help veterans at Concord Court. Victor Montero had built this townhome bridge community for veterans to keep an eye on his oldest daughter, Reyna, but Brisa had found her calling here. Veterans throughout southern Florida were lucky because of it. "What did you tell your friend about me?"

Brisa set her clipboard down. He hadn't seen her without it lately. "I don't know if I'd call her a friend, exactly. We went to school together. I dated her brother for half a minute when I was seventeen, we once spent too much of our fathers' money in Europe, but she's the kind of 'friend' who never loses a contact, right? Somehow, she heard I was hiring a coordinator for the business lab and called to apply. Over the phone. She closed her boutique in the Design District so has time on her hands."

Peter sighed. "Oh, she was going with the whole 'you gotta know somebody to get ahead' philosophy."

"Exactly," Brisa said as she put hands to hips and grinned. "But you will be happy. So will she."

Peter relaxed fractionally. For some reason, he got nervous before every first date, wondering if that nerdy, awkward kid had reappeared somehow when he wasn't watching. "Because she's beautiful? Is that the reason you set us up?"

Brisa wrinkled her nose. "It definitely doesn't hurt."

It also didn't fill him with hope for the evening. If they had nothing in common, he'd be stuck discussing the weather. At least the dating apps started with basic questions to see if there was anything to talk about, not that they helped much in his experience. He was beginning to think the first woman who helped him carry a conversation would get a proposal and a ring…someday. He wasn't ready for that yet.

"You asked me to give this a shot, remember?" Brisa asked.

"That's not exactly how I remember it. You said you could find a better match for me than I was doing for myself." Peter tapped his chest. "And I said there was nothing wrong with the women I've found to date. I don't want to get serious right away. I want to focus on me for a while, what I enjoy, what I want. Does that ring any bells with you?"

She pretended to think back and studied the ceiling. He knew her tactics. "Vaguely. I guess we'll see who is right tonight. I told her to meet you there and that the reservation is in your name." Her shoulders slumped as she picked up her clipboard. "Do not mention the business lab job, though. Had to let her down easy. She wasn't qualified. I'm desperate for real help, someone who knows contracts and finance and business. Candace could help with the people part of what's required, but she isn't the organized, attention-to-detail type."

Apart from morning runs, Brisa never seemed to stop working for Concord Court. When he'd moved into the town house complex, it had been presented as a place to stay for two years, rent free, while he adjusted to his new civilian life. Leaving the air force had been easy in some ways, more difficult in others. The only rules here were find a satisfying job or go back to school.

Having the time and breathing room to work through law school had made the choice simple for Peter.

But since then, the services available at Concord Court had expanded, thanks mainly to Brisa's vision and drive. For months, she'd been hunting for the right person to lead the business lab that would support veterans who wanted to open small businesses.

"Are you sure I can't talk you into taking it? Just while you're in law school. When you're ready to go into business for yourself, I'll find someone new. Smart guy like you wouldn't have trouble managing both, would he?" Brisa chuckled and innocently fluttered her eyelashes at him. Sixteen-year-old Peter had fallen for similar tactics, and even now he struggled to say no.

"Sorry. Can't do it." He needed time to live, not just study law. That was the whole point behind Concord Court.

She sighed. "I don't really blame you. I mean, I totally blame you, but I won't hold it against you." She gave him a quick hug. "Don't tell Wade about this conversation, otherwise he'll lecture me about working too hard and I have it memorized. Also, if you can think of anyone who would be right for the job, send them my way. I will sell this job like it's the last car on the lot, and if you help me, I will owe you one." She brightened. "I could set you up again, this time with one of my best friends!" So he'd only rated a setup with an acquaintance tonight? If it didn't work out, and Peter was almost certain it wouldn't, he'd move up a tier into Brisa's inner circle.

Her excitement made him laugh…and also fear for how his evening was going to go. She really wasn't great at this matchmaking thing.

"Someone better than Candace, huh?" he asked as he opened the door for her.

"Candace might be perfect for you. She doesn't take anything too seriously." Brisa shrugged. "Besides, you already know all my best friends. They're your friends, too. Have a good time and tell me all about the meal the next time I see you, okay?"

Peter nodded and waved as she hurried off.

It was a beautiful night for dinner on the terrace, warm but not as humid as normal. When he arrived at Las Estrellas, Candace was already seated as he made his way to the table.

"I hope you haven't been waiting too long," he said as he pulled out the chair across from her and sat. Candace was beautiful, for sure. Her dark hair was swept up to show a graceful neck and bare shoulders.

Peter scanned the terrace and had to admit that Brisa knew what she was doing when she picked the restaurant. The terrace jutted out over the water, leaving the hustle, bustle and neon lights of the street level behind. The setting sun cast a pink glow over everything, and the discreet fans located around the deck's edge stirred a breeze and made a gentle background noise for conversation. He could hear faint music from one of the clubs down the block, but it only added to the atmosphere.

"Only long enough to order a glass of the most expensive red on the menu." She picked up her wineglass. "I hope you don't mind that I started without you."

Peter nodded at the waiter who approached with the bottle. As he poured, Peter said, "Of course not. I always admire initiative." When his glass was full, he picked it up to toast her. "Here's to a fun evening."

"Good company and beautiful surroundings." Candace sipped and then asked, "I know what I'm doing here. After a divorce and closing one chapter, I'm ready to start fresh. I was looking for a job when I called Brisa, but she suggested something better. You." She tapped his hand. "What brings you out on a blind date?"

Brisa had left out that important detail, the divorce piece, but it wasn't important. Being judged better than a new job? Peter wasn't sure how that made him feel or the right answer for that, so he said, "Being set up by a good friend has to be better than a dating app."

Her vigorous nod propped up his confidence. Maybe this was going to go better than he imagined. They ordered and made small talk about the usual suspects: the weather, Miami traffic, tourists and how they knew Brisa Montero.

"How is the paella?" he asked after she finished a story about a girls' trip to Europe where she and Brisa had spent an adventurous spring break. He hoped her answer would distract him from the alarms going off in his head. Illustrating how different their backgrounds were could not be easier than comparing her story with his normal school break occupation: doing inventory in his mom's bookstore. It had been a sweet job, but it was still a job.

"So good. It might be my new favorite," Candace said. "And the fish dish? What was it called again?"

"Bacalao. I can't remember the name of the sauce, but it's excellent. Garlicky. I've never had anything like this." That had been why he'd chosen it. He'd always gone for the new and different; Candace stuck with what she knew.

Which was definitely not a deal breaker, but it made him think of all the other things he wanted to see and do and try now that he had the time and ability to do it.

"We should go to Spain sometime! I haven't been there in years," Candace gushed, and he realized that a lot of his list of "somedays" might have already been crossed off by his date.

"I'd love to see Barcelona," he said without committing to the trip one way or the other.

"Do you ever think about how your life would be different if you'd gone straight to law school, skipped the military altogether? You could be partner in a firm by now, making the big bucks, and planning trips for you and your wife." She raised her wineglass. "You could even be on your second wife by now! The first marriage is like the first pancake. It's only practice!" Her grin told him she was making a joke about the wife part, but he wasn't sure the whole comment was a joke.

"You might be right about the money, but I joined the air force for myself. I'm glad I did. It's made all the difference in my life and I wouldn't give that up for anything." He watched her smile fade, as if she'd realized she might have said something he didn't appreciate.

It was hard to hold comments like hers against civilians who had no idea what went into military life, but it didn't ease the sting. He'd sacrificed a lot more than income by making that choice, but what he'd gained was hard to put into words.

Candace put her spoon down and said carefully, "Of course. Thank you for your service." Peter had the impression that she was the one offended by his offense, no matter how gently he'd stated it.

"The dinner was excellent. I definitely owe Brisa a big favor for setting it up for us," Candace said as he paid the check.

"I've been trying to get reservations here for a couple of months, so she worked some magic." Peter moved around the table to pull Candace's chair out for her to stand and then offered her his arm as he led them out of the restaurant. She might not be impressed with his service to his country, but his manners were going to be impeccable until she got in her car and drove away.

Every date was practice until the one that mattered; that's what he told himself whenever a first date fizzled like this one. Someday, he'd meet the right woman and everything would click.

"I'd love to go out again, handsome," Candace said as she pressed her lips to his cheek and then handed the valet her ticket. Peter silently urged the valet to hurry as he evaluated what would be the best answer.

When he didn't immediately respond with enthusiasm, her expression changed from expectant to resigned. "Well, when you change your mind, you know how to find me."

"Be careful on the way home," Peter said, and handed the valet his own ticket. He shoved his hands in his pockets as he watched her car merge with city traffic.

"She wasn't the one, huh?" The kid leaning against the valet stand stared after Candace. "Too bad."

"Plenty of fish in the sea and all that," Peter said. He waved at the kid, tipped his valet well and drove home.

He'd been operating on the whole "lots of opportunity will lead to the right person eventually" strategy, and admitted he was in no hurry to get to the end of the journey. He was enjoying every minute of it. Even that night, it was hard to regret a fantastic dinner at a new restaurant with a beautiful woman, even if she wasn't the one for him and vice versa.

"Better to know now." The real problem was how to tell Brisa her match had fallen flat again. On paper, this one made sense. The problem with her matches and the apps was the part that couldn't be measured, the spark that turned into a flame.

He should ask Brisa to keep looking. In the meantime, he'd focus on winning Lauren Duncan over to his side. For some reason, that sounded more like fun than hard work. He was already looking forward to seeing her again.

CHAPTER FOUR

"WHAT ARE YOU doing, Lauren?" she mumbled to herself as she stopped in front of the Cutler Bay Club's guard hut. Driving through the highly manicured, lush green golf course with peekaboo views of water had intensified the dread and near certainty that spending the day with Peter Kim was a mistake. Golf might be the lawyer's best networking game, but she didn't belong here. Why hadn't she turned around before she had an audience?

Lauren pasted on a smile and pretended to be a person who knew exactly what she was doing. That woman totally belonged at the private club and she'd brought along a big, floppy straw hat to prove it.

For some reason, when Lauren imagined the women who embarked at the Cutler Bay Club marina, they wore flowing dresses and exceptionally large hats, knew how to throw elegant parties and laughed knowingly as they sailed away on yachts named *Seas the Day* or *Midship Crisis*.

The guard on duty was either highly suspicious by nature or Lauren was failing at her pretense or both because all she got in response was a terse "Name, please."

"Lauren Duncan. I'm here to meet Peter Kim." When the guard held out her hand, Lauren slipped her driver's license into it, impressed at the top-notch security of the fancy club and curious as to whether it was necessary. She'd never had the kind of money that made belonging to a private club possible, had she? Were there a lot of security threats to the golf course, marina and clubhouse with a world-class chef in residence and spectacular water views? Those were the amenities listed on the website. Lauren always did her best to hunt up details about any unfamiliar territory through extensive web searches. Going in unprepared would have made her twice as anxious.

Meeting Peter Kim for a day out on the water qualified as extremely unfamiliar. Uncharted waters? The pun would have made her smile if she hadn't been nervously chewing her bottom lip.

Nerves were meant to be carefully hidden away, so Lauren fussed with the folds of the skirt of the vibrant blue sundress she'd settled on after an invasion of her closet that morning. To find her bed again, she'd have to clean up that mess when she got home.

"Thank you, Ms. Duncan. Mr. Kim has added you to his guest list. He's asked that you meet him in the marina parking lot." The guard handed back Lauren's ID. "Have a nice day." Her lips curled but there was no display of teeth. Polite but never far away from dangerous, either. The Cutler Bay Club hired professionals.

Lauren nodded and watched the gate rise. Her heart beat faster the closer she got to the marina.

Allowing Peter Kim any more time to convince her to take his nephew's case was a terrible idea. He was persuasive and she didn't have much of a foundation to lean against as she was currently jobless, planless and bored. She'd almost resigned herself to helping out in the name of… It wasn't exactly friendship, but it was close enough.

After Peter left her condo, Lauren ate three pieces of pizza, flipped through all the channels and failed to find anything interesting to watch on TV. Then, she'd given in to her curiosity and called in some favors to get email copies of the police report and the public defender's case notes.

She had a better picture of the case now. It would be fairly simple, a pretrial hearing where she would do her best to prevent the case moving forward to a full trial.

Or a good lawyer would make that her goal.

If Lauren told Peter she'd be that lawyer before she got on his boat, then she could avoid spending too much time with the irritating rival who'd only gotten better-looking with time. That was so unfair.

Unfortunately, she'd also miss out on a chance to sail away from her troubles for a few hours.

Those troubles were getting louder, more insistent, instead of fading. Insomnia had led to more internet searching when she should have been getting her beauty sleep. First, she'd visited job sites to see who was hiring lawyers. If personal injury had been her passion, she would have been set. She'd taken three quizzes to determine her perfect career; two of them were certain she should be a lawyer. Then she'd searched local real estate for available office space. How much money would she have to bring in to cover the costs of business day to day? When she added a salary for herself and anyone she'd hire on top of office rental…

That last search had been so discouraging that she'd given up on sleep completely and moved to watching the sunrise. On nights like that and with problems that big, Lauren always wished one of her parents was the wise counselor who could guide her through such tough decisions. Instead, Lauren had always been the one to make the tough choices for them and all on her own.

The truth was, Peter was her best shot for keeping a firm grip on reality. She'd watched three movies back to back the night before, and she'd already been to the beach. That had exhausted her list of staycation activities. Peter had always excelled at commanding attention. He would be able to push everything but him out of her mind.

She pulled into an empty space near the marina and watched Peter straighten up from where he'd been lounging in the shade of the small building on the edge of the water. He was talking with an older guy who leaned out the window. If someone had asked her to describe a sailor, Lauren would have started there: wisps of white hair curled around his ears, his skin was tanned from days in the sun, his cap was indeterminately splotchy gray and he grinned as if he'd never seen a rain cloud. How he clapped Peter on the shoulder before he disappeared inside made Lauren believe they were friends. That surprised her. It was easy to picture Peter in an expensive suit with a sharp tie, commanding a courtroom or even swinging a golf club and laughing heartily with clients on the golf course. Instead, he was wearing board shorts, a faded T-shirt and dark sunglasses. Maybe with his sailor friend was exactly where Peter fit.

Had she ever tried to guess whom Peter would hang out with? In her mind, he stood alone.

Before she could again waste time and breath asking herself why she'd come here, Lauren grabbed her tote, stared hard at the cell phone on the seat next to her, tossed it in her bag before she could change her mind and slid out of the car.

Wind caught the edges of her hat, but Lauren managed to clamp one hand over it before it escaped. She wasn't sure she was truly reflecting the country club aesthetic with one hand clutched to her head and a grocery store tote bag dangling off her shoulder.

But she was here. There was nothing to be done now, so she tried to smile.

"I wasn't sure you were going to meet me today," Peter said, his lips curling slightly. His eyes swept from her hat to her sandals, but she couldn't read his expression.

"Me, either," Lauren said before a nervous laugh left her lips. "I considered a U-turn but I decided the extremely efficient guard protecting the club might think that was suspicious. I didn't want to get into a high-speed chase with a golf cart this morning." The strap of her tote bag cut into her shoulder, so she shifted it but forced herself to stop fiddling with it, and to leave her hat alone. She'd meet his stare head-on, make it through this without doing something silly like rekindling the "it's not a crush" part of the love-hate relationship she'd battled for four years as an undergrad.

Peter Kim had been close to her league then, the nerdy overachievers' league.

Now? He moved in a different world. Military hero, she'd bet. He would have accepted nothing less. Athletic. Soon-to-be lawyer. Boat owner. Country club member. Family guy. They had almost nothing in common. They'd both come a long way, but she wondered if he'd left her in his wake.

When he reached over to take the tote off her shoulder, Lauren protested, but he shook his head. "Let me carry it for you. I've already loaded all my stuff on the boat." Then he grinned. "You've got your hands full with that hat. Literally." It was a huge, happy grin. Lauren hadn't ever seen that expression on his face, and it was powerful. He'd won a lot of their face-offs, but this teasing was… It made her feel like that kid again whenever a cute guy smiled at her. Which made a lot of sense, actually.

"Sun safety, you know." Lauren walked beside him, conscious of the way her shoes slapped the dock with each step. Could she walk less loudly? "You seem…different today."

He nodded and then pointed at a boat. It

was longer and taller than she expected, but he slowed to a stop and then held out his hand to help her step onto the deck. His hand on hers was steady, solid. She trusted he would keep her safe. "Yeah, I've gotten pretty good at compartmentalizing worries over the years. Military intelligence sort of requires that. Getting out on the water fixes everything, I promise. Step down with your right foot first."

As she followed his instruction, Lauren asked, "Is that a safety requirement?"

When they were both on board, he let go of her hand but slowly so that his fingers trailed across hers. "Nah, superstition. Just in case there's anything to it, it's bad luck to step on with your left foot first." He winked. "We old sea dogs know that boats require lots of superstitions. The sea is a jealous lover and all that. Let me give you a tour."

Lauren huffed out a breath at his teasing, but she tightened her fingers into a fist to chase away the feeling of his skin against hers.

"Up here, you can see the equipment, the electronics that help with navigation," Peter said as he waved generally at a seat with a steering wheel in front of it. From there, the view of the water would be perfect. "Comfortable seating. I've got the bimini on for shade but I can remove it if you'd rather. I wasn't counting on your impressive and powerful hat." He knelt and pulled up a section of the deck. "Machinery and storage in here. I've got rods if you're interested in fishing."

Lauren was searching for a strong, independent way to ask if he would bait her hook for her when he pressed his hand to her shoulder to urge her to step out of the way so he could open a…door? Hatch? She was going to have to learn some real boat terms if this became a habit, but he disappeared inside the narrow opening and then motioned her to follow.

Below deck was a tight but efficiently laid out…galley? Kitchen? It was a kitchen with a microwave, a small fridge and a hot plate. She could see that he'd brought in food containers. They were secured to the small counter with cords. The walls were lined with shallow cupboards that latched shut. There was a small table and a booth wrapped around it for seating.

"Bathroom with a shower in kind of a wet

room situation over here, and if you need a place to sleep, there's a pretty good-sized bed," Peter told her as he knelt and lifted another smaller hatch-thing. When Lauren bent down, she could see a mattress covered with a sheet and a blanket folded along the end. There might be five feet top to bottom, so whoever made it into that hatch better be... "You can't be claustrophobic if you're going to sleep on my boat."

"How often have you slept on your boat?" Lauren asked.

Because if she had any other choice, she'd go with that one, not the boat box contraption.

"A few times, but I slept out on deck. Under the stars. Much more comfortable. Making this bed nearly killed me, so I've been hesitant to get back in there. Trying to put a sheet on a mattress while you're lying on it and the deck is about three inches from your head requires more patience than I have." Peter stood. "I like day trips better anyway."

"So it all works out for you, then," Lauren said with a grin. When she realized how quickly she'd forgotten her nerves with Peter, she understood that she was in trouble. He was charming. He was handsome. She knew he was one of the smartest guys she'd ever met.

And now he was bouncing in excitement to show off his boat.

Being adorable on top of all the rest could be her doom.

"Were you a yes or no on fishing?" Peter asked.

Good. Good! She'd be typically girlie, make a grossed-out face about baiting her hook, he'd give her a hard time and then she'd be back on level land.

"Only if you'll do the hard part." Lauren grimaced. "I can't bait my own hook."

His comical response was twice as violent as hers. "Ew, no way. I have lures for that very reason. Plastic. Metal. No wriggling bait." Then he tipped his head to the side and grinned as she chuckled. She couldn't help it. Everything about him was adorable right now.

"Let's see if we can get down to the Keys, find a good spot to fish, then we'll decide." Peter waited for her agreement, then motioned over his shoulder back up to the deck. "I hope you brought your suit. We can also swim. If you didn't, I might have one that would fit you. Join me in the cockpit. That's the best view in the house."

After Peter had walked out of her condo, Lauren had tried to imagine how this day would go. She'd pictured awkward silences, uncomfortable small talk and occasional hard sells by Peter to convince her to accept the case.

Instead, Peter motioned her to a shaded seat next to his located behind the steering wheel and handed her sunscreen. "It's reef safe. I wasn't sure if you had any, but you'll burn before you know it even with the covering."

While Lauren studied the covering that protected the exposed cockpit and wondered if that was what a bimini might be, Peter disappeared. One quick glance caught him pulling in the lines that had anchored them to the dock.

He was whistling as he climbed the three steps back to his chair, where he turned and clicked a variety of dials and switches on the control panel next to the steering wheel. Lauren could hear a faint motor start up, and they began to ease away from the dock. His focused frown was back as he maneuvered out of the boat slip and slowly entered the marina's waters, so she was afraid to shatter his concentration.

Once they made it past the sign floating in the water that read No Wake Zone, he eased back in his chair, turned to her with a happy grin and declared, "Success."

A light breeze brushed through his dark hair, and the boy she knew was staring back at her.

"Let it go, whatever it is." Peter grinned. "That problem is stuck on dry land." Then he pushed a lever and the engines engaged. The speed, salty air and the sunshine combined to wash over Lauren. Her hat immediately flapped giant wings around her ears so she was giggling as she yanked it off and shoved it in her tote. Boat days required messy hair.

"You're going to have to teach me everything I don't know about boating," Lauren said as she climbed up next to him. "For example, is this called a cockpit? Isn't that airplanes?"

Peter blinked. "You're lucky I didn't tell you it's the crow's nest or something like that. I call it the cockpit." He held one hand over his chest. "I believe that is considered accurate, but just in case, I would caution you not to trot out the term in front of a pirate or sailor or other nautical expert. I cannot be held responsible for future embarrassment."

Lauren narrowed her eyes at him. "Yes, I remember the whole 'who can pick up the bedposts' conversation from our ill-fated bowling team in college."

"Oh, yes, bowling for a physical education credit. That was a good decision for both of us, wasn't it?" He laughed. "Hey, it's not my fault that you'd challenge whatever I said, even if you didn't know that was picking up a seven-ten split, hardest split in the game." He tilted his head back. "Who won that bet?"

Lauren crossed her arms over her chest. "You did, which you obviously expected to."

He clapped his hand to his cheek as if he was surprised at the memory. "You were the captain of that team and could have chosen anyone in the whole bowling class. Why'd you pick me?"

"I wanted to pass," Lauren said.

He bent his head closer to hers as if he was studying her face under a magnifying glass. "Try again. We all showed up, so we all passed."

Lauren rolled her eyes. "Okay, fine, I wanted to win the tournament. I like trophies."

"And you thought I'd assist with that," he drawled.

"You were great, although little did I know you'd be goading me into silly bets," Lauren said. "I thought bedposts were names for any pins."

"Couldn't you have asked me for clarification before agreeing to the bet?" Peter bit his lip as he waited for her answer.

"Obviously not," Lauren said reluctantly before laughing. It was silly now, but she'd been irate at the time. The fact that he remembered it, too, was surprising.

"Come on. Buying me a chili dog wasn't so bad, was it?" He bumped her shoulder with his.

"Swallowing my loud boasts for all to hear was the worst part, but you were always a pretty good winner. You didn't gloat. Proper sportsmanship and all that," Lauren grumbled.

"That is the nicest thing you've ever said to me, Duncan." He motioned between them. "You know what this is? Growth."

They were both grinning when he turned back to the water.

She'd made the right decision joining Peter today. Whatever his concerns were, in addition to his nephew's case, Peter knew how to let the sea carry them away, even if it was only for a while.

If she could learn to do the same, this time spent with Peter Kim would be priceless.

CHAPTER FIVE

As PETER HAD waited for Lauren at the marina, he'd wavered between hoping that she didn't show up so that he could enjoy his day on the water and hoping that she did because... Well, he hadn't wanted to consider why it mattered so much if she met him. He could always track her down again and make his case if she didn't follow through, but for some reason, it had been too easy to picture Lauren seated next to him.

When Frank had stuck his head out the window to ask him what he was doing there, loitering next to the marina's one-stop shop for food, beverage, bait, tackle and sundries, he'd replied that he was waiting for a friend.

Lauren wasn't exactly a friend, but what was she?

He hadn't had to come up with a better answer. When Lauren slid out of her car, all sunny and elegant in a bright blue dress,

Frank had smacked him on the shoulder, chuckled as if it was clear why he'd been waiting and wished him luck before disappearing inside the store.

And as she was walking across the parking lot toward him? Peter had realized there was something different about spending a day on the water with Lauren, an added level of anticipation that made him restless. Peter didn't make a habit of inviting company along on his fishing trips. Solitude was still so sweet that he guarded it closely. He was proud of his boat, for sure. It was the measure of hard work and sacrifice and his hopes for the second part of his life, but having her see it added something he couldn't quite identify.

When he was back on solid ground and had all the time in the world to worry about things he couldn't control or even understand, he'd analyze what her presence brought to the day and what it meant. Today was about pleasure, and having her in the cockpit seat next to him was sweet.

"How about a boating lesson?" Peter asked. Conversation had been his worry. As a teenager, making small talk with someone like Lauren would have twisted him up in knots.

Practice helped, but so had her stroll down memory lane.

"Stick with approved terminology, please," she drawled. "If you don't know, don't make it up."

He rolled his eyes. "Where's the fun in that?" Then he held up his hands in surrender. "Fine. If I don't know the answer—" he shivered as if the idea was too scary to imagine "—I'll say 'I don't know.'"

If he actually did that, they might both fall overboard from shock.

"What's this?" Lauren asked as she leaned closer, her shoulder brushing his; the smell of sunscreen mingled with Lauren's perfume and went straight to his head. Peter had to re-engage his brain before he noticed she was pointing at the electronics on the dash.

He nodded. "Very important if you want to become the first mate on this vessel. That is the chart plotter, the fish finder, a valuable piece of equipment for all sailors." He tapped the screen. "Here, I've saved the coordinates of one of my favorite spots. See how it's marked? A dot on the grid? The GPS helps me navigate there and find my way home again."

"So, it works like the GPS in my *car*," Lauren said slowly. "Got it." Before he could react, her grin blossomed, and it was impossible to be annoyed by her smart answer.

"But with no roads or landmarks, madam." She was right about the GPS pretty much being the same on land or sea, but it was still possible to show off a bit. "Fine. What's this one do?" He pointed at the screen to the right of the steering wheel.

Her hair drifted across his chest, thanks to the breeze, as she leaned across him to study it closely before reading. "That is your basic multifunction display."

Peter realized he should have chosen something else. No way would she miss the label running right across the center of the screen. Failing to impress her was fast becoming a possibility since most of the controls were set up so that anyone, even a green sailor like him, could use them. "It's sort of like the screen on your phone. You can control all the boat's systems from here. Electrical. Marine. So lighting, air, sound." Peter decided not to give her any other openings and quickly pointed as he named what things were. "Gauges that monitor the boat's performance, fuel level, engine temperature, like we have in our *cars*. This is a VHF radio, which we can use if there's an emergency. That's important since cell coverage is spotty out here." Peter pulled the throttle back to show her how the engines responded. "Throttle determines how hard the engines work and moves us in reverse."

Lauren nodded as if she was absorbing his impromptu boating lesson. "What's this called?" She tapped the steering wheel next to his hand, the quick brush of her skin against his more exciting than he expected.

"That is a steering wheel," Peter said carefully as he bumped her shoulder. "Your car also has one of these. It turns the boat. I hope that's the technical term."

Lauren rolled her eyes. In that moment, she might have been a college junior again, the expression was so familiar. "In official boat talk, please."

Peter laughed. "Boat talk." He cleared his throat. "Aye, matey, to impress sea dogs and scallywags alike, call that the helm. The kitchen is the galley. The bathroom is the head. They'll never know you're a landlubber."

"Well, shiver me timbers." Lauren pretended to scrawl notes furiously on her hand. "Aye, aye, Captain." When she glanced up at him, they were both laughing.

Peter shook his head and realized that it might be that they'd been on separate paths for years, but when they came back together, he and Lauren were still in sync, step for step. She might thrust with a teasing comment, but he could parry and they'd move across the floor.

Why was this so much more satisfying than his first-date conversation with Candace or any of the other women he'd done his best to impress? Lauren wasn't there to be charmed. Maybe that's why.

As she relaxed next to him, it was tempting to watch her face as she enjoyed the speed and the waves and being free of land. When he realized he was doing that instead of using all his fancy equipment to get them where he wanted to go, he put his attention to the blue water in front of them.

"If you're thirsty, I have cold drinks down in the galley," he said, already certain of how she'd react to the "suggestion." The thing about tangling with Lauren was that knowing the outcome, how she'd react, had never dampened the fun.

Lauren narrowed her eyes at him. "Are you telling me that you would like a drink? Oh, and while I'm getting that for you, I'm welcome to get one for myself?"

Of course he had been. "You must be hearing things. I'm only doing my best to be a welcoming host." He raised his eyebrows. "However, we only have room for first mates with strong initiative here on the *Hardly Working*."

Watching her absorb everything had always been one of his favorite pastimes. She blinked slowly while her brain made lightning-fast connections. "Two things," she said as her lips twitched.

Peter settled back and crossed his arms over his chest.

She held up a finger. "I'm onto you. I haven't forgotten how smooth you were at suggesting things and making me think they were my idea. I'm older now and I have a lot of training reading between the lines."

Peter nodded sagely and managed to keep a straight face. He believed her but it was hard to ignore how adorable she was with her firm, mean expression as the wind tossed her blond hair over her shoulders. Also, he was fairly sure she was still going to get him a drink when she was ready to admit defeat. "And second?"

"You named your boat *Hardly Working*." It wasn't a question and it was clearly the part that confused her. "I hope that's not about her seaworthiness as we are out on the *sea* right now. Deep water. Lots of deep water all around."

Peter shook his head. "No. That's the name she came with. It's kind of a long story. Want to hear it?"

Oh, she was struggling. She had to have gotten better at controlling the way emotions splashed across her face to win in court, but he could read the curiosity and the desire not to give him what he wanted.

"Okay. Let me get a drink first," she muttered.

Peter didn't react. "Will you grab me one, too?" He made sure his face was perfectly still.

Lauren tried a mean glare. "Yes. Sure. Absolutely. I'm a good first mate, after all."

Peter nodded solemnly and watched her

spin on her heel. She wanted to stomp away. It was almost impossible to stomp anywhere on a boat this size so she maneuvered carefully down to the galley but made sure to shoot him a final threatening stare before she ducked below.

He couldn't help the chuckle that was brushed away by the breeze as he turned back to the GPS and steered the boat. If he knew her at all, she was furiously thinking of a comeback while she was below deck.

After all this time, one thing hadn't changed. Whether it was good or bad, Peter was anxious to hear what Lauren would say next.

LAUREN WAS MUTTERING to herself as she opened all the tiny doors and hatches in the galley-slash-kitchen, but the urge to smile was strong. Peter had always been fun to spar with, mainly because he was so audaciously cheeky about the whole thing. He knew he was manipulating and he also knew that she knew his tactics, but that was no reason to back down because he would also argue his case cleverly.

When she realized her lips were twitching

with stifled amusement at his maneuvering, Lauren placed both hands on the tiny counter. "You have got to get a hold of yourself. This is not a date. He's not a cute boy that you'd like to have a crush on if you weren't obligated to *crush* his test scores. Not anymore. You're here because he wants something, and it's something you don't want to do, so…" Lauren waited for her brain to supply the rest of that sentence but nothing came. It was a difficult problem to solve. Agreeing to his request would end this back-and-forth between them. A wise woman would remind herself that he was doing what he needed to do to win her agreement, but nothing good could come out of going back into the courtroom before she was ready.

And the danger of falling for Peter Kim?

Much scarier, especially since this little adventure was strategy, a way to win her over, and he'd always excelled at that piece of their competition. She remembered most of his playbook. He was buying time, softening her, to get the answer he wanted. There was no romantic intent on his side, and if she was as smart as she'd always prided herself on being, she'd remember that. It was about winning, nothing else.

"Fine. Good. We're back to old times already, Lauren. Pep talks on not being charmed by the most charming boy in the world, I see," she muttered as she grabbed two water bottles, the box of snack crackers she'd thrown in her tote bag and the cheddar from Peter's tiny fridge.

Because she was hungry.

Not because he might be.

"That whole 'he teases you because he likes you' narrative? It's old-fashioned, out of date and should never have taken root in the first place. He teases because he enjoys it." Lauren refused to consider too closely what it meant that she enjoyed it, too.

When Lauren spotted the plates strapped into a small alcove next to the sink, she grabbed those, too, because she was not coming back down to this galley because Peter remembered something else that might be nice for *his guest* to have.

Having plates because she found them on her own initiative was one thing.

Letting Peter catch her off guard and send her back down to get them would never do.

It was the principle of the thing.

As she navigated the steps back to the cockpit, she breathed deeply of the sea air. It would be almost impossible to hold on to any irritation here. Minor ones evaporated, so when Peter glanced up at her over his sunglasses, Lauren smiled easily.

"Water, because I was thirsty." Lauren plopped down his bottle in front of him. "And some snacks in case I get hungry." She put one of the plates down on the small console next to the steering wheel and tipped out some crackers for him before offering him the cheddar package.

"Strong initiative. You might make a successful first mate yet," Peter said as he pointed across the bow of the boat. "What do you think of this spot?"

Lauren eased down next to him, shaded her eyes with one hand and rotated slowly in a half circle. "Looks like a lot of water. Surely there are fish here somewhere."

"Surely," he agreed, and tapped one of the electronic displays.

Lauren leaned closer. "Blobs. I see blobs. They're moving. Are those fish?"

Peter wrapped an arm around her shoulder

and said solemnly, "I really hope so. Otherwise, this has turned into a horror movie because something is swimming under this boat."

Lauren turned her head to roll her eyes at him and wanted to be sure he saw it, but his face was close. So close. She could see the warm gleam in his eyes. It would be so easy to lean forward and press her lips…

She jerked back. "Are we going to catch dinner?" The loud crunch of her plastic water bottle convinced her to loosen her grip while she grabbed a hold of whatever strange impulse was calculating kissing distances.

Peter's arm slowly slipped away but she couldn't face him to see what he might think about the situation. She retreated a safe distance and continued twisting her water bottle until Peter stood. "Fish don't like that noise, Duncan." He motioned her down the steps toward the platform on the back of the boat and muttered, "And neither do I." Then he knelt, lifted a hatch and pulled out two fishing rods and a large plastic box.

Lauren followed him to the platform and took the seat he folded down for her. "You'll have to teach me everything. I've never been fishing before." She'd never wanted to go fishing, either, but as she watched him open the box and poke through multicolored lures, Lauren realized she'd spent half a day without worrying about what she would do to fill her time or what kind of job she'd need to find. Fishing could have been the answer all along?

Or worrying about Peter and his reentry into her life had crowded out her other concerns.

"Teaching you what I know won't take long." Peter offered her a lure. It was bright pink with feathery pieces that blew in the breeze. It was also as big as her hand. If she managed to hook a fish that would go for a meal that size, would she be able to get it on the boat? "Hold the rod and I'll put on the lure." He fiddled with the end where she assumed the hook would be. Then he did the same with his rod. His was a darker purple but had the same feathery pieces. After he effortlessly pulled the rod back and flicked it forward, the lure landed in the water with a plop. "Cast it into the water." When he turned to smile at her, Lauren realized the power of his attention when focused on her. She'd been focused on the lure and on absorbing his every move so that she could replicate it and avoid looking like a fool.

But while he watched her, the best she could manage was an awkward swing that almost caught her water bottle and an alley-oop toss into the low rolling waves. Visibly cringing at not excelling would never do. She couldn't let him know she knew she was not a natural-born angler, so she said, "May need some practice."

He shrugged. "Sure. Don't we all." With that he easily wiped away her awkwardness.

Then he slipped his rod into a silver holder on the rail next to him. "We let the rod holder do the hard work while we watch the end of the rod. If it moves, we reel in the lure. Maybe there's a fish on the end, maybe there isn't. This is how we fish." Peter stretched his legs out and then reclined the seat to fold his arms above his head. "You can pick the music if you like. Or no music is fine, too."

His attitude showed that he could wait all day long right there and be happy to do so.

Lauren expected more work, more technique, something to do to make sure she was successful in landing a fish. Did fish prefer a certain kind of music? Shouldn't he already know these things?

"That's it? That's all you know about fishing?" Lauren frowned as she slipped her rod into the holder.

"So far, yes." Peter sighed happily. "Isn't this the perfect way to spend a day?"

"The entire day?" Lauren asked doubtfully. The to-do list of things she should be accomplishing with this much free time began to take over her brain.

Lauren wanted to ask for more steps to fish successfully or volunteer for busywork that she could do while she watched for the end of her rod to move. Didn't boats have barnacles that needed to be scrubbed or lines to unknot or something? Peter held up a hand. "Stop making lists, Duncan. That stuff stays on dry land."

Lauren did her best to mimic his pose. She kicked off her sandals and stretched out her legs to wiggle her toes in the breeze. This should be comfortable. He seemed so relaxed. When she realized she was staring at the end of her rod as if it meant life or death, she said, "Tell me about the *Hardly Working* and how you came to own her."

She needed a distraction that didn't involve her fishing rod or Peter Kim. Neither was relaxing.

"Did you see that?" He pointed quickly, excitement in his voice. "I think it's a—"

Before he could finish, Lauren saw a dolphin make a low leap out of the water. Two more followed, but they were moving away quickly. "Dolphins! Do you see dolphins every time?" When she heard the excitement in her own voice, it was like that of a five-year-old in a toy store. Lauren forced herself to settle back in her chair slowly. She should be cooler about this, shouldn't she?

Peter was grinning. She knew it; she didn't look. She didn't have to. She could feel his amusement.

"There's always something to get excited about out here. Never gets old," Peter said. He wasn't interested in playing it cool, and it made sense. That was why he made the escape to his boat when he could and why she'd been unable to say no to his offer to bring her even though she understood why he was doing it. This day was special. Seeing those dolphins didn't happen all the time or for everyone lucky enough to be out on the water, and there was every reason to be excited about being in the right place at the right time.

Playing it cool around Peter might be sound strategy, but not even Lauren could blame herself for letting her game face slip under these circumstances.

Lauren nodded maturely. "Your story, please."

"Okay," he drawled, "well, you know how some people like to shop real estate listings for homes they can never afford or in places they'll never move to?"

At that, Lauren faced him. "No." People didn't do that, did they? Her last investigation of real estate online had been depressing. The fees she'd have to charge to keep an office open and the lights on if she decided to go out on her own were enough to stop that plan in its tracks. Shouldering that responsibility would bury her no matter what kinds of cases being her own boss would allow her to take. "Real estate for fun?" She didn't get it.

He blinked slowly at her answer before sighing. "You have so much to learn." He reached over to straighten the rod that hadn't moved in its holder. "Some people—" he shot her a side-eye "—escape the real world by imagining life in outrageously expensive real estate. Thanks to the power of the World Wide Web, homes in big cities and small towns and your hometown and your last vacation spot are easily searchable. They all have photos. That makes it easy to snoop inside and imagine an alternate universe where you can afford that move or that house. You also get to see some truly weird and sometimes cool decorating." He pressed a hand to his chest. "I preferred boat shopping as my escape. When the pressures of the job were overwhelming, I could take fifteen minutes out, pull up listings on my phone and daydream about owning one."

Lauren studied his profile. This time he didn't face her. Would he answer if she asked more about the stresses of his job?

"I should have tried that instead of quitting," Lauren said softly.

He chuckled. "Yeah, I'm not sure it's strong enough to stand up to the public defender's office, but military intelligence…" He sighed. "Are you going to make the joke here?"

Lauren frowned. Was this the time for a joke? Did she have one?

"About military intelligence being an oxymoron," he said as if he'd heard it a million times before and this was her one shot to get it out. "Like jumbo shrimp."

"Seems like that would get old fast." Lauren cleared her throat. "I'll skip it if you can refrain from any of the myriad of 'how many lawyers does it take' options out there."

He sighed. "I've never heard a good lawyer joke. Since I'm going to be one someday, I should start building up a tolerance for those, too."

Lauren pretended to think hard. "The only one I can remember is 'old lawyers never die, they just lose their appeal.'"

He winced. "I'm sorry that one stuck with you. It's bad." Then he nudged his sunglasses down. "Not that either one of the lawyers on this boat have to worry about losing any appeal." Then he gave her a broad wink that made her giggle. Out loud. She literally giggled.

She was in so much trouble.

"So I understand how you came to own a boat. Found the right deal? Is that how you and the *Hardly Working* teamed up?" Lauren asked, determined to get them back on track.

At that point, he did turn toward her. "No, I found the right person. The old guy who listed her likes to renovate and resell boats. He buys wrecks and rebuilds them as a hobby. Part of the ad was about her history. She'd been recovered as part of an estate sale. The previous owner had died without leaving instructions for her. Air force like me. Career military. He bought her as soon as he retired." He patted the railing. "If you trust in signs from the universe, it was all right there. Frank, the guy who sold it to me, was more than happy to include the fees to hold it long enough for me to get back to Miami. Even offered to rename her, but it was meant to be. It's my goal in a nutshell—hardly working, just living every day as I want, possibly on a boat."

Lauren watched the waves ripple against the boat and wondered whether she should say the cynical thought that popped into her head. What if Frank had told Peter the story he needed to hear to make the sale? Was any of it true?

"I can hear your thoughts, Duncan," he drawled, "and the truth is that it doesn't matter. True or not true, Frank and his boat were exactly what I needed to make it back to Miami in one piece."

She smiled. They had both taken knowing their enemies to heart in college. Apparently he really did remember her. "I'm glad you made it back in one piece, and I can tell she makes you happy. That's the important part."

Peter grunted.

When her amusement faded, she decided to press her luck. "Tell me about the job."

He grimaced. "You think the biggest danger in military service is battle, and it is, the life-and-death part. I didn't see much of that, but the day-to-day of intelligence…" He turned his face toward the sun. "On the one hand, you're buried with information, phone calls, emails, tiny bits and bytes of so many lives that don't add up to much, not until you can find the pattern. Then, on the other hand, you've got the resources of the United States military, governments, embassies, civilians living and working in the country…the safety, the costs, the lives, all hinging on how well you sift through data and find good information and it just…" He stared off at the horizon. "To be in absolutely no danger but running on adrenaline more often than not… It's hard to explain."

"I imagine your brain rebels at the volume and the everyday normalcy while also battling the pressure of 'what if,' and I can see how that tension needs a break, a boat break," Lauren said as she smiled at him.

"I don't talk about it much because so many people don't understand that, the pressure. No one is shooting at me." He scrubbed his hand through his hair. "What is there to worry about, right? I sat at a desk, stared at monitors, drafted reports, translated calls. Mundane life, you know?"

"But there are still people in the line of fire, and they're depending on you," Lauren said softly. "I get that. I do. I was never under threat of jail time or worse, but people trusted me to help them, to save them or someone they loved. The job was about juggling resources to do the most good overall, but how do I tell that to the woman who would lose her kid with any kind of conviction? 'I'm sorry that this will go on your record and endanger custody of your children, but they're offering time served and that's good enough for me. Aren't you happy you won't go to jail?' Low stakes in the overall scheme of things, but shattering her world. Minute details that add up to so much pressure over time."

Lauren closed her eyes, felt the waves and the lurch of the boat, and immediately opened them. Getting seasick would put an end to this happy escape.

"If it makes you feel any better, I understand needing to walk away," Peter said as he gripped her shoulder. "Yes, you're the best. I was good at my job, but I was never perfect. Living with those misses made getting back up again harder every day. Retiring was one of those decisions that I struggled with because… I guess I always believed I could do the job well so I should do it or who would do it if I didn't?"

"What made you decide it was time to go?" Lauren asked, surprised that she understood him this well. Maybe there was more to his story that could help her.

"It's hard to describe." Peter clamped his hands together. "Phone calls with my parents and my sister and my nephew reminded me that there was this other world that was going on without me. I was missing it. I worked with some good people who were still battling, and I had this sensation that I was losing something I couldn't get back." He met her stare. "Eventually, we step out of the ring and hope we can put ourselves back together."

When their eyes were locked like that and he was speaking from the heart about his experience, Lauren knew that he understood her. They had connected on this point, on two very different jobs with unique stresses and worlds apart, but their personalities, their commitment to being the best and doing everything they could was the same.

"Is there any chance you're taking that knowledge into criminal law after you graduate?" she asked. It would be easier to let go if she could depend on someone as smart and wily as Peter to step up.

"Estate planning. Low pressure. Free time. That's the plan," he said.

"I have a hard time picturing you mediating family feuds over the heirlooms, Peter." Lauren pointed. "On the other hand, I have no trouble at all imagining you in a sharp suit, marching up and down in front of a jury, and yelling 'I object!'"

"Really, how often do you get to object like

that?" Peter asked skeptically. "That's only on television."

Lauren refused to answer that she had never once slapped the table and yelled anything dramatic in a courtroom. Peter could get away with it even if she couldn't.

"How did you pick criminal law in the first place?" he asked.

Lauren had two answers for this question. The first, the cocktail party answer, was that she'd become a lawyer because she trusted in the justice system. It would be easy enough to trot out here and Peter would let her.

This close, she could see some of the changes in Peter Kim's face. His eyes were the same, reflecting his sharp intelligence and usually gleaming with laughter, but the rest of him bore the signs of years spent fighting for others. Maturity. Fatigue. Worry. And yet he had the energy to keep getting up.

Lauren wanted to say…something, but she couldn't put her emotions into words.

Which was just as well.

That only left her with the truth. "My father was arrested for armed robbery when I was in high school." And for smaller crimes before that and since, but she didn't have to tell the whole truth. "He had court-appointed attorneys who did fine, but young Lauren believed she might have done more because she loved him."

Usually, speaking the truth led to awkward silence and a stilted conversational recovery of some sort, but Peter wrapped his hand around her shoulder and squeezed. He didn't know the right words because there were none, but it meant a lot that he didn't fumble around and toss out a cliché that did nothing to reassure or comfort.

Lauren wasn't sure how to tell him that, not without slipping into a shaky voice and the threat of tears. At some point, that hurt would fade, but she was still waiting, decades later.

Then, out of the corner of her eye, she saw the tip of her rod bend sharply. "Did you see that?"

Peter frowned as if that wasn't what he expected from her. She knew the feeling. "What?"

"My rod. It moved!" She jumped up to grab the rod. "Help me reel in this fish!"

CHAPTER SIX

PETER WATCHED LAUREN bounce up and down, motioning excitedly at her fishing rod. It took a beat longer than he liked to check back into reality. One second, he'd been staring into Lauren's eyes, connecting with her on a level that could only be improved one way: with a kiss. He'd never heard about her father when they were at Sawgrass and he never would have guessed she'd experienced what had to have been traumatic. Young Lauren had been tough and determined, even invulnerable.

Or so he'd thought.

As a kid, he'd been guilty of believing everyone had been as comfortable as he was. His family had it easy: two jobs, two cars, two kids. Since then, he'd seen more of the world and understood his good luck.

Lauren had pushed herself through college and law school to do something important with it all, so it made perfect sense that she'd been driving herself to help more and do more for her clients and their families. His goals? As a kid, he wanted to make money. Sometime between his high school graduation and his college graduation, he'd learned that there were other reasons to work, that the career he chose could change who he was, and he'd wanted to be more. The air force had given him that, but the lesson hadn't been without costs.

He admired what Lauren accomplished. She'd understood why her work mattered from the beginning.

But how could he say any of that to her? His brain was too slow to process the right words.

Then she was gone and yelling and jumping up and down.

Lauren grabbed his arm. "Peter, help me! I don't know what to do!" She wrestled the rod out of the holder, a grimace contorting her face. The rod whipped down, pressing Peter into action.

"Sorry, okay," Peter said as he wrapped his arms around her. Her back immediately settled against his chest as he gripped the handle between her fingers. "Hold tight. We wait for the fish to stop fighting. Keep the tip of the rod up."

Lauren relaxed, but the fish fought a few moments longer. Peter did his best to focus on the rod, not the perfection of holding her, how their bodies fit together as if they'd been made to stand there like that. "Now, pull the rod back, then tilt down and turn the reel." Peter guided her arms and waited for her to follow his direction. "And we repeat until we lose the fish or…"

"We do not lose this fish," Lauren muttered through clenched teeth.

Peter laughed as he braced her and added his strength to the up-and-down motions. No matter what happened, he admired the spirit. No way would he have imagined Lauren catching anything with his spotty teaching, indifferent fishing techniques and whatever lures he'd put out, but it made perfect sense. She never had been one to back down from a fight, not even one she couldn't win.

When the fish cleared the water, Lauren yelled in triumph. "I don't know what that is, but it's the most beautiful fish ever."

Peter had to scramble to grab the net to pull it onto the boat. When he had the fish on the deck, Lauren jumped up and down until the boat lurched on the waves. "What is it? What is it?"

The golden gleam along the fish's scales made it easy to identify. "Congratulations on catching your first amberjack." He bent to cut the hook out of the fish's mouth. "Want to hold it?" He wished he had brought his phone this time. Having a souvenir of this moment would be amazing.

"Yes," she shouted, but she scrambled across the deck and back up to the cockpit. "Let me get my phone! I want a picture of this!"

Peter shook his head while he waited. When she bounded back down on the swim platform, he said, "The rule is no phone, Duncan. I thought that was clear. That is how we do this correctly."

"I know, but I can't go anywhere without a phone. I promise, I haven't thought of it once until now." Her voice was a happy high-pitched squeal and she was nearly vibrating with excitement. "Show me how to hold this baby and then take my picture. Now. Hurry. Now!"

Was she going to hold the wet, slimy fish?

A live fish? A squirming, pretty good-sized amberjack?

He carefully handed the amberjack over, ready to make a quick grab if there was any yelling or squeamishness. Instead, Lauren shoved the phone into his shorts pocket before taking control of the fish, cradling it lovingly against her chest.

"Hurry. Get the photo. Come on, Peter." Her lips were twisted in a smile, but each flip of the fish made her twitch, too.

He was laughing as he pulled out her phone and quickly opened the camera. "Smile."

Her proud grin was beautiful, but he had to move fast. The fish jerked, Lauren made a choked squeak, and the moment was over. "What do I do with it now?"

Peter grimaced. "If I'd known you were going to catch something, we would have already discussed this, but I'm shocked and impressed at your catch."

A scowl flitted across her face. "You didn't think I could do it?"

He crossed his arms over his chest and watched her subdue the flopping fish. "I never catch anything."

Her eyebrows shot up.

"I mean, that's how I prefer it. I'm not about cleaning fish, you know?" Peter was grossed out by the idea. "But if you are, I have a well. We'll drop it in. Just don't expect me to help. I order my fish from restaurants and let professionals handle all the messy prep."

He wasn't sure she was following him at first, but eventually she said, "You come out here to fish all the time." The fish jerked, inching closer to freedom.

He nodded.

"But you don't catch any fish."

He nodded again.

"But I caught one."

He shrugged.

"I don't want to kill this fish or clean it!" she said loudly.

Relieved, Peter pulled up the phone again, switched the camera to video and motioned with his head to the swim platform. "Then let that beauty go."

Her face was a wild mixture of emotion. Regret. Irritation. Relief? Then she motioned with her chin at the phone. "Make sure you get this. I want proof that I'm better at fishing than you are."

Peter chuckled as he watched her press her

lips to the fish and then fling it back into the water, where it immediately disappeared under the waves. The fella was now on his way to tell his friends in the amberjack school about the weird adventure he'd been on and how it ended with a kiss.

That was one amazing fish story, for sure.

"Let me see." Lauren held her hand out to take the phone as a text message flashed on the screen.

Did you block my calls? We need to talk about when you're coming back to work.

Peter bent closer to Lauren and sniffed loudly. "You're a little…fishy. You sure you want this back right now?" He ran his thumb over the screen to wipe the message away as Lauren narrowed her eyes.

"After I go to the bathroom and wash my hands, I want to see," she muttered as she moved toward the galley.

"A real first mate would call it the head," Peter called, and grinned as her glare intensified. He was almost certain her lips were twitching, too. There was something about her expression that convinced him she was enjoying herself.

Which might be ruined when she found out she'd missed three calls, he thought.

Apparently, the cell service satellites were strong and powerful that day. He quickly texted himself the picture of Lauren and her first catch. It was something he didn't want to forget.

"I am de-fished," Lauren announced as she held her hands up in front of Peter's nose, "although the facilities here lean more toward industrial-strength bleach than rosy fragrances."

"Upgrading the amenities, that's the first mate's responsibility." Peter pressed his lips to her palm and watched her eyebrows shoot up before she curled her hands defensively against her chest.

That answered that. He was not going to be getting a kiss anytime soon.

Before she could say anything else, Peter held out her phone to her. "The problem with ignoring the rules, the most important of all being leaving the phone at home, is that the magic of the *Hardly Working* fails when it's interrupted by your boss's phone calls or multiple texts." He tilted his head to the side. "Even if he has to work for it by using someone else's phone."

Lauren frowned. There were several different angry directions she could go in if she wanted to.

He could picture her demanding to know who he thought he was and why he believed he could tell her to leave her phone anywhere.

Or why he was reading her messages.

Or how he expected the lecture to work out in his favor.

Or when had they become kissing friends or friends at all, for that matter.

It was easy enough to come up with a counterargument for all but that last point.

Lauren snatched her phone and quickly scanned the texts. "My phone was secure in my bag, Peter. It wasn't bothering me, nor was anyone else, so I'd say we accomplished the goal of the *Hardly Working*." She pulled up the video and bit her lip as she watched it. Her delight was easy to see. "Also, I caught a fish. You didn't. And I have the proof."

There was also an overwhelming temptation to bend down and press a real kiss against her curving, happy smile. When she looked up, Peter realized his stare must have grown intense. She rolled her eyes. "Let it go. Who cares about the messages? I'll block that number, too. Talk to me about how hard it is to become a professional amberjack fisherman." She frowned. "Fisherperson?"

The breeze caught a lock of hair and whipped it across her lips. What would she do if he smoothed it back?

She waved a hand slowly in front of his face. How long had he been staring at her lips?

"Angler? That seems gender neutral." Peter ticked the steps off on his finger. "Step one has to be learning how to bait your own hook. Step two could be getting a boat."

"Or I could borrow one from a friend." She tapped his shoulder in case he had any doubt whom she had in mind.

So, she had called him a *friend*. Did that put him in his place or was it a step up from where she'd had him slotted before this boat trip?

"Step three…" He pretended to think. "I guess that's it. Step three is profit. Although it is only the one fish. Still, we found your next career!"

Lauren stared down at the picture of her proudly holding her catch. "At some point, I'll have to figure out how to keep the fish instead of throwing it back in." Her eyes darted to his, warm happiness and something else reflected there. "That seems critical to the 'profit' piece of the equation."

As waves buffeted the boat, Peter understood that he was enjoying himself more in that moment there with her than with any other woman in…a long time. What did that mean?

And more importantly, what should he do about it?

"I could hire a first mate to take care of that part for me." She pretended to type. "'Wanted—boat-haver who likes to bait hooks and clean fish. Must also choose pleasing toiletries for the bathroom and work for free.'"

Pete laughed. "Or we could keep looking for your next career. The problem with turning something you love into the thing that pays the bills is that you never love it quite as much again. I'd hate to see that happen to you and all the amberjacks in your future."

"Good advice," Lauren said as she strolled

toward the cockpit. "I'll put this problematic phone away now that I'm satisfied you captured me and my fish in all our glory." Her lips were curved as she sat down next to him. "I like the no-phone rule and I get the reason why. It's like this invisible string that ties me to all my problems, but I have you. I haven't considered those one time today, not since I forced myself to climb out of my car at the marina."

Peter pulled her rod out of the holder to check the lure and hook before offering it to her. "Try casting again for the practice. Do not catch a fish this time. My heart can't handle that twice in one day."

Her chuckle lifted on the breeze and floated back to him. Sweet.

This time, she was a fraction less awkward. Hitting the pro-fishing circuit was a long way away.

When they'd settled in their spots again, Peter asked, "Why did you say *force*? You didn't want to come out with me today?" He propped his feet up, fully content with his life and every decision that had led him to this spot.

She sighed. "This probably never happens to you. I can't imagine suave, charming Peter Kim experiencing any social anxiety, but I was afraid we'd have tense silence and strained, albeit polite conversation. I had forgotten that you are never polite." She stuck her tongue out when he glanced over, ready to argue. "Kidding. You know what I mean. We don't know each other well, haven't talked in years. It was hard to imagine what we'd have in common."

Peter nodded. "Makes sense." He wasn't going to admit that he'd had the same concerns. That had everything to do with being called "suave" and "charming" because that felt too good to dismiss. He wished he could go back and tell sixteen-year-old Peter that his time was coming in just…a few short decades, when an amazing woman would call him suave and charming. "We never had trouble talking before."

"We were always ready to argue before. Not the same thing." Lauren copied his pose and crossed her hands over her stomach. "I also never expected that the Peter Kim, the boy who had to be the top, the best, the first in every class and assignment would ever accept being less than that at anything, even fishing."

"I like to win. Always have." Peter studied the clouds gathering on the horizon as he considered that. "But I have learned that not everything has a winning side and a losing side. There's so much gray in the middle. That might be the difference. I'm good at the pieces of fishing that I like and I don't do the parts I don't like. To me, that's winning." He turned to meet her stare. "I'm the best and first at picking battles I will win."

She sat up. "Teach me your ways."

He stretched his arms widely, thoroughly satisfied with how the day was shaping up. "Okay, the next thing is to decide whether to swim, nap or read." He pointed at her. "Today, I'm not even doing that. It'll be guest's choice. Like I said, I have extra clothes if you didn't bring a suit."

Lauren peered over the side of the boat. "My friend Jack is long gone, but there are other fish down there. Gigantic fish. You showed me the blobs, remember?" When she glanced at him, he could read the "no way, no how" all over her face.

"Yes, and you were holding one in your

hands," Peter said slowly. Was he missing something? "You pressed your lips to Jack and his gross scales, remember?"

"In the boat, I have the advantage." Lauren pointed. "Out there? I'm at their mercy, and I can't even see them coming." She shook her head. "You swim. I'll nap. We can divide duties and accomplish twice as much."

Every bit of her body language screamed he'd have to toss her overboard for her to end up in the water, so that made things easier. "Okay, we can read while we check the rods that will definitely not catch any more fish today. I have a little library, just my favorites, stored under the banquette." He pulled his current book out of the small compartment next to his seat and sighed happily.

Her laughter distracted him. "What?"

"That sigh. I never would have guessed you were so...domesticated." Lauren eased past him to check out his collection of titles. "Although, that quality doesn't quite match having *extra* women's swimsuits on board, just in case. On the one hand, nerd who speaks my language. On the other?" She hummed as she considered the right word. "Playboy on a cruiser?"

Peter wanted to catch her expression, but she was staring at his books. When she finally picked one and returned to her seat with her gigantic straw hat in place against the sun, he held out his hand to see what she'd chosen. Spy thriller and one of his favorite rereads. Interesting. As he handed it back, he confessed, "I never said they were women's suits. I have extra trunks, T-shirts, that kind of thing. I've never had a woman on my precious *Hardly Working*." He raised an eyebrow at her. "You're the first."

Her mouth dropped open. "What?"

"It's my place. My buddy Marcus comes out now and then, but I like to spend time here, being quiet." Peter sniffed. "Besides, women are bad luck on boats. Ask any sailor."

This time she rolled her eyes. "One of those all-important superstitions, I guess."

"Right. They cause unrest in the crew, so the fewer women, the better. That's the way I've always heard it," Peter joked.

"Unrest. In the crew," she repeated slowly. "Of two. And one of them, the first mate, is me. A woman." She motioned slowly at his lounging position. "This is not the picture of unrest."

She had him there. "You are surprisingly entertaining and a calming influence, Duncan, a combo I never imagined I'd find in one person."

That stopped her in her tracks. The color in her cheeks might be from the heat or too much sun, but he'd bet that it was embarrassment. He also hoped there was some pleasure, too. He meant it as a compliment.

"As long as I promise not to catch any more fish, or at least not to ask you to clean any of them," she said and flashed him a grin before she opened the cover on his paperback.

"And return that book when you're done."

"I will. You don't let me sleep through more than twenty minutes of my time out here with you. On the *water*."

He laughed. "And since you tossed back our only catch, I'd suggest we stop at the Plank and Anchor on the way home. Are you feeling adventurous?"

The way she instantly straightened pleased him.

It was as if she was ready to step up next to him and take on anything.

As if the two of them were a team and she'd back his play, no matter what.

Or she was prepared to give anything new a try as long as they were together.

That last part might be a dream.

Or it might describe what he was feeling. It was impossible to imagine enjoying his beautiful boat more than he had today with Lauren. When he was on land and had the time to turn over problems in his mind, he would take a hard look at why he'd connected with her rather than any of the first dates he'd had like Candace. Their backgrounds were as dissimilar as his and Candace's, but there was something else, something that was a part of them, that was very much the same.

The fact that he couldn't figure it out in his safe, sweet boat of no worries convinced him that she'd find it hard to do, too.

"I will follow your lead," Lauren said, her beautiful smile flashing under the brim of her enormous hat. "I'm ready for my next adventure."

Lauren was a match for that side of himself he was just getting to know.

What should he do about that?

CHAPTER SEVEN

THE PLANK AND ANCHOR. It was a name that conjured up visions of a pirate-themed chain restaurant with its own birthday song and T-shirts for sale, or perhaps a run-down joint that served whatever the seafaring equivalent of a greasy diner might be. The food would be grilled hot and delicious. The floor would be dark and slightly sticky. In Lauren's mind, that version of the Plank and Anchor would definitely have a pool table, a jukebox and a regular at one end of the bar.

Instead, Peter maneuvered the boat carefully into what looked like a drive-in for any sort of water transportation.

It was also a mash-up of both scenarios, themed-restaurant experience and hole-in-the-wall atmosphere.

Lauren was immediately in love.

Pulsing pink neon trim outlined the roofline and the order windows. Strings of multicolored lights stretched from the building to the end of the docks, forming a semicircle in front. Music blared from speakers, mostly classic rock. Worn wood contributed to the dilapidated decor, but that might have been part of the plan. The sign they passed as they were docking advertised "Craft Brews on Tap." Lauren couldn't see a pool table, but there were two volleyball courts in use, complete with hot pink volleyballs being served.

Peter maneuvered close to the end of the center dock and tossed a line to a guy wearing black swim trunks with a ragged edge and nothing else to perfectly display the tattoo sleeve on his right arm. The pinup model on his biceps was easy to make out, but everything else blended together.

After the *Hardly Working* was secured to the cleats, the man said, "Ahoy, there, Cookie's in the galley today. What'll it be?"

Delighted and confused, Lauren turned to Peter. "Is *this* a pirate restaurant?"

The guy immediately shushed her loudly and made the keep-it-down motion. "Scalawags abound 'round these parts. Never catch their attention. They'll steal your booty."

Then he pulled up a tablet. "Can I get you folks two specials?"

Peter nodded. "And some of Cookie's finest ale, please."

"Dark or light?" He bent forward as if he had a secret to share. "Better go with light unless you have a day or two to recover from the headache."

"Light, then." Peter tapped Lauren's arm. "My lady here has made a fine catch."

"I'll need some proof," the pirate said with a suspicious stare.

At first, Lauren's brain stuttered at hearing Peter call her "my lady," but she soon realized it was part of the pirate patter. Then she wondered why he would brag about her skill to a stranger, but the even bigger question was why the waiter would pretend to be interested.

Still confused, and even more delighted, Lauren said, "I have proof!" Then she scrambled to the cockpit to grab her phone. She was out of breath when she skidded to a stop next to Peter, who braced her with one hand to keep her from bumping into the railing. She grinned at him as she waved the phone with the fish photo at their pirate-slash-waiter. What was the equivalent of a carhop? A boat hop?

The pirate bent to peer closely at her phone. "Aye, that's a fine amberjack. I'll ask Cookie to toss in the boon he reserves for the finest treasures." He pointed at the large clock in the center of the sundial of docks. The hands were pink, and a giant squid was perched on top with one arm waving a hat. "Cookie's running about twenty minutes now. Swab yer deck while you wait."

Then he marched down the dock to where another boat was slowly approaching.

"We eat on the boat? Somehow food comes out to us?" Lauren asked as she watched Peter assemble a table that fit perfectly between the cockpit and the swim platform. "The special is food, right?" And what was the boon? Light ale was beer, wasn't it? Did pirates understand the difference between light and dark beer? Didn't they prefer rum? "I have so many questions!"

Peter's grin was huge as he slid onto the banquette on the opposite side of the table. "I have no idea how this mash-up of themes came to be, but it's sort of as if pirates took over a fifties drive-in and all the cars are boats. You can only order the special, which is usually some kind of combination of fish, fries, slaw and more hush puppies than any family of four should ever eat. The owner is a brewmaster who likes to tinker, so there are always two choices of beer, but there's no way to know what they are. They will serve sodas, but no other alcoholic beverages, so it's not a bar exactly." He stretched his arms across the back of the cushion. "You can reserve the volleyball court for your own use or join a pickup game. In twenty minutes or so, another pirate will deliver our glorious food in a cardboard box. This place is not about fine dining. In fact, there are no chairs, even if we wanted to go up to the window."

Lauren clasped her hands in front of her, the thrill of experiencing such a weird place too much to contain. "I love it. I love it so much."

"I'm glad." Peter wrapped his hand around her clenched fingers and wiggled to convince her to loosen them. "I wasn't sure you'd be okay with anything this…out there, but the food is good. The beer is usually, too. And the treat they give you for showing off your catch of the day…" He made the chef's kiss motion.

"What is it?" Lauren asked breathlessly, uncertain if she could stand the surprise.

"You'll have to wait and see, but I hope you like chocolate." He raised his eyebrows.

"I do. I really do love chocolate." Lauren had to laugh when she heard how breathless her voice was. Chocolate was a blessing and her favorite guilty pleasure, but that tone was about miracles and wonders.

"During the busier summer months, you can barely get close to this place. They run a second operation in a cove not too far away, where they have this huge screen set up. Staff on a boat deliver to all the boats that show up to watch the movie, selling boxes and ale as they go." One side of Peter's mouth curled and Lauren knew she was gaping in wonder again. "Maybe we'll come back and try that."

She was nodding enthusiastically before she realized what he was saying and what she was agreeing to.

That this day wasn't going to be the last time they went out together on his boat.

It wasn't a one-shot deal if they were making plans for the future, was it?

It would be easy enough to let this drop. He'd forget the offer soon enough.

But she wanted to do that and she definitely wanted another chance to spend time on Peter's boat.

With Peter.

"I'd like that," she said before she could second-guess the decision. Most of the time, she preferred to play it safe, especially in relationships. If she never showed all her cards, no one could call her a liar when she said she understood if friends or dates got tired of waiting for her schedule to open up or quiet down to leave room for them.

If no one got close, she didn't have to deal with her father's story and the messy emotions that some holidays stirred up. Pretending that she was unaffected when things fell apart made it all easier to handle.

But she wanted this too much to pretend she didn't.

"Me, too," Peter said softly, a small frown wrinkling his forehead. "This surprises me. Your enthusiasm over catching that amberjack and this place..." He shook his head. "I love it. Watching *you* love it makes me happy."

Lauren wanted to put them back on firm

ground. This was dangerous territory, but the words wouldn't come.

The arrival of another pirate, this one wearing a patch shoved up on his forehead, saved her from any awkwardness. She realized the delivery box that Peter had mentioned earlier was decorated like… It was too much. "You didn't tell me it was a treasure chest," she squealed before she covered her mouth in embarrassment and delight.

When had she ever had such a silly, amazing dinner? Never!

Peter was chortling when he accepted the delivery. The pirate saluted with a fake hook for a hand and then trotted away.

"Best criminal defense attorney in the metropolis of Miami. Annoyingly smart, strategic and clever whenever called for." Peter slid the box on the table. "I assumed you'd be all about fine dining. Restaurants with a grand view of the ocean or sparkling city lights." He shrugged. "Tickets to the ballet. I don't know. Something like that is what I expected. The last time I heard that high-pitched noise you made was…" He stared off in the distance as if he were struggling to remember.

Lauren pressed closer to the box, desperate to find out what other surprises might be inside. "Boring Lauren Duncan would totally sneer at this place, wouldn't she? Not really. She didn't have time for either high society or theme restaurants, but vacation Lauren is fully into every single minute of this experience." She waved a hand to move him along. "Open the chest. Hurry."

Peter met her stare across the box. "I like both Laurens, but I will never forget seeing you like this. I'm glad I talked you into it."

She wanted to look down, look away, let the moment pass. Instead, determined to try something new, she said softly, "Me, too."

Peter smiled before he turned the tab on the front of the box and lifted the lid. Lauren saw baskets of fish, fries and hush puppies, a bag of condiments, a container of slaw and a smaller box that shined like gold. "Catch of the Day" was stamped across the front.

"Can I open that?" Lauren asked, almost hopping in her seat. She should eat dinner while it was warm, but she needed to know what she'd won by catching her first fish.

Peter lifted it out and set it in front of her. "No rules on the *Hardly Working*," Peter said before muttering, "except leaving the phone at home, but I guess that one was meant to be broken."

Lauren nodded and carefully lifted the top of the box to reveal...

"Molten chocolate lava cake," she said breathlessly, "with whipped cream." It was perfection. She reached for one of the plastic forks but Peter stopped her. "Before you dive in, make sure you see what shape it's in."

Lauren frowned as she dug her phone out. "Better, I'll take a picture. I don't want to forget this." After she took the photo, she frowned down at the cake. "Is it a bird?"

"It's a pirate's bird, a parrot," Peter said as he pointed out the beak.

When her eyes snapped up to meet his, Lauren knew they were wide. "I love this place. You have to bring me back."

His loud chuckles didn't stop her from cutting into the parrot for one delicious bite of the cake. It was dark, sweet, warm and absolutely perfect. She pointed her fork at him. "If you don't catch fish, you don't get the treat. Lucky for you, I'm generous enough to share."

Peter popped a fry into his mouth before he pointed back at her. "It's free with a catch of the day, but I'm a rich boat owner, so I bought my own piece of parrot perfection on my first visit. I go for the gusto always."

Lauren giggled as she chose a hush puppy out of the basket and bit into it. "I believe it, Peter Kim. You have always been filled with gusto. I'm glad you showed up on my front step."

He pretended to bow. "Some things are meant to be."

Their conversation died down as they did their best to eat every bit of the Plank and Anchor's special of the day. By the time they'd split the chocolate cake, Lauren was full, sleepy and satisfied with how she'd spent her day.

"Sun's setting. I better get us back to the marina," Peter said after he'd gathered up their trash and stowed it in the galley. "Come sit with me." The pirate on the dock untied the lines and they were ready to sail home.

Lauren scooted onto the seat next to his in the cockpit and watched as he went through the motions of easing the boat away from the dock and into open water. The trip back to the Cutler Bay Marina took longer because Peter was clearly in no rush. The sun was slowly dropping toward the horizon by the time he carefully slipped *Hardly Working* into its spot. An easy silence had settled between them that Lauren hesitated to break.

She wasn't quite ready to wake up from the dream.

"The next time we do this, I'll give you first mate lessons, let you drive, for instance. What do you think of that?" Peter asked, his voice hushed in the quiet around them.

"I'd like that, Captain," Lauren said in the same tone. After she'd gathered her things and he'd secured everything on the boat, Peter stepped onto the dock and offered her his hand. Lauren slipped hers inside and realized how right it felt to accept his help, to rely on his experience and guidance all day long.

He tangled his fingers through hers instead of letting them slip away and she held on tight.

They walked slowly back toward the marina parking lot as the darkness grew. Night sounds were a nice backdrop.

"I didn't worry about my job once today," Lauren said. "You kept your end of the bargain."

She waited for him to press her for an answer on his nephew's case. What would it hurt to take it on? She had the time.

"You can't decide yet. This was only your first visit." He shoved his hands in his pockets. The gleam in his eyes almost convinced her that he knew she was going to agree to help his family, but he wanted to…spend more time together?

"I can't think of anything else in this world that could entertain me as well as a day on your boat and dinner at the Plank and Anchor. You set the bar too high." Lauren held her hand out for the tote bag he'd insisted on carrying for her.

"That sounds like a dare," he drawled. "Don't you remember what happened when you insisted I couldn't beat your score on that presentation we had to do about a Florida historical figure who deserved a statue in the Capitol?"

"Oh, I remember. I had never even heard of Benjamin Green. No one had," Lauren answered, amused at how proud of himself he still was, years later.

"The inventor of sunscreen? Right here in Miami? Think of what a difference he made to tourism and even health care, and not only here, but everywhere the sun shines." Peter rocked back on his heels, a picture of glee and satisfaction.

"It didn't hurt that you came with a surf-board and dressed in swim trunks," Lauren added. "I did this whole multimedia presentation on Dr. John Gorrie, who created air-conditioning. I had music. Animation. It was air-conditioning, Peter." She waited for him to acknowledge the lifesaving properties of air-conditioning. "You dressed for the beach."

"But you remember it, don't you?" Peter bent closer to her, the teasing gleam in his eyes tempting her to grin back at him.

She nodded. "Yeah, you pulled out all the stops to win. I remember."

He sighed as if content. "It's always nice to know I left an impression on a beautiful woman."

Lauren blinked. Beautiful? He thought she was beautiful? She would have said that was impossible but…

The thrill stole her breath. When she'd thought he was bragging about her fish, the spark of excitement had come and gone quickly as she puzzled through his motivation, but calling her a beautiful woman…

What could be the ulterior motive there? Flattery was a solid tactic, but he'd know she would see through that, wouldn't he? The other option was that he'd meant it. There was no strategy behind it.

If that was the case…

Could she trust it? Was she succumbing to a Peter Kim crush already?

"What's one touristy thing that Lauren Duncan, hometown girl, has never done?" Peter asked. "We'll do that tomorrow to keep the job worries and the legal negotiations at bay."

In a flash, the realization of what she was feeling and where she desperately wanted this to be going crashed over her. The entire day had become the best date she'd ever been on…and Peter had never intended it to be a date. He was softening her up to get what he wanted. She knew that. How could she be falling for this?

Peter had never lost sight of his goal.

So many times they'd stood right here when they were younger: him with a plan, her distracted by his technique. She owed it to herself to be on guard, to watch out for her interests.

"Can't tomorrow. I have something I need to do," Lauren said as she unlocked her car door.

"Oh, okay." Peter opened her car door for her, but she wasn't brave enough to read his face for clues. "That gives us time to think, then. I'll text you. If you want to…do something anyway, after, or later, let me know. Okay?"

Lauren nodded but didn't meet his gaze as she slid into the driver's seat. After she backed out and drove the winding path past the guard hut, she muttered, "What are you doing, Lauren?"

Falling for his clever strategy. Like she always had, she answered silently. Learning to protect herself had taken time and experience; forgetting that here would hurt.

And she'd have nobody to blame for that hurt but herself. Peter wasn't the one changing directions; she was letting romance cloud her vision.

When she gave Peter Kim what he wanted, agreed to help his nephew, he'd go back to his own life that included fun and relaxation and pirates. If she got used to the taste of adventure, especially with Peter by her side, where would that leave her?

CHAPTER EIGHT

PETER WISHED HE'D followed Lauren home from the marina. Was it silly to be concerned about a woman who had been navigating the world effectively on her own for years without his help? Probably. That didn't stop him from pulling out his cell phone to stare at the picture he'd taken on the boat. Lauren's sunny grin as she gripped the amberjack made him smile. He quickly added her contact information to his phone with that photo for the display.

He shook his head, called himself a fool and typed, Are you home yet?

Then he realized that message might not convey his concern and added, Just want to make sure you made it in safely. The way they'd said good-night made him uneasy for some reason. He could pinpoint the instant everything changed between them, but he hadn't been able to figure out why during the drive home.

One second, he'd been ending the best day he could remember in a long time, and the next, they were separated by a gulf and neither one of them had taken a step.

When the dots immediately popped up to show she was typing, he leaned against his kitchen counter and waited. The message finally popped up. I'm home safe and sound. Thank you for a wonderful day. Truly. I could not have asked for a better way to forget work.

Peter brushed a hand over his mouth as he considered what to send to keep the conversation going.

The emotion he'd been experiencing might have been vague worry over her safety mixed with confusion about the change in the atmosphere between them, but the dominant feeling was regret that the day was over.

Which was weird.

He'd been happy to wave goodbye to Candace at Las Estrellas' valet stand. Tonight, all he wanted to know was when he would see Lauren again. How long had it been since he'd experienced that at the end of a date?

"Not a date," he muttered. He should say

good-night and put the phone down before he got weirder.

But the dots were flashing. It would be rude not to find out what she had to say.

Unless she was texting him to tell him she'd made up her mind that she wasn't taking his nephew's case and she didn't want to see him again. That had been her first response, and he understood it after they'd talked. She'd tell him whom to hire and this reunion would be over.

Why did that thought hit him in the gut?

"Because you are getting wrapped up in this and it's not smart," he told himself.

He read, Today was great. Very relaxing. I'll take Davey's case because I want to help, no need to continue convincing me. Set up a meeting for next week and then text me the details, okay?

Regret was his immediate response.

"That makes no sense." She was giving him exactly what he'd asked for. He was winning and it had been so easy. All the demands on his time had magically been resolved, and he was back to his own plan of doing as he pleased.

There, in his town house, all he could think

of was all the excitement and grins and floppy hats he was going to miss out on because she'd agreed so quickly. It didn't follow that he should regret winning, did it?

On the drive home from the marina, he'd considered how to impress her on their second date. Something he'd never done and always wanted to do flashed in his mind. Kayaking in the Everglades had been on his bucket list forever, but finding a woman who would enjoy that seemed tricky. For that matter, he'd never met a guy who wanted to get that close to Florida wildlife, either. His best friend, Marcus, had laughed as if Peter had told him a killer joke when he'd suggested they take a Saturday and go.

But she'd loved the Plank and Anchor.

And she was already a more committed angler than he was.

She might be the person to take a chance on something like kayaking. Lauren could be the right friend to take along.

"Friends don't go on dates, Peter." He closed his eyes. His mind was a mess after one day with her. What would more hours with Lauren Duncan do to it?

There was only one sensible answer, but his

arms were heavy as he picked up his phone to text, Thank you, Lauren. I appreciate this.

After he hit Send, he stared hard at his phone, willing more dots to appear.

When he realized she wasn't going to respond, Peter slowly set his phone down, relieved but…unsettled? It was hard to name the emotion. He'd gotten what he wanted, but it might as well have been a major loss with the way fatigue and disappointment settled over him.

Why did this seem so wrong and so very important?

He huffed out a noisy breath and considered his options. It was too early for bed, but he wouldn't sleep anyway. TV might distract him, but he wouldn't remember anything he watched.

With no better options, Peter picked up the remote, found a replay of an old college bowl game and stretched out on the couch. He stuck with it until the daily recap show began with all the sports highlights. He'd thought he was watching, but every now and then he realized Lauren was playing in his mind. Reliving their afternoon together and deciphering her every reaction would occupy him for the rest of the night.

Or he could head out to the pool area to see if anyone from the unofficial therapy group was having a session and might benefit from his excellent advice on matters of life. Although, since every one of his friends had turned into a cooing lovebird, he'd sort of reached the end of his expertise.

The veterans who drifted out to the closed pool area late at night needed a distraction or understanding and even sometimes a wake-up call about life after the military.

Peter knew the friendships he'd built at Concord Court were important, but he always counted himself lucky because he didn't have scars from his time in the air force, physical or emotional. He knew what he wanted to do, didn't need career guidance, and he'd solved his own problem of the suffocating weight of his job responsibilities by refusing to have any going forward. His friends liked to pick at his relationship status, just as his parents did routinely, but it was easy to ignore since there were no problems to solve there, either.

This thing with Lauren and his feelings about tonight...

Was this the night he asked for advice?

Peter locked his front door and made the quick trip to the pool using the shortcut between the buildings. The night was humid, as always, but cooler than normal. Almost pleasant. The stars were faint against the clouds, but everything was right there at Concord Court.

It had felt like home almost from the first moment he arrived.

Leaving it would be tough. He'd built a family here, so moving out when his two years were up would be another adjustment. Loneliness might be a problem.

When he made it to the wrought iron fence that surrounded the pool, he was happy to see Marcus Bryant in his usual chair with his feet propped up on the cooler. They'd been best friends ever since they'd met here. When Marcus joined the lovebird crew, his presence most nights became a little iffier than normal.

"Hey, man, it's been a minute," Peter said as he took his usual seat. When Marcus lifted his feet, Peter reached into the cooler to grab a bottle of water. Beer might hit the spot, but they'd all embraced water after one of the regulars, Wade McNally, had explained he was sober.

"Evening." He squeezed Mira's shoulder. Mira Peters was the unofficial leader of their ragged band, the one who kept them moving forward. She was also the first to leave the townhome complex after her time was up. She'd stayed in the neighborhood, though, much to their relief, and showed up to make sure they stuck together and kept up with their running.

Sean Wakefield saluted him with his bottle. "We were just talking about you, Peter." He pointed. "What to *do* about you."

Peter frowned as he puzzled what that could mean. His life was fine.

"Really?" Peter asked doubtfully. "What's wrong with me?"

"That's how I know you're off your game." Sean's grin stretched from ear to ear. "You lob me a soft pitch like that, and you don't even see how I could smash it out of the park, listing all the things *wrong* with you." He mimicked a baseball home run and the crowd going wild.

When no one said anything else, he turned to Mira. "Spit it out. You're the only one here with the guts to tell me what you guys have been saying."

Mira laughed. "Remember when we were telling Marcus to open his eyes and realize he was in love with the girl next door?" She tapped her chin as if she was thinking. "Who was that who hit him right between the eyebrows with the suggestion that the reason he might have trouble with women was because he'd already fallen for one?"

He'd been that guy. No one needed him to say so because no one had forgotten. He never let them forget when he was right. Peter sipped his water.

"If you don't want to answer her question, what did you say when we were leaving the pool that night?" Marcus asked. "Don't bother pretending like you don't know. You said if Cassie and I figured things out, you'd be the only one left single."

"Thanks to you, Cassie and Marcus seem to be making excellent progress in all things romantic." Sean grinned. "We promised there and then to focus the rest of our attention on you and your love life, so here we are. Focusing. We haven't made it to solving yet, but we will."

Peter scrubbed his face with both hands. He should have gone with TV or even staring at the wall.

"At least Brisa isn't here," he muttered. Their resident matchmaker had been eyeing him on their morning runs as if she was mentally paging through a file of eligible women. She hadn't given up on him yet. Soon he'd run out of time, and she'd corner him for details to help her revise her search.

"I don't need help finding a date," Peter said. They knew that. The multitude of women he had dinner with was something they enjoyed giving him grief about.

"Is that what's been keeping you busy lately?" Marcus sat up in his chair. "Haven't seen you out here in more than a week. That's too long."

Peter met his stare and nodded. "It is too long, but no." Was he going to tell them about his nephew? There wasn't much reason to. He had a plan. He'd done all he could. No need to burden anyone else, especially now that Lauren was on the job. In cases like this, Peter was always successful in shoving any other concerns deep down and locking the box. He liked to take care of his issues on his own.

When Mira shifted in her chair, Peter knew she was preparing her familiar lecture about how they should ask for help when it was needed. To head that off, he said, "My nephew was arrested on drug charges." He hesitated. That was enough information, right?

Mira made the "keep going" motion with her hand. "Use words. Don't turn into the strong, silent type now, Peter Kim. That's not who you are."

Should he be insulted by that? Peter pondered it for a half a second before he let it go. That's who he was here, the one with the answers. That's who he was comfortable being now, but he'd done that for too long. Holding everything inside had robbed him of air.

"He was arrested. It was the first time, and I believe him when he says the stuff wasn't his." Peter leaned forward. "Ever since I've been back in Miami, I've tried to be more… involved with my family. My parents have always expected me to look out for my sister. Her son, Davey, called me from the police station because I'm in law school. He hoped I could get him out or help. All I could imagine was how I would feel if I had to tell my family something like that, if I had to call my parents and ask them to get me out of jail. So I went and bailed out the kid, stayed with him to tell my sister and parents, and promised to get him the best lawyer I could find. I've been hunting her down."

They were quiet until Sean softly said, "I'm sorry to hear that, man. Did you ask Brisa and Reyna for lawyer recommendations? You know a well-connected guy like their dad could provide some high-power names." Then he frowned. "They have high price tags, too, but we'll figure out how to pay the bill later."

Sean had said "we." His friends would help him find the answers and even the funds if necessary. Surprise, gratitude and appreciation showered down on Peter and he had to take a minute to catch his breath. That was the kind of friendship he'd forged around this table. Even if they viewed him as Mr. Lonely Heart at the moment, he was lucky to have them.

"Never occurred to you to ask for their help, though," Mira drawled, "did it?"

Uneasy that she had called him out like

that, Peter cleared his throat. "Thanks, man. I had a good plan. I started with the public defender who represented Davey at his arraignment, but I didn't like the firm he recommended. Then I asked around at the police station and got the name of a defender who had left the office but had an impressive reputation. Then, thanks to the power of the World Wide Web, I tracked her to her house, made my pitch to hire her and did it well enough that she didn't call the police on the strange guy loitering on her steps, and now..." How did he explain this bargain he'd entered into? Or that he was all out of sorts because his strategy had worked so well? Maybe he wouldn't have to. They would never let it go if he tipped them off that Lauren had captured his attention.

Then he felt the weight of Mira's stare. "And?"

Peter raised his eyebrows. "And what?" Bluffing never worked with Mira, but a man without options used what he had.

"Why are you out here tonight?" she asked sweetly. When Mira used a friendly tone like that, they'd all learned she could see right through them to the truth underneath. There was no sense in trying to stonewall her.

His hesitation was reasonable, however. If he described his last two encounters with Lauren Duncan, they would immediately know that there was something different about her.

Then their "focus" on him would shift from kind interest to true plotting. The group had proved itself effective in the sort of strategy that led to happily-ever-after.

He wasn't in the market for that. Not yet. His life was everything he'd dreamed of at the moment, or it would be after Davey's case was over.

As long as he didn't think about being unable to sleep because Lauren had prematurely conceded.

Peter was saved when the gate opened and Wade McNally and Brisa joined them at the table. They would divert the conversation. All Peter had to do was wait it out.

"Have you gotten him to say what's wrong yet?" Wade asked as he took the bottle Marcus handed him. "Sorry we're late. Emergency surgery popped up." The ex-navy surgeon had moved to Miami and Concord Court after he'd accepted a position as a trauma surgeon at the hospital. His hours were unpredictable, but he'd become a steady part of their group. Wade pulled up a chair for Brisa and one for himself and they both sat.

"He was about to tell us everything," Mira said. Everyone at the table watched him as if he might make a run for the gate at any moment. What would they do if he did? Mira was faster than he was.

"The lawyer is someone I knew from undergraduate days. She was the thorn in my side that propelled me to the top of some classes, and I have no doubt that she is the best person to defend Davey. All I had to do was convince her to take this last case. She quit her job without notice a week ago, and she was pretty determined not to go back." Peter sipped his water and tried to telegraph that his story was finished.

The way everyone leaned slightly forward in their seats was unnerving, like predators locking in on juicy prey.

"So I did that. The end." Peter shifted uncomfortably in the chair and tried to meet every stare evenly.

Mira raised her eyebrows.

If he held his ground, could he get by with pretending that was the end of the story?

The silence stretched around the table in a clear "no."

"I asked her to let me help her fill the vacation she's forcing herself to take. She's recuperating from the grind of the public defender's office. I figured that way I'd have more time to convince her." Peter stopped to see if that was enough.

Mira nodded. "So, you've been..."

"I took her out on the boat today." Peter focused on the lid of his water bottle. He had no hope that they'd fail to see something in that admission.

"She made it onto your boat before I did," Mira said slowly. "How long have we been friends now? Almost two years, right?"

"Hadn't you mentioned that women on boats were considered bad luck?" Wade added.

"That was a joke," Peter muttered. Not a good one, but he'd tried to deflect their conversation then so he wouldn't have to explain why he preferred solo trips to company on the *Hardly Working*.

"And none of the women he's been dating

have been on the boat, either," Sean tacked on helpfully. "Wade, have you been out with Peter?"

The surgeon shook his head.

Sean placed a hand over his heart. "Neither have I. Since I loathe fishing and I've made that clear, I can let that pass. Marcus?"

Peter watched his best friend frown at the table in front of him. "Yeah, I've been out on the boat." Marcus shrugged. "He asked for a fishing lesson. Just one, though."

"Aha!" Sean said accusingly as he pointed at Peter. "I knew it."

Before they could demand answers, Peter said, "You're all invited. You tell me when you're available. I'll go out as many times as you like. It's been this…thing, an escape, but my best friends are welcome." Peter made eye contact with each of them to make sure they understood him.

"Someone else can show him how to clean all the fish you catch," Marcus spoke with a grimace. "I didn't make it that far."

Mira shook her head. "More fish for me, then." She punched Peter lightly in the arm. "My dad taught me how to fish and clean them before I could ride a bicycle."

Peter rubbed the spot where he assumed a bruise would now be. "Sorry. Next time, you can show me."

Mira tipped her head back to study the stars and breathe deeply. Sometimes she did that.

"All right, your best friends haven't made it onto the boat, but she has. How did it go?" she asked. Apparently she was tired of leading them slowly to the point. Her patience did have a limit.

"Really well. It was a great day. I was worried about what we'd talk about, but it was easy to get reacquainted." In fact, he hadn't wanted the day to end. He couldn't add that. It would be chum in the water for these sharks.

Mira's victory punch into the air confirmed his suspicions that they'd read between the lines effectively.

"And the next time you're going to see her is…" Mira tilted her head expectantly.

"I don't know." Somehow she'd led him to the problem he was going to keep buried. Why had he even hoped he could? "I was thinking of tomorrow, but she has plans, but then tonight out of the blue she texted to say she'd decided to take the case. Just let her know when she can meet with Davey and his parents to get the details. No need to plan any other distractions."

Sean said slowly, "So…you won. That's… nice." Peter could hear the grin in his voice. "Isn't that nice?"

"Not if one date made a man start thinking of ways to set up the next date before the first one was even over," Wade said slowly. "That's next-level nice."

"Was I this annoying when all of you were fighting the inevitable?" Peter asked as he straightened in his chair. "Because I don't want to be paired off. I still have so many things I want to do. Don't start imagining wedding bells yet."

"Wedding bells," Sean murmured before he whistled quietly. "Wow. You've jumped ahead of yourself now."

Peter glared across the table at him but knew it was diminished by the dark corner.

Brisa daintily cleared her throat in a way that was definitely not like her usual grab-the-center-of-attention self.

"Yes, darling," Wade drawled. "Did you have something to say?"

"While we're evaluating the current situation of Peter Kim and his lawyer," Brisa said, "I would like more details on the blind date that I labored to set up at the hottest restaurant in Miami." She crossed her legs and settled back in her chair with an expectant attitude.

"It was fine. Nice. Food was amazing. Company was…okay." Peter searched for more details but they'd blended into a fuzzy atmosphere of "okay." "We didn't connect."

Brisa wasn't satisfied with that level of reporting. "Candace called to let me know that if you changed your mind about a second date, she would be ecstatic. That was her word. *Ecstatic.* Ecstasy, Peter, and all you have to do is go out again."

"Is this about your reputation as a matchmaker or…" Sean let the sentence trail off.

"This is about Peter's problem, which we are all here to solve," Brisa said sweetly. "And also to shore up my name, thank you."

Peter fiddled with the water bottle for a second. "On paper, the evening was perfect, but there's something…" He inhaled. He was about to get honest. They weren't going to know what hit them. "There's something more important than hobbies and experiences, you know? Something about who you are, what you value or..." He shook his head. "Candace asked me if I ever regretted going into the air force because I would be a partner making big bucks if I'd skipped that and gone to law school directly. It's hard to put into words, but... We aren't the same kind of person, does that make sense?"

This time, he got nods and felt slightly vindicated.

Wade said, "I get that. It's not just about where you're alike but where the places that you're different fit together." Wade tangled his fingers with Brisa's.

The urge to groan as they traded intense love stares was strong, but Peter had learned to keep the noise down at the midnight pool sessions.

"I'm not sure I know anybody who's been successful with 'dating,'" Marcus said. "You can answer many questions, but you don't know a person until you spend time with them." He held up a finger as if he'd made an important discovery. "Cassie and I were best friends forever. I fell in love while decorating a smelly high school gym. Twice."

Peter laughed. The guy had a point.

"Watching Reyna Montero disco at a street party changed my universe," Sean said.

"Rob and I? It was love at first sight, but we couldn't make that work. Love at second sight?" Mira said. "I watched him scramble up the side of a large inflatable slide in the middle of the ocean because he was sure a shark was about to get him." She laughed. "Did he rescue me? No, but he said he would have, and I almost believe him. I'm just happy it wasn't really a shark."

"For me? It was Brisa's terrible sculling at her first synchronized swim routine practice. My daughter saw potential, but I was already hooked," Wade said.

"What about you, Brisa?" Mira asked.

"It had to be the room he built for that same lovely daughter. Stars everywhere for the astronaut-to-be," she said softly. "Who wouldn't fall for a guy like that?"

Peter made choking sounds. All the love in the air was making it difficult to breathe.

Sean grunted. "Just wait. Your time is coming, hotshot."

"You mentioned hobbies. I'm guessing you

don't share any of those in common," Mira said. "But something else is there. You can see kindness or creativity or loyalty or generosity, a trait that draws you to her. That's what I hear from these stories."

"I always admired her brain. So brilliant. And determined. The more I learn about her, the more impressive all that is, but today, her absolute joy over little things…" He paused. He was saying too much.

"Take it from a friend," Marcus said, "don't drop this. If you're still thinking about her now, hours later, you gotta find out more. Whatever you were planning for your next vacation day together, talk her into it. You're good at that."

"Kayaking in the mangrove tunnels. Bugs. Alligators. Nothing romantic. That was my idea." Peter realized his mistake almost as soon as he said it.

"To me, this sounds like a person you want to share doing some of the 'many things' you still want to do. Not go on dates to impress, like at expensive restaurants with champagne and valet parking," Marcus said. "Interesting." The fact that he didn't yell "aha" like a detective solving a murder mystery had to be due to the late hour and the setting.

"She loved the Plank and Anchor," Peter said.

Marcus whistled. "She might be your soul mate, then." He and Marcus had discovered the place together and Marcus had not been impressed.

Which had made Lauren's reaction that much sweeter.

"She's also made it to a second date in his mind." Sean's grin was easy to hear in his voice. He did enjoy teasing anyone when he had the chance. "The solution to Peter's problem is at hand. All we have to do is convince them both of that second date."

"Not a date," Peter muttered, but he knew it was a lost cause.

"You keep telling yourself that." Mira patted his shoulder.

As they all stood and tucked in their chairs, Brisa said, "Thanks for letting me crash the party tonight. I couldn't sleep."

Wade squeezed her shoulders. "Too much Concord Court planning running through her mind."

"I've got to get someone hired soon, and

this outreach event we've got coming up is big." Brisa ran her hands over her face. "All of you are on the list of volunteers. I don't know what your jobs are yet, but this is going to be a huge splash for our veterans and the new ones we want to reach. We'll bring several of Sean's service dogs, Jason will be there to talk about Sawgrass University programs and job assistance, Marcus will represent our business lab. Everyone has a task."

Peter wouldn't consider skipping the event, but it was clear she was struggling with everything on her plate. "We could cancel our morning runs until things calm down."

Mira immediately shook her head and Brisa followed. "No, I need to run. I also need more people and hours in the day."

"You could bring your friend, ask her to volunteer. We want to meet her, and think of all the positive spin you'll get from having such awesome friends." Sean framed his face with his hands.

"I don't need positive spin. I need her help with my nephew's case. Frankly, Lauren Duncan may be ready to go back to forgetting I exist." Peter tried to make it sound as if that would have no effect on him.

But he wasn't certain he believed it.

Mira patted his shoulder. "The clock's ticking then. Sounds like you better make effective use of the time you have. I will gladly fish and clean what we catch. Any woman that will agree to go kayaking with you in Florida's swampy alligator waters? She's a keeper."

CHAPTER NINE

ON SATURDAY MORNING, Lauren was wired from too much caffeine. She stared through the car's windshield at the door to the South Florida Correctional Facility. For seventy miles, she'd had time to think and drink coffee, and it showed in the nerves that made it difficult to let go of the steering wheel.

All of the relaxation she'd managed to claim while out on the water with Peter had worn away after a long night and the morning's drive.

"What is your problem? You've done this a hundred times before." Lauren forced herself to reach up to flip down the visor and check her reflection. Yep. Pale. Tense. Jittery. Not her best choice for visiting hours, but it had been a month since she'd seen her dad and she had absolutely no excuses to miss another chance.

She knew the procedure. Her clothes, a

plain crew neck pink T-shirt and blue jeans, had already passed inspection on other visits. Her purse was locked in the trunk, and she'd counted the cash before slipping it in her pocket to make sure she was under the facility's limit.

"Put the key in your pocket with your driver's license and go inside." Lauren rolled her head slowly on her shoulders to ease the tight muscles there before leaving the car. The parking lot was not as full as she'd expected. Walking into the facility always caused the knot in her stomach to tighten, but Lauren pasted on a smile as she approached the window.

"Good morning. I'm here to see Michael Duncan." She slipped her driver's license through the gap in the window. "Lauren Duncan." She waited while the guard typed in her information to check the list of approved visitors and did her best not to fidget. At one time, she'd had her father's information memorized down to the number assigned by the Department of Corrections, but that had been the last stay, not this one.

"You know the rules, right?" the guard said as he passed her license back. "No touching. Do not give the inmate anything. Do not speak to any other inmate. Do you have questions?"

Lauren licked her lips nervously, feeling on the spot. Why did she think she needed a question? "I can still buy my dad things from the vending machine, can't I? He can have them…later."

Something in the guard's eyes eased. Lauren heard the buzz of the door release and smiled at him before stepping back. When she entered the big room with evenly spaced metal tables, she found an empty spot and slid onto the bench. The nervous bounce of her leg made a rhythmic squeaking noise, thanks to the high polish on the floor and the rubber sole of her sneakers. The only things to focus on in the room were other visitors and inmates, the signs listing all the rules in case anyone had forgotten and a couple of bored guards. Then she remembered the vending machine and stood back up to see what was available. Something chocolate. Her father loved chocolate. They had that in common.

While Lauren was working her way methodically through the vending machines and her wad of cash, the door opened and a guard escorted her father in. Every time she saw him, Lauren was afraid to find signs of a hard life behind bars. Slumped shoulders. New wrinkles on his face or scars. Instead, he grinned happily and held out his arms as if he would hug her. The guard grunted. Lauren nodded her understanding and moved to one of the tables to dump candy bars and chips out of her arms. "Hey, Dad. You look good."

His eyes lit up as he saw the chocolate bar with almonds, his favorite. She'd bought three of those. "You know I love talking with you on the phone, but candy? Nothing beats my daughter in person bearing candy." He touched one of the bars. "Is one of these for you?"

"Nope, all you, Daddy. If Larry's still your cellmate, save the one with coconut for him. You told me he doesn't get any visitors." Lauren smiled as he stacked them up and stared at his treasure. She realized she'd stared at the Plank and Anchor's chocolate cake with the same expression.

"My sweet daughter, remembering Larry. He'll appreciate that. To what do I owe this visit?" he asked. "Isn't there some important case you should be working on instead of running the interstate?"

Lauren was never sure how to interpret comments like that. Did he think she should come more often? Was she letting him down by visiting infrequently?

Or did he not want her to come at all? As long as she kept depositing money, he could have treats and phone calls, and he seemed to be doing fine. Would Larry miss her more if she stopped coming?

"It's been too long. I wanted to see you." Lauren shoved a strand of hair behind one ear. "How have you been? Mama said she was here last weekend and you had a cold."

Her father stopped fiddling with the paper on the chocolate bar. "You worried about a little cold? Got to see a doctor quicker than I ever would have on the outside." He shook his head. "How many times have I told you both to relax? I'm okay. I know my way here. Nothing to fret over."

Nothing to fret over. That's what he'd told her when she was a teenager, too, and the police had come to the door to ask questions about stolen cars. Since her father had recently been on a spending spree, with trips for her to the mall, Lauren had had no difficulty jumping to the right conclusion. The math had been simple. It usually was with her father. Almost like he had calculated in his mind how long it would take for the police to track him down. He never struggled or got emotional.

To him, it was nothing to fret over.

Eventually, her mother had learned to follow his lead. He'd go to jail, she'd do her own thing, he'd get out and they would get back together until the cycle started again.

Her father wasn't violent or mean.

He also never changed.

Mike Duncan was the best-natured criminal she'd ever met, and Lauren had spent some time with criminals.

Not a one of them confused her like he did.

"You keep saying it. We'll keep ignoring you." Lauren tried to smile. She'd put as much distance between herself and her father and mother as she could allow. She was close enough to make sure they were okay, but they couldn't turn her life upside down anymore. "And when you get out in a few months, we'll stop worrying."

He nodded. "Yes, your mama already mentioned how she repainted the kitchen in the condo. I'm looking forward to seeing that bright yellow."

"It's pretty. Cheerful." Lauren made a special effort not to glance around them at the walls that had been white at one point but had aged into a blah beige. "What else are you looking forward to?"

He frowned as he considered her question. "Gotta get to the beach. Need to put my toes in the water." Since that had been her first impulse with new freedom, Lauren understood that.

"I'm going to look for a job, too. This time will be different," her father said, and caught her stare to make sure she knew he meant it. That was how it always went.

"Yeah? What would you like to do, Daddy? If you could do anything," Lauren asked. This was something they'd never talked about. Why hadn't it occurred to her to wonder about what he'd wanted for his own life at one point?

"Win the lottery," he said with a grin and then waved a hand. "No, to be serious, I always wanted to teach." He pretended to blow a whistle. "To coach football, maybe,

and teach something light, like study hall."
His eyes twinkled. "That's why I joined the
army, money to go to college, but that didn't
work out. Can't keep up with construction
anymore, so I'll have to do some hunting this
time."

Her mother had gotten pregnant, and he
couldn't afford school and a baby. That much
she remembered from the story. Construction
had been good money, but not consistently,
and he'd always been the fan of fast money.

Anxious to change the subject, Lauren
said, "I do have news. I quit my job. Had
enough and walked out. I am unemployed.
Like father, like daughter. Finally?"

Her father whistled low under his breath.
"Well, now, that is big. You've been employed, sometimes overemployed, ever since
you were sixteen. What brought this on? I
thought the courage of your convictions pow-
ered your career."

There it was again, that tone that tempted
her to read between the lines and hear a jab
instead of innocent conversation. "I was pow-
ered by my beliefs. I want everyone to have a
fair defense, but that's not possible with the
system the way it is." Did he understand why

that mattered so much to her? Had she ever told him? "I needed a break before it broke me."

He nodded. "Too many criminals, I guess."

Lauren clenched her hands together as she considered that. "Not enough lawyers who will take on the defense." That had been the problem all along in her mind, but sitting across from her father made her wonder. The prison system that was supposed to rehabilitate him had failed, but he seemed completely unbothered by his circumstances. Who carried more of the fault in his case?

How much of her life had she sacrificed trying to change this situation? A lot.

"How long do you think it'll be before you're back in the defender's office?" her father asked. "Duncans? We stick to what we know. I expect you're already considering how to convince your boss to rehire you. If you aren't, you will. As soon as you start to worry about who'll cover the payment on your condo or your mama's place if you can't do it, you'll jump to what you know. We don't change our spots even if we sometimes want to."

Since she'd already accepted a case, the one to help Peter, that hit too close to home.

There was no reason to tell her father that. It would be over and done by the next time she came to visit.

Was that what happened in his mind? When he got out, he usually did fine for a while and made good on the promise to change, but then something derailed that. Was the fast-money scheme that landed him back in jail his return to what he knew?

Whatever her father said, they could both change. Lauren wanted to take a chance on him again because she wanted to believe she could do it, too.

"I won't be asking for my old job. I'm going to make a change, do something easier now. I've sacrificed enough. It's time to look out for me." It felt wrong to think that. It felt worse to say it to her father. In her mind, she carried the weight of his jail time, too. She wanted to change things for him.

Maybe more than he wanted to change them for himself.

He pursed his lips as he studied her face. "I almost believe you." The corner of his mouth curled. "You know, when I was in the army,

I had this buddy. He would volunteer for the worst duty and even when I would draw the short straw, he'd turn up, ready to pitch in. Nobody ordered him to, or even asked him to. He was a good guy. Worked harder than anyone else and was an easy mark, but he never changed. You remind me of him sometimes. I worry."

"You fret about me?" Lauren asked, amazed to hear him say it. He was the original "no worries" example.

"I do. When you give your all to something, a person or a job or a government, like in the case of my buddy, and then no one is there to give it back to you when you need it, what happens? You're all tapped out. He had no place to go when he left the army, got hooked on some bad stuff and stayed on the streets for a while, until I lost track of him. All that work he did for other people when he should have been looking out for his own future, you know? Taking care of yourself is important." His smile faded. "Especially when no one else is there to pick you up."

Right. Her father was never going to be the one to help her up.

She'd given so much. Whom did she have to call on now?

For some reason, Peter Kim flashed in her mind, the guy who had tracked her through time and across town to help his nephew.

Because he could and he wanted to and he'd done what he set out to do. Davey could depend on his uncle.

Lauren didn't have anyone like that. Never had.

The envy, disappointment and sadness that overwhelmed her made it difficult to pretend that everything was fine. But if her father was never ruffled by his surroundings, she would always try for upbeat. That's who they were in this relationship.

"So far, I've been to the beach and spent time fishing on the ocean. I'm taking to life after criminal defense pretty well," Lauren said. "I'm considering opening my own office, making the switch to real estate law or something like that." Saying it out loud brought the low-level panic of her real estate search back. How would she guarantee enough income to cover the expenses of her own office? Where she'd have to hire people and do payroll and pay insurance, and who even knew what else would come up?

That sounded almost as exhausting as her old job.

Her father tapped the table in a rhythm she almost recognized as he considered her. "You'll end up working more hours doing that than you did defending criminals. Being your own boss means you'll work around the clock because you can. Was that the plan?"

Lauren blinked. Going into business for herself had been the second-to-last thing she would have imagined. Her father giving sound career advice would have to be the very last.

"No, not the plan. Living a life where there's beach time and boat time is the plan." She stared at her father, who returned the look.

"Better keep thinking, then, baby. You haven't found the right answer yet." He tapped out a pattern on the metal table. Was he amused? There was a glint of something in his eyes that she couldn't label.

In that second, whatever had snapped in Blake Bennings's office when she'd slid her resignation across his desk splintered again.

Suddenly, she couldn't stand the questions anymore. If his comments were veiled criticism, it was time to take off the veil. Her heart was in danger, but she needed to know the answer. "Daddy, if you could have anything in the world, what would it be? Should I come every week? Should I stop coming altogether? What can I do for you?"

He closed his eyes. "I want you to be happy. First, last. That's the list. I love you. I'm proud of you. You'll never understand me. I can see that on your face and hear it in your voice on the phone, but you shouldn't have to. I understand you." He moved as if he wanted to take her hands but glanced at the guard who was watching them, and leaned back. "I said Duncans don't change their spots. That much is true. You're going to keep doing too much for me, feeling too much responsibility for the universe, but you can learn to care for yourself the same way." He sighed. "Or I hope you can."

Uncomfortable tears sprang up. Lauren might cry after she left her father, but she didn't let them show while they were together. She quickly wiped them away. "Right. We don't understand each other. That's okay."

He nodded. "You bet it is. Means we're family. But I love you, I'm proud of all you've accomplished for yourself, and I hope that when I get out in a few months, you'll have found the thing that makes you happy, too."

"I'm going to." Her firm tone was reassuring. Did she have any idea where or what that might be? No, but she'd worked her way through harder things.

"Good. Get out of here. Go catch me a fish," her father said.

"Oh, Daddy, I caught an amberjack! That was my first fish! When you get out, I'll show you the photo," Lauren said, and desperately missed the phone she'd had to leave in the car.

He pointed. "That's my girl. Let's cook it up for our first family meal. We'll get your mother to make some of her famous coleslaw, too." Then he stood and nodded to the guard. Her father was gone before she had to confess that she'd tossed it back in the ocean.

When she made it to the car, she got her purse out and pulled out her phone to see the photo with the fish again. She didn't know what her future held. That was true.

But with this picture, she had a vision of what it might look like.

And today? She needed the help of someone who was ahead of her on the road to give her some much-needed instruction. Only one person came to mind.

"So, I know I agreed to help already, but until I meet with your family, I'm lost." She stared at the keyboard as she tried to figure out what to text. No way was she sending that to Peter Kim. Admitting she needed his help was going to restore balance between them and she wanted to hold on to her advantage for whatever fleeting time she could.

As if thinking of him had the power to summon Peter, dots appeared before she could start to type her message.

Family meeting is set for Monday night. Is my parents' house okay? Lauren read and then checked the address. She didn't recognize it, but it seemed easy enough.

Absolutely. After she hit Send, Lauren chewed her lip as she tried to figure out where to go to keep the conversation rolling. What she needed was to suggest to Peter that he distract her with something and make him think it was his own idea.

Are you busy tomorrow? he asked.

Her eyebrows shot up. Was her brain more

powerful than she knew? Somehow she was thinking these things into existence.

No. Do you need more help? Lauren wondered if she was pressing her luck with the message, but it fit their pattern.

He sent the rolling eyes emoji. I booked a kayak trip. It's probably not your kind of thing, but the buddy I asked had something come up. Do you want to see some alligators?

Did she? Lauren was certain her grimace was the correct answer.

As she sat there, she weighed alligators and kayaking against sitting in her condo and worrying. I do, but if one eats me, I will come back to haunt your boat. You will catch so many fish you will be forced to clean them.

When the phone rang, she immediately dropped it between the seat and the center console and had to dig it out to answer breathlessly. "Hello?"

"If an alligator eats you, he eats me, too. I never leave a friend behind," Peter said, laughter in his voice. "Besides, I'm afraid of ghosts and cleaning fish, so that threat was too violent. Think of something less gross, at least."

As she stared at the front of the correctional facility, Lauren laughed and everything was better.

Because Peter Kim had thought of her, texted her, called her.

Because Peter had included her, life immediately seemed better.

What was she doing? The hurt he could cause was scary, worse than close encounters with alligators, but there was no second-guessing her decision. This was the right thing for her.

"I'll pick you up in the morning. Don't forget bug spray."

When she hung up, Lauren was relieved. Friendly. That was a friendly way to end the conversation. There was no romance in alligators and bug spray. Maybe she could make it through one more day with Peter without falling for him.

CHAPTER TEN

ALL THE KNOWING glances his friends had traded as he'd talked about Lauren at the pool made perfect sense. By the time Lauren had snapped her seat belt shut in Peter's passenger seat on Sunday morning, he saw it himself. If he compared the warm glow of pleasure he got every time he sat across from a beautiful woman in a fancy restaurant with the surge of raw excitement at the sight of Lauren trotting down her front steps, wearing shorts and a long-sleeved T-shirt with a baseball cap and her short ponytail… Yeah, it was embarrassing to be this happy. Lauren Duncan was dressed practically, not for seduction, and the way his heart thudded worried him.

"Good morning." She tugged her hat down. "Am I ready for this kayak trip or what? Come at me, bugs!"

Peter nodded. "The only thing missing is gator repellent."

"Doesn't exist. I looked." Lauren waved her cell phone. "Sleepless nights plus a handheld computer always within arm's reach means plenty of time for random research. Apparently, a legitimate alligator deterrent has not yet been invented."

Peter glanced at her but she was staring out the window. When people cracked a door that revealed they weren't quite as fine as they seemed, like mentioning insomnia, he always wondered whether he should shove it wide open or let the person make that decision. Years of intelligence work had convinced him that prying the information out wasn't necessarily the most effective solution.

"Thinking about the future? Is that what's keeping you up?" he asked, and directed his attention to the interstate in front of him. If she wanted to talk, she would. If she didn't, he'd go with that. What he wasn't quite as clear about was why he wanted to know. Was he going to try to solve her problems? That was the exact opposite of his plan to take life easy, avoid all entanglements.

For that matter, every minute he spent with her was unraveling that plan.

In for a penny, might as well go for the whole pound.

"Sort of." She pulled out her phone again and entered a search. He assumed she wasn't going to say any more about it and started hunting for small talk. "I went to see my father yesterday." She turned toward him. "In jail. Visiting hours. That always affects me. I was glad to see your text. Today would have been a long, exhausting day all by myself."

Peter wanted to hold that shot of satisfaction close. Lauren was strong. She'd done a lot of hard things all by herself, but managing to be there when she needed him felt like a win.

"He's getting out in a few months, so we talked about that and about quitting my job. He's pretty sure I'll return to my old job as soon as the threat of not paying my bills or my mother's rent kicks in. He might be right."

Of course she was taking care of her mother. Why wouldn't she also have that unbelievable pressure to work through? Peter tilted his head up and realized he was angry at her parents on her behalf.

"He doesn't have to be. There's no reason for him to be right. You can do anything you want."

Lauren gasped. "Anything? Anything I want? Wow." She tapped her chin. "I want to be born an heiress."

Peter rolled his eyes. "You know what I mean. Anything that doesn't require a time machine or a fairy godmother."

She laughed. "Okay. Maybe you're right." Then she looked down at her phone.

"What are you researching now?" Peter asked.

"Well, last night I was on a survival kick. How to escape an alligator. What to do if a python gets a hold of you. How many alligator bites there are in Florida every year." She wrinkled her nose. "Twelve last year."

"Is that more or less than you expected?" Peter asked. He wasn't sure how to respond.

"If I weren't headed out in a kayak to see alligators? I'd feel pretty safe. As it is…"

"You're going to haunt me. I remember. I won't let anything get you. So what is the topic you're researching today?" Peter smiled as he realized how easy it was to slip into a comfortable rhythm with her. Hard things, silly things, they came up in their conversation and both of them rolled with it. It was nice. Nothing felt too scary to talk about with Lauren.

"Kayaking videos." She showed him the screen where he could see paddles flashing. "I've never done this before."

"The people who run the place are going to demonstrate how, Duncan," he drawled. "Lots of people don't know everything about everything." He'd never been kayaking before, either, but it had never occurred to him to study up on techniques in advance. That might be one key difference between them. At this point, he found it charming. Would that always be true?

"I like to have an idea of the basics. I don't want to slow the rest of the group down because I can't keep up." Out of the corner of his eye, Peter could see that she was chewing her bottom lip. Was that unconscious or a sign of nerves? Both?

"We'll be together. I'll paddle. Blame any holdup on me." Peter wasn't worried. These guides taught tourists all day, every day. No way could he be the worst they'd ever seen.

Lauren patted his arm, there right below his elbow. Her hand on his skin was brief, but he would remember it. That she'd done all this research about surviving Florida wildlife and how to be a superstar kayaker convinced him she wasn't as positive about this experience as she had been about catching fish or theme restaurants. She wasn't complaining, either, which was encouraging.

"You don't seem to be regretting your decision yet, which is good," Peter said as he parked.

Lauren grinned. "I've never done this. When I tell people I did it, they will be shocked, amazed and impressed. And if I die, I'm going to be haunting a boat. I don't see a downside here."

Interesting. Peter would not have guessed an outlook could be filled with both fatal dread and optimistic excitement, but she'd nailed it, somehow.

They left the car and approached a short dock and boat landing. Lauren's smile was open, cheerful. Not even the cloud of bug repellent surrounding the four other members of their tour and the two guides seemed to faze her. Lauren took the spray, doused herself and him and then handed it back to the guide.

He watched her listen intently to the safety

lecture that included tips on how to paddle properly, what to do if they got stuck in the mangroves, how to stop the kayak and move in reverse. If there was a test coming, she would ace it.

Everything was going well until one of the other guests, a large guy with a camera slung around his neck, said, "I have heard that Florida is the Australia of the United States. Is this true? Are all the animals out to kill you here?" Uncomfortable chuckles from the rest of the group filled the silence until one of the guides waved away the comment.

"Now, now, if we're talking about the alligators and the crocodiles, because Florida is the only place lucky to have both..." He paused. "It's easy enough to deal with them. Just keep away. If you see one, get moving. If one surprises you, do not return the favor. The kayak should be bigger than he is, so he'll leave you alone. Do *not* dangle any hands or feet out of the boat, either."

Lauren shot him a glance over her shoulder. Peter wondered what she'd do if he chickened out. Honestly, he was here for a nice, easy adventure, not an epic battle against murderous dinosaurs.

No one else seemed inclined to back out. He definitely would not be the first.

The other guide, a woman who'd introduced herself as Kirstie, a conservation biologist working in the Everglades, added, "Don't fall out of the boat." She frowned. "If you do fall out, get back in. Quickly. The kayak is the key to safety and success here. Oh, and for the record, we haven't lost one tour member yet."

When Lauren inched closer, until the fold of her shirt brushed his abdomen, Peter inhaled deeply and enjoyed the moment. They might be covered in bug spray, but it was the two of them together, braving it as a team. Thanks mainly to the threat she'd hung over his head. Why did that make him happy?

Had he been out in the sunshine for too long?

"What about the pythons? Apparently, they are everywhere," Mr. Helpful continued. "I saw a news story about the epic bounty on these snakes. This year, the largest was sixteen feet long!" His absolute delight in the fact convinced Peter they should all keep an eye on him.

Lauren turned her head to whisper, "If we are caught in some kind of battle for survival, he's the first one to go." Her eyes met his. The laughter there reassured him. She might be scared, but if they survived this, they were going to laugh about it together.

"They are definitely a danger to small mammals, but we don't have any of those on this tour, so we should be fine," Kirstie said. She pointed at Peter and Lauren. "You two look like you're ready. Should we get you in your kayak?"

Before he could answer, Lauren said, "Let's do this." Because she didn't back down once she was committed. Her shoulders were tense enough to snap with the wrong pressure applied, but she was going on the tour.

Kirstie motioned them to get closer to the water. "I'm assuming you want to go out as a duo. If not, we can put you in individual kayaks. That way, you both get the full effect."

Lauren immediately shook her head. "No, Kirstie, this is great. We'll stick together."

"Okay, hop in. Back seat generally paddles, but you can switch off if you prefer." Kirstie held the edge of the kayak to steady it so Lauren could get in.

Lauren patted him on the shoulder. "Go right ahead, back seat."

"I like Captain better." Laughing made it harder for him to clamber into the back seat and get his legs situated, but he wasn't going to argue.

Kirstie was laughing, too. "Front seat, you're the lookout. You see anything with teeth, tell him to stop paddling."

"Oh, I will definitely be watching for teeth, Kirstie. And that won't be the only thing I tell him," Lauren muttered. Peter wasn't sure that Kirstie got the full effect because she gave them a shove to send them out onto the water.

"Practice with the paddle while we're loading everyone in," Kirstie called, and then turned away for her next kayakers.

Peter practiced a bit with the paddle until he saw Lauren relax against the seat. "You don't want to be first mate of the kayak?"

She glanced back at him. "I will pick out all the hand soaps. Otherwise, you're the crew."

Peter nodded. "Yes, ma'am."

The lack of small talk got easier once all the kayaks were in the water. The two tour guides kept up a running stream of interesting facts about Florida's mangroves and the ecosystem unique to the Everglades. The long, thin roots, trunks and leafy branches of the mangroves grew denser the farther they traveled. A canopy formed overhead and a lot of noise faded. All Peter could hear was the plop of paddles in the water, rustling of the wind through the mangroves and occasional sounds that were definitely wildlife of some kind.

Kirstie was excited to point out birds here and there. The tricolored heron made his passenger "ooooh," and she pulled out her phone to take pictures. He lost track of all the birds, but when Kirstie noted a bald eagle nested high above them, every kayak stopped for passengers to take photos. He relaxed in his seat to enjoy the shade and how good it felt to do something he'd wanted to do for a long time but never made a priority.

"Are you happy? You look happy," Lauren asked as she aimed her phone at him for a picture.

"I hope you mean rugged or strong, a certified winner in the battle of man against nature," Peter said as he held up the paddle and tried a mean expression. Her soft laughter pleased him.

"Oh, definitely, that, too." Lauren's jaw dropped and she pointed silently before whispering, "Teeth. Alligator. Murder log. Nine o'clock."

Peter calmly turned his head to see a pair of eyes on what might have been a log but definitely was not a log. It was tempting to say the alligator was too far away to be dangerous but just in case, he said, "Hey, Kirstie, there's an alligator over here and we're going to move away from it."

Kirstie stood from her spot in the last kayak. "Yep, you spotted the first gator. Excellent job, front seat. Back seat, go ahead and move away. You aren't in any danger, I promise."

Peter trusted Kirstie. He did. And this had been his idea, but the way his heart raced as he paddled slowly away from the alligator made him wonder if he should have done his own research. Then he realized Lauren was videoing their getaway and hoped his face didn't reflect the immediate panic when his fight-or-flight response kicked in. He was 100 percent all-in for flight and had to battle through freezing up at the beginning. When Lauren never acted as if imminent death were stalking them and they'd put some water between them and the alligator, Peter forced his heart rate to return to normal.

"Good job, back seat," Lauren murmured. "You saved us." Her eyes met his, and he knew she was teasing but something about the exchange flipped the switch in his head from "this was a terrible idea, you maniac" to "another fine strategy by Peter Kim."

"Couldn't have done it without you, front seat. Excellent eyes make a keen advance warning system," Peter said.

"We make a good team, I guess." She turned to get a shot of the loggerhead turtle Kirstie gestured to. Neither one of them wanted to interrupt the tour, so Peter paddled, Lauren took pictures and they made it safely through the mangroves to a clearing where the water turned brackish—Kirstie's word—or saltwater mixed with fresh. The species of birds changed, and Peter could see more fish moving in the water. Some of the heat and humidity lifted and the last part of the tour was pleasant, not a single sighting of anything with teeth. When they arrived at the marina's landing, Kirstie helped everyone pull the kayaks in.

"Are you disappointed you didn't see any

pythons?" Kirstie asked Lauren when they were both out of the water.

Lauren immediately shook her head. "That alligator covered the price of admission."

Kirstie laughed. "I swear, we have one on every tour, some lonely gator who wants to make sure everyone is scared. I call it the 'haunted house' effect. It's easier to be scared if you're already scared when you go in, you know?"

Peter watched Lauren consider that. "That makes sense, but you did such a great job. This isn't about scares, but about taking in the beauty of a place not many people get to see." Then she tipped her head from side to side. "Plus, occasional floating logs with eyes and teeth."

"Right. I'm glad you didn't ask for any kind of proof that alligator had teeth." Kirstie nodded at the van where other members of the group were collecting. "When you have someone on the tour like the guy with the questions, it's almost a fifty-fifty shot he'll decide to move closer instead of away."

Mr. Helpful was trying to convince the others getting in the van that he'd caught a picture of a python in a tree. Peter grinned.

Neither he nor Lauren needed to see that photo. As long as it remained unproven, he could relegate it to Kirstie's "haunted house" theory.

Lauren was quiet as they pulled out of the parking lot, and he wasn't sure how to break the silence. Eventually, she began looking at her phone. "Are you interested in eating alligator? It looks like there's a popular restaurant coming up that has options. It's called Gourmet Gator." Lauren glanced over at him. Her lips were twitching, but it was hard to read what she expected him to say.

"Do you want to eat gator?" he asked. Did his voice go up at the end in a weird squeak? Yes. He hadn't fully committed to this experience obviously.

She wrinkled her nose. "I'm hungry. I could go for a regular burger. They also have those at Gourmet Gator, but we'd be missing out on some of the experience."

Relieved, Peter relaxed. "Lead on, front seat. I'm all in for that."

Lauren laughed. "All day long I've been trying to figure out how I ended up in a kayak with you paddling. Tell me about this friend that backed out at the last minute. I need to know who, other than you, skips Sunday brunch for adventure."

Peter exited where she pointed and wondered if he could stall long enough to let the restaurant derail the conversation. Then he realized he needed to be honest with her. Whatever this was between them, it deserved that.

"I lied," he said, and noticed her head whip toward him. Her mouth dropped open, probably at the blunt truth coming from him for once, but he wanted it that way. "I've wanted to do this for a long time, but I couldn't get anyone to go with me. My best friend, Marcus, is up for most things, especially days out on the water, but if he'd heard that guy talking about pythons…" Marcus would have stolen Peter's keys and left him there to walk home after that conversation. He tried to picture Sean or any of his other friends from Concord Court even making it that far, and the image wouldn't form.

When the violent green building loomed up on the left side of the road, Peter pulled into the parking lot of Gourmet Gator. How did he know it was the right spot? The sign. So many signs. One that should be visible from space announced the name and ran from one side of the building to the other. All the driveways had Gourmet Gator signs pointing in. From his spot, he could see a stand with souvenir shirts, hats and no telling what else with the Gourmet Gator mascot.

"I believe we've arrived," he said dryly, and was immediately rewarded when giggles erupted from his passenger. For some reason, that made him feel like a conqueror. He'd successfully followed her directions to arrive at this place. That was it, but he was proud he'd gotten the response from her.

"I'm not letting you off the hook that easily," Lauren said. "Why me? Did you think to yourself 'I bet Lauren is game for bugs, mud and danger' or was that an afterthought?"

Peter slipped the keys out of the ignition. "The truth is… I didn't want to say goodnight there in the marina. I wanted to make more plans with you. Why this kayak thing?" He shrugged. "I've always wanted to do it, and given how much you seemed to enjoy the Plank and Anchor, it made me wonder if we might have as much fun together here." He sighed. "The Plank and Anchor is not to everyone's taste, but we both love it."

When he turned to gauge her reaction, her

frown was adorable. "You've taken other people to our place?"

Our place? Why did that hit him in the abdomen and spread out in a glow?

"My best friend, Marcus. His opinion? His mother makes better chocolate cake," Peter said.

"That might be true, but is it parrot-shaped and delivered in a treasure chest? I doubt it." Lauren bumped his shoulder. "I can honestly say you are the first person who has ever taken a look at me and said, 'She'd be fun to outrun alligators with,' so thank you." Then she got out of the car.

The chummy shoulder bump wasn't exactly the bit of physical contact he wanted.

Peter had to hurry to catch her as she marched down the sidewalk. "Wait," he said, and grabbed her hand to pull her to a stop. "Are you mad at me?"

Lauren met his stare. He could see her take a deep breath, likely to calm herself. "No, I'm not mad, or I'm not mad at *you*, I guess. Me? A little bit."

"Why are you mad at you?" Peter asked as he held both her hands now.

"I know better than to spend time with you.

You're dangerous. You get in my head!" She tried to yank both hands free, but he didn't let go.

"How?" he asked. This was something he needed to understand. It was the key to the change in the atmosphere between them after the day out on the boat. It was also the reason his whole mood had dropped when she'd agreed to represent his nephew, and thus, to forgo more time with him.

"I know you've got a strategy in mind, that you're working on winning, whenever we're together. I know it. I tell myself to watch out for it, but then I find myself slipping into this…" She shook her head. "I don't know what to call it, but I start to look at you like…" She stopped talking and forced a smile. "Doesn't matter. You always remind me where we stand, so let's go get some burgers. We'll talk about the temperature and whether it will rain and nothing else. Don't be charming."

Lauren jerked her hands out of his and opened the door to the restaurant.

Don't be charming?

Like he was purposely deciding to pretend… something with Lauren?

The blast of cool air-conditioning caught his attention and he followed her inside. There was no way to untangle that short blip of conversation yet. He needed more information. Peter slid into the vivid green booth across from Lauren and took the alligator-shaped menu from the stack on the table.

"They have crayons in a cup," Lauren said as she pointed toward the napkins and condiments on the table. "This is our kind of place." She waited for him to smile and then returned to the menu.

They were both going to pretend, then. Acquaintances. Sort of friends. Definitely not more. The emptiness that accompanied every single one of Peter's first dates settled between them.

After they ordered, they both stared out the window until the waiter slid a basket of "gator nuggets" and three sauces between them.

Lauren raised dubious eyes to him before returning her attention to the basket. "When in Rome…" Peter was fascinated as she carefully chose the smallest bite and dipped it into what looked like ranch dressing before popping it in her mouth. He propped his chin on his hand as he watched her chew. "Well?"

After she swallowed, Lauren sipped the tea the waiter had delivered. "Tastes like chicken," she said as she wrinkled her nose, "but it's definitely not chicken." Then she leaned forward. "You aren't going to let me lord it over your head, are you? That I'm the only one brave enough to try those."

He couldn't allow that. After carefully eyeing the choices, he picked the largest nugget and went for barbecue sauce. Chewing was the only challenge, but he made it through and bent his head closer to hers. "You might have been first, but I chose the biggest bite. And you're right. It's definitely not chicken."

Her smile was sweet, but there was something missing in her eyes.

"Instead of the weather, let's try another direction for our next conversation. I know why I asked you today. Why did you agree?" Peter sipped his tea. If he could understand this, he could unknot his complicated emotions regarding...everything right now.

"Simple. I didn't want to be alone today." She smiled up at the waiter who deposited their burgers. "If I had known the full extent of the offer, I might have reconsidered that."

Lauren let loose a laugh and waved her hands about. "But then I would have missed out on fun, so I hope I wouldn't have gator-ed out." She raised an eyebrow. "Did you see what I did there?"

"As opposed to chickened out. Yeah, I got it." Peter snorted and took a bite of his burger. This had definitely been the right decision. Gourmet Gator made a nice hamburger. "Tell me more about your visit to your dad."

Her head snapped up before she glanced away. She was uncomfortable here. That meant he desperately wanted to know.

"I try to make visiting hours once a month." Lauren twirled the straw in her drink and watched the tea spin as if it was a fascinating show. "He's been in other facilities that made seeing him in person harder, so it's good he is where he is, I guess."

Peter set his burger down.

Lauren bit her lip. "It's part of a cycle. Right now, he's planning his future, and it sounds promising, like this time we'll see a change from him when he gets out. Then he'll get out, won't be able to find or keep a job, and will have this inspiration for easy money, aka illegal money. The cops, who also know his pattern, will eventually track him down. There will be a trial where I do my best to represent him fairly against overwhelming evidence, followed by jail time." She smiled but it didn't meet her eyes. "It's Mike Duncan's version of lather, rinse, repeat. I've been through it enough that the exciting highs are not as high and the devastating lows aren't as low. He's not bothered by it, so I try not to be."

That's what she thought, but her face told a different story. He could read the confusion in her eyes. Peter reached across the table to squeeze her hand.

Lauren dropped her gaze. "I don't know why I'm telling you this. Here I am handing over my secrets to my sworn competition!" She returned the squeeze before reaching for the ketchup. As she smacked the bottom of the bottle, she said, "Duncans don't change their spots. Nothing to fret about. Duncan philosophy right there. I walked out feeling defeated and yet…" She rolled her eyes. "I still desperately wanted to show him my amberjack. I wanted my dad to see my fish. Can you believe that?"

Peter could believe it. He understood it well.

"He also told me he loved me. And that he was proud of me, and wanted me to be happy more than anything else in the world. It was kind of a mixed message overall." Lauren shoved a fry in her mouth. "Aren't you glad you asked?" Her slightly high-pitched hysterical laugh was intended to lighten the mood, but it was hard to follow her lead. He knew she wasn't feeling any lighter.

"I don't think your spots have anything to do with your job," Peter said slowly as he worked carefully through her words. "Hard-working. Determined. Someone who helps others. You can take those spots anywhere you want." He waited for her to meet his eyes. "And your dad could have used all the things you love about him and done something with those spots instead of landing in jail. You make different decisions than he does, even if you have a lot in common to start with."

When she didn't say anything else, Peter returned to his lunch and finished his burger. "No comment?"

Her huff of breath made him grin. "I'm right, Duncan. You hate it when I'm right."

"You think you're always right, nothing new there," she muttered. "But this time, I appreciate it. I don't know if I can get there, but this is a new way to think about what he said, and I needed that. Do we ever get to the point where our parents and their opinions don't matter?"

Peter tilted his head to the side as he considered that. "Nope. Or I haven't reached it. My parents were proud of my air force career, but when I started talking retirement, they wanted to know what my next idea was. It couldn't be actual retirement. No stopping for Peter Kim. There's always more to be done." He dropped his credit card on the bill the server left on the table. He was glad to see she swiped it up before Lauren could argue about him paying. "So...law degree. That makes them happy. It was always my plan, but I wouldn't say it's a passion."

"I'm glad I'm not alone with the whole 'my parents don't get me' at forty years old." Lauren snickered when he groaned.

They stood and Peter put his card back into his wallet. Lauren said, "Thank you for lunch and kayaking and the time on your boat and that delicious cake. You've gone above and beyond to win over the best criminal defense lawyer in Miami. Your parents should be proud."

She stepped outside and held the door open for him. Peter followed her to the car and wondered if he should explain that that's where he'd started out but not where he'd ended up. He was having fun being with her.

Though it occurred to him that nothing had changed. He was going to spend as much time as he wanted doing exactly what he wanted and he could only do that as long as there was no one else close enough to be impacted by those decisions. It wasn't the time to get serious about Lauren Duncan because there was no doubt in his mind that she would change his whole plan. Keeping it friendly between them without the hint of anything more serious was the only route to do both, keep his plan and enjoy time with Lauren.

Then she did a very Lauren thing.

"Oh, Peter, we have to," she said as she hurried to the side of the restaurant. There was a photo op set up, including a stage with wooden cutouts of one alligator with a blue bowtie, and another alligator with a pink hat. It was perfect. People stepped up and put their faces in the cut out holes. A family of four had finished their photos when Lauren trotted up to them. Peter joined them in time to hear her say, "...group shot? I'll be happy to if you'll do the same for us."

Amused, Peter watched her give direction so that the kids were the gators and Mom and Dad were frightened for their lives. Then she made the "hurry up" motion to get him moving. "Pick your spot, Peter. Hurry!"

Peter was laughing as he stuck his face under the pink hat and batted his eyelashes. Lauren hurried up to stand next to him, and the family watching them chuckled at whatever she was doing. When the photo was done, Lauren reclaimed her phone and waved to the family before she tugged him over to a shaded bench next to a creek that ran behind the restaurant. "If you see anything with teeth, let me know." Then she pulled up the photo and giggled. "Oh, man. This is priceless."

Peter stared down at the photo. Lauren was glaring as if she was a tough alligator and he was staring in her direction…almost as if he were in love.

Or his alligator character was in love with hers.

"I'll send it to you," Lauren said as she chuckled.

If they'd gotten straight into the car, he might not have thought to do it. If they'd only headed home and resumed their normal schedules with the trial and all that to work on, Peter would have been okay.

But when she looked up at him, with her stubby ponytail and her hat and the bug spray and the laughter through it all, he bent forward and pressed a kiss to her lips. Her gasp caught his attention so he eased back to see surprise and confusion on her face.

Her hand immediately covered her lips and she stood.

"I'm sorry. I didn't mean to…" What? Catch her off guard? Kiss her when she didn't want to be kissed? He hadn't asked permission. He hadn't even thought it through. That wasn't like him and it certainly wasn't like her.

"No problem. We're friends. I know that." She shook her head. "It must be the romantic ambience of this place." She slugged his shoulder and headed back to the car.

Peter stared at the water for a second as he tried to make sense of his kiss and her reaction, but the pieces didn't fit together. Maybe the long drive home would give him time to figure out the answer.

CHAPTER ELEVEN

LAUREN FACED THE door of Peter's parents' house for too long as the nerve she'd slowly built up on the drive to suburban Miami Gardens quickly drained away. All the things she'd told herself had been true. They wanted a good lawyer; she was the best public defender in the office. Peter trusted her because he knew what she was capable of; his family would trust her, too. Defending Davey would come as second nature. The muscle memory would kick in and she'd do everything she could.

Every bit of it was true.

But the building pressure to pull out a win so that faith was deserved was taking her right back to her breaking point in Blake Bennings's office.

Then there was the kiss she'd successfully avoided talking about during the silent drive home from Gourmet Gator. At some point, she would need to address it, but she hadn't come up with any coherent thoughts so far.

Peter might have been using charm and flirtation to win her over, but now that she'd agreed to take the case, it was harder to find a good reason for anything more than their usual banter. Friends bantered. *They* bantered. Friends did not kiss, so chalking that up to an impulse made sense, even if Gourmet Gator didn't count as a romantic atmosphere.

Standing in front of the door wasn't solving anything, but if she knocked, she'd be face-to-face with Peter again, and her tongue was ready to tie itself in knots already.

"Listen, if you want to leave, I'll go with you. I know a place that serves excellent martinis and it's always happy hour for ladies," murmured a woman who had stepped up beside Lauren while she was staring at the doorbell. "And if we're going drinking, let's introduce ourselves. Nicole Kim." She held out her hand. A streak of yellow paint covered one of her knuckles. "That paint is dry. Don't worry."

Lauren inhaled slowly as she shook Nicole's hand. "I can't leave, but I will never betray your presence if you need to escape. You can trust me. I'm a lawyer. Lauren Duncan."

Nicole nodded. "I figured you must be Lauren. We're all glad you're here. Peter has done an excellent job of talking you up. I expect part of that is to reassure Davey, but he said he'd find the best and he always comes through. As my mother says, 'thank heavens for Peter.'"

Lauren ran her hand through her hair. She'd gone for business casual since they were nowhere near a courtroom, but she was suddenly wishing she could pull off adorable buns on either side of her head like Nicole. Her jeans were dappled with paint, too, but it seemed more like a choice than an accident.

"I was about to ring the doorbell." Lauren smiled as Nicole raised a skeptical eyebrow.

"Door's open. It always is. No matter how many times I or even the Chosen One tell them to lock it, they never do," Nicole said as she pointed at the knob. "The Chosen One is my nickname for Peter. Feel free to use it. He hates it. After you." Then she rocked back on her heels.

Lauren laughed. "I came along at the right time, didn't I?"

"You mean, I did!" Nicole said. "Walking in alone makes me nervous."

"I'm sure your brother's case is going to go well. Peter said Davey has a spotless record. This should be open-and-shut." Lauren knew it wouldn't be quite that easy, since she'd been in front of the judge who'd be hearing the case. The judge showed little leniency for drug crimes, but this would be as simple as it could be.

"My brother? Peter would never! And Davey…" She shook her head. "My son is even less likely to flout the law of the land than my brother, although I have no idea how that could be possible. Both of them are uber-law-abiding citizens."

Her son? Lauren did her best not to gape, but she couldn't make the math work. Nicole might as well be a college student, not mother to a college student.

"Don't let the hairdo fool you," Nicole said with a grin. "I still get carded at bars, but not by anyone who knows me. Davey was a surprise, although my parents were ready after I dropped out of college to backpack through Europe at eighteen. Best piece of kismet in my life."

Lauren processed Nicole's confessions as quickly as she could, but it was clear Peter's sister's brain worked as quickly as his did but not in quite the same way. It would take a second to catch up.

Nicole reached over to open the door. "Fine. I'll be brave. Follow me." She straightened her shoulders and stepped inside. The floors were cool tile and the walls of the entryway were painted a cheerful yellow and lined with photos. "I call this the gallery. I'll give you a tour later if you'd like to meet all the ancestors, but if we don't go and let my mother know we're here, we're going to be in trouble, me more than you, but I don't think you'll escape her wrath."

Lauren nodded. "I'm right behind you."

Nicole took off through the living room, which was cluttered with stacks of books and more plants, but inviting. It was easy to tell this had been the Kims' home for years and they were comfortable here. No modern, stylish pieces, but plush furniture gathered around the television. "I imagine they're outside. My parents are renovating the kitchen right now, so cooking in there annoys my mother."

She stopped in the doorway of a galley kitchen. The flooring had been removed along with all the cabinet doors, and the counters were covered in plastic. "I don't blame her. That would bother me, too."

As Nicole entered the sunroom, Lauren could hear voices. When they walked out onto the covered patio, she could see an older couple stretched out on loungers while Peter manned the grill and a younger version of Peter set the table.

"When Lauren gets here, remember to tell her everything you told me," Peter said over his shoulder. "And make sure you ask all your questions. She's good at this and she'll know the answers. If you wait to ask, I'll have to call her and get the information later, so cut out the middleman."

"Good advice, Peter," Nicole said as she came forward. "Did you get all that, Lauren?"

All eyes were on Lauren as she tripped on the threshold. "I'm better at law than I am at walking, obviously." Her joke fell flat as everyone but Peter frowned at her.

"Hey, you should have texted me you were here. I would never abandon you to Nic's clutches first thing." He handed Davey, she presumed, the tongs he'd been using to turn the meat and hurried to put his hand on her arm. "Eomma, Appa, this is Lauren."

"That means Mom and Dad. Don't call them that," Nicole muttered in her ear before she bent to give her parents a peck on the cheek before wrestling her son into a bear hug while he protested.

"Are you okay?" Peter asked. "She didn't say anything weird, did she?" He sighed. "Okay, not too weird?"

Lauren laughed. "We were plotting an escape for martinis but thought better of it."

"We should have done this at my house. Everyone acts better when we get away from the home Nic and I waged battle in through our teenage years, but my mother insisted, something about family matters being taken care of at home." His helpless shrug was cute. It might have been the oven mitt still covering his hand. It was shaped like a fish.

She pointed at it. "Do they know your aversion to actual fishing?"

He shot her a guilty glance. "That's our little secret."

They both laughed and Lauren realized that everyone else was watching them with extreme interest. Every face, except for perhaps Davey's, was telegraphing curiosity and differing levels of delight.

"Mr. Kim. Mrs. Kim. It's a pleasure to meet you. You have a lovely home. Who is the gardener?" Lauren asked as she shook their hands. "The pots in the front are beautiful."

"Please, call me Anna," Peter's mother said. "I do like my plants, but I'm not sure it counts as gardening if they're all in pots. Don't gardeners need plots of land?"

"Certainly, it counts," her husband said as he patted her back. "In books and plants, my wife is the expert." He pointed to his chest. "I'm Tim. I tore up the kitchen. I have to confess now because it's going to come out at one point or another tonight. Might as well lay all my cards out on the table."

Lauren laughed at the way he ducked his head when Anna glared at him.

She turned to Peter's nephew. "And you must be Davey."

She could see the nerves and the youth in his eyes. He swallowed audibly and said, "Actually, it's David, if you don't mind. I can't get anyone else here to change a childhood nickname, but I'd rather not have the judge hear my lawyer call me Davey."

"Smart. Very smart. Presenting the right image is part of the successful attorney's defense strategy," Lauren said. "Have you considered law school?"

He ran his hand over his forehead. "That was the plan, but with this on my record…"

Lauren's surprise lasted only a second, but Nicole filled the silence. "That's it! The Kims will build a law dynasty." Then she brushed at the dried paint on her fingers. "Just not me."

"Two is not a dynasty, Nic," Peter grumbled as he moved his nephew out of the way to check the barbecue. Lauren could tell pressure was straining his nerves when Peter forced a smile. "I thought we could eat and then discuss the case, if that's okay? Davey, grab the stuff from inside for me. Nic, go help him."

His sister rolled her eyes behind his back but followed directions. It was interesting to see Peter here, surrounded by his family. Mom and Dad were comfortable resting while he took charge.

Lauren watched them go. "Can I help with anything?"

"You are a guest. Please take a seat," Anna said from her comfortable spot on the lounge.

When Peter's eyes met hers, Lauren swallowed the laugh, but it was adorable to see him in these circumstances. No one here was impressed with the facade of the smooth, charming Peter Kim that she knew.

After all the food was on the table and everyone was situated, they ate and made the usual small talk. Lauren was amazed to hear about all the changes the Kims had witnessed over the years in their neighborhood. New people moving in, raising grandkids, previous neighbors who had stopped by to visit while they were visiting the area, updates on the teenagers Peter and Nicole had run around with in high school.

Peter and Nicole had grown up in that house; there were a lot of memories connected to it. That kind of continuity sounded ideal to Lauren, who'd moved in and out of random apartments, depending on her father being in jail or out of jail and her mother's ability to cope. The neighborhoods had always stayed pretty much the same, but she'd love to have a welcoming home to return to each day.

It was a sharp display of the differences between Lauren and Peter, too.

His teasing, open family was what she dreamed of. What would they think about her background?

As a lawyer, it might be fine or even a bonus, but if Peter had brought her home as a friend or…a person he kissed often, they would likely have a different opinion. Nothing to fret about, Lauren reminded herself. That was not important here.

Tonight she had a job to do.

After David, Peter and Nicole cleared the table, Lauren reached for her notebook. "Now's the time to tell me everything and ask all the questions."

RELIEVED TO MOVE on to the elephant in the room, or on the patio to be exact, Peter picked up the folder he'd put together and tried to smooth the crumpled edges before he slid it in front of her. "I started a case file. All I have in it right now are the police report and Nicole's copies of every report card in Davey's academic history." Had he asked for those? No. They would carry little weight, but his family had been doing nothing but coming up with what they hoped were ironclad defenses ever since Davey's arraignment.

Peter was relieved all over again that the outcome of this trial was out of his hands. No way did he want to carry all that responsibility.

As Lauren flipped through the papers he'd gathered, he realized that was what she'd been saying to him all along. That responsibility was the crushing piece of the job, not the work itself.

And he'd convinced her to put herself back under the weight. The realization sat heavy on his shoulders.

"He's a good student. That should be mentioned in his defense. Honor roll. Scholarship. There has never been a Kim in trouble with the law, and there is no way this one would be the first." His mother sniffed as if everyone would agree with that. Even Peter's law school classes would not stand up against what his mother considered common sense, so he sent Lauren a silent message to skip any reasonable explanation of why the defendant's elementary school marks for arithmetic did little to prove his character before a judge.

"Of course it should, Mrs. Kim." Lauren

smiled at Peter before she pulled out the police report. "Thanks. You got the case started for me."

Her approval...

Peter had made it through two years of law school already. His grades were good and he had the respect of his peers and his professors. None of that was as powerful as Lauren's expression.

His parents had always treated him like the sun rose on his command, at least until Davey came along and showed them what a real student looked like. His bratty little sister looked up to him, too, although she'd never admit it. The way Nic kept shifting her attention between him and Lauren while she nervously chewed her bottom lip telegraphed both her worry and her faith.

But Lauren's smile? The warm glow of pleasure and pride was silly but it spread through his middle anyway.

Lauren scanned the report and turned to Davey. "David, tell me in your own words what happened."

"I was driving home after work, a night shift at the hospital, and I ran a stop sign." Davey squeezed his fingers together so tightly that his knuckles were white. "When the police officers pulled me over, I expected a ticket that I'd never tell anyone about and pick up extra shifts at the hospital to cover. They always need more janitorial staff at night. I didn't stop, that's true. I was distracted and someone could have been hurt, so I deserved that ticket."

"What reason did the officers give you when they requested to search your car?" Lauren asked.

Davey rubbed his forehead. "They just told me to get out of the car. That's when I realized something else might happen. Not a ticket. Worse."

"Does the reason matter?" Peter asked.

Lauren blinked at him. Had she forgotten he was sitting next to her? That punched a hole in his ego, for sure. "For a warrantless search, the officers should have had David's okay before they started looking and a reasonable suspicion that they might find something. First-time offender..." She clicked her pen. "This traffic stop was after midnight on a Thursday night. Residential area. True, it's near the college but a pretty quiet spot nonetheless. Why were the police there at all?"

She clicked her pen several more times before scribbling something on her notepad. "If there's a pattern, it might not mean anything other than they've had other drug busts there or neighbors have registered complaints or… It might be a sign that they are targeting college kids." She checked the address. "I'm not familiar with the Royale Apartments. Are most of your neighbors also college kids? Rent's not terrible but not the lowest, either?"

"Yeah," Davey said, "I couldn't afford it myself, but I share an apartment with two other guys and it's not bad." Then his head snapped up. "Two guys in my study group have been pulled over. They live there, too."

Lauren nodded. "Not a known location for frequent arrests as far as I'm aware, so if it's a pattern, we need to find out why."

Peter glanced at Lauren, who was now scribbling more notes on her pad. That frenzy to get everything down, he'd seen that before in a classroom setting. Her shoulders were climbing toward her ears as she wrote, one hand anchoring her pad to keep it from sliding away. She'd been the most serious student in their class, and she hadn't shaken it. Why did he find that so appealing?

"What are you writing?" he asked when she showed no signs of letting up.

"We can raise the question of whether the officer had probable cause for a search." Lauren grimaced. "The problem is almost all judges are going to say yes, they do have enough cause, most of the time, but it's never a guarantee. We can work with that, even if it's not a sure thing." She gave a brief nod and looked straight at Davey. "Did you know you had drugs in the car, David?"

"No, ma'am, I did not. I don't use drugs. I don't sell drugs, but now I'm wondering if my roommate does. He asked to borrow my car to drive to class that day and barely made it back before I left for my night shift. I'm the only one in the apartment with a car, so the guys borrow it to make store runs now and then," David said.

This is what Peter had been hanging on to. The only thing David had done was trust the wrong people and everyone was guilty of that at one time or another. All they had to do was get Davey through this one episode without it ruining the kid's life, and he might learn a valuable lesson.

"We moved him home as soon as he was released on bail," Peter's mother said firmly.

Nicole cleared her throat. "To clarify, David moved here, with his grandparents, instead of back home to the modern loft over my art studio in Wynwood where he was raised." Nicole smiled but it didn't reach her eyes. "Everyone thought it would be a better environment."

"Not everyone," Davey muttered.

"Okay. I've got ideas on what we need to do to win." No one replied but Peter could see a wave of shoulders relax down the lineup of chairs on the patio. "I need names and phone numbers of the other two students who were stopped to confirm it's the same officers. I might be able to get the information from the police station."

Davey didn't hesitate but wrote the names she demanded.

When she took the notepad back and slipped it into her bag, she smiled at Davey. "I don't want to get your hopes up. At the pretrial hearing, the prosecutor will offer you a plea deal that we'll discuss, but we're going to do our best to make it clear that would be a waste of time."

"You mean I'd plead guilty? And that

would go on my record?" Davey's horrified tone and the glitter of tears in his eyes twisted the knot in Peter's stomach again. He'd told the kid more than once that, no matter what happened, his life would go on and his family would support him.

Still, it was impossible to blame his nephew for failing to trust that when he was faced with something none of them had ever come up against.

As Peter watched Lauren calmly reach across the table to clench Davey's hands, he felt a warmth overtake him. He was grateful she was here.

"The plea is something we'll talk about only if we get there. We'll plead not guilty and build a persuasive case. We'll keep your options open. I'm good at my job." She wrinkled her nose. "Okay, it's not my job anymore, but never doubt I'm the best."

She waited patiently for Davey to signal that he was hearing her.

When he nodded, so did Peter.

"I'll verify the date of your pretrial hearing and be in touch." Lauren pulled out cards. "Okay, these are almost useless." She shook her head and scribbled her cell number on the back. "You can call me anytime you have questions before then. That will save Peter a phone call."

Lauren stood but before she could walk out, his parents wrapped their arms around her in a group hug. Her eyes met his over his mother's shoulder as if to ask, "What is happening?" Her bewildered frown and gentle pats were sweet. Apparently, she wasn't used to instant gratitude from most of her clients.

When his parents let her go, Nicole slipped her arm through Lauren's. "You can't leave yet. Let's finish the tour." Her wicked grin as she led Lauren inside convinced Peter that his sister was about to make sure Lauren saw every single awkward photo of him that his parents refused to take down. He wanted to follow, but he also wanted his sister to have time to say whatever was on her mind to Lauren. Davey was afraid, but his mother was terrified, even if she'd never admit it.

"Davey, let's clean up the dishes," Peter said, and grinned as Davey grumbled. It reassured him that the kid grumbled like a normal boy. "I'll wash, you dry."

They worked quickly, putting the leftovers away and clearing all the dishes. Through the kitchen window, Peter could see his parents. His mother's head was resting on his father's shoulder while they talked. That was nice. He knew they were concerned; meeting with Lauren should help them cope.

When he handed Davey the last pan, he asked, "How are you feeling now?"

The kid frowned as he dried. "Better, maybe. I'm not sure. Knowing that we aren't alone helps."

"Lauren had good ideas to track down, so that's progress." Peter crossed his arms as he leaned back against the counter. "How is it going here?"

Davey rolled his eyes. "They act like I was living a wild life. All I did was work and go to school and sleep and work." He shook his head. "The food is better here, but I can't imagine spending two more years in your old bedroom."

Since Peter had been forced to do that for about a month before he could move into Concord Court, he understood Davey. Family was nice, but they were usually even better at a distance.

"On the bright side, if you go to law school at Sawgrass, too, you won't have to pay rent.

You'll always have a room with your grand-parents," Peter said, and laughed as he tossed the dish towel over Davey's head. "Listen, make it to the trial. When that's settled, we'll work on Halmoni and Harebeoji. Check on the deadline for on-campus housing. If we can get you back in the dorms, I'll get every-one else to agree to that."

Davey yanked the dish towel away. "I love you, Uncle Peter. If I ever told you I didn't, I was wrong. If you manage to fix this, I will forget the time that you missed sending my birthday gift."

"You were eleven. Holding a grudge this long? That's impressive, kid." Peter wrapped Davey in a headlock and messed up his care-fully styled hair before he said, "Fair enough. I'll hold you to it. Go study or something."

Davey was still trying to fix his hair when Peter got brave and tracked down his sis-ter, who was pointing at what appeared to be Peter's high school sophomore yearbook picture. It was a glossy eight-by-ten-inch framed photo on the wall. "As you can see, my brother never was very good-looking."

Lauren's jaw suddenly dropped, which con-vinced him that his sister had been restrained until he turned up. Lauren laughed. "Does his shirt say 'Math Hero' or..." Lauren shook her head. There was nothing else that it could have said. The skinny arms and legs had been part of growing up, but Peter couldn't blame his clothing choice on anything other than a bad decision. "It's nice to know Peter Kim had an awkward phase, even if some of us never managed to grow out of it like he did."

His sister snorted and Peter knew exactly why. His parents were equal-opportunity embarrassers, so her freshman-year photo was right next to his.

"Was this for Halloween?" Lauren asked, completely innocent to the style parade his sister had led through the years. "How did you get your hair to do that?"

"Black dye. Cans of hairspray. Iron will," Nicole answered. "That was my punk phase. I was the only representative at our school, so I had to do it justice."

"Oh, I'm sorry. I didn't mean..." Lauren's stricken face as she turned and spied him reminded Peter that she was a genuinely nice person, too. No way would she have meant to embarrass or insult anyone.

Nicole sighed. "No, it's fair. I went through a lot of phases before I figured myself out."

"Whereas I've just had one phase and needed time to catch up to all my good looks," Peter said from his spot down the hall.

"Do not agree with him. His head barely fits through the door as it is," Nicole muttered. "There aren't any pictures of him being shoved into lockers but it did happen, and I try to make sure everyone who enters the Kim house knows about it. I was the only witness, but I take my job as Kim family historian seriously."

"I don't believe that," Lauren said, creases wrinkling her forehead. "Charming Peter Kim stuck in a locker?"

His sister groaned. "Everybody says that, but it's true. Before he learned to handle all this *charm*, he ticked people off. Large people. Angry people." She pointed a finger at Lauren. "The next time I see you, I'm bringing the family albums out. You'll believe me then. My theory is that he found a magic lamp somewhere between high school and college and used all three wishes to improve his personality." Nicole marched up to him, instantly putting Peter on guard. His sister stretched up on her tiptoes to kiss his cheek. She whispered, "I like her. A lot. Don't mess this up." Then she waved at Lauren and said she was off to find her son.

"I'll walk you out," Peter said, and opened the front door. As they stood on the stone walkway, he said, "I don't know how to thank you."

"Just doing my job, Peter." Lauren brushed her hair over her shoulder. Was he making her nervous? Or was the kiss on her mind, too?

"I realized today what I was asking you to do, by continuing to do this job, I mean. I get the heavy responsibility so much better. I owe you. Big." Peter had no idea how he would pay her back, either.

"I'll start a tab for you," Lauren said.

That response made him wonder how many other people owed her favors. It was right there, on the tip of her tongue, to brush off his debt.

"Your family is great, Peter. I'm happy to help." She motioned at the neat driveway and his mother's colorful pots. "I had no idea I was walking into the home I dreamed about as a kid, but it's so sweet to see your roots. Those pictures..." Her eyes were huge.

"When you get your law degree, you might consider suing your parents for keeping all that on display. Emotional damages. Pain and suffering, something like that. I don't know as much about civil litigation, but you and Nicole have grounds for some kind of monetary payout, I'd say."

Peter stepped closer to her. "I'll keep that in mind. I try to view it as a sign of how much they love us, but knowing my mother, it's also to keep us humble."

She did the cute thing with her hair again. "I see that. It's sweet, whatever it is."

"If I can help with anything, I want to. Research or tracking down people. I seem to be pretty good at that." Peter didn't want her to leave. That was becoming a habit.

"I may take you up on the offer if I can get more information from the police station. That's on my agenda for tomorrow, and I'm going to swing by the prosecutor's office to test the waters," Lauren said as she shifted her bag to the opposite shoulder.

Peter reached to take the bag for her and dropped it inside her car on the passenger seat. When she tangled her fingers together, he wondered if that had been nerves, too.

"I hope you will. Or if you need some distraction, Concord Court has a pool. There are zero fish in the water there, although it is sometimes home for synchronized swimming practice. You might enjoy that." Peter reached for her hand and smoothed his thumb over her knuckles.

"I would, yes, even if I have no idea what that means." The way she studied their hands made him wonder if he was about to be sorry for pushing his luck.

"What's your strategy now, Peter?" Lauren asked. Her confusion was easy to read. "I've agreed to help. You don't have to do this." She lifted their tangled hands.

The urge to pretend he had no idea what she meant came and went.

This was the problem he kept circling, too. "Honestly? I wanted to touch you. No strategy. No plan. I wanted to so I did. Are you familiar with the concept?"

Lauren inhaled slowly. "Run it past me again. Draw a diagram. I need the basics."

Peter nodded. "Yeah, I've gotten fairly good at that. It's the whole guiding philosophy of my life, the reason for a focus on wills and estates in law school and dating for fun instead of the future. I had so many strategies and long-term plans and responsibilities for such a long time that this was supposed to be my break. You wanted two weeks of vacation, but I decided to make that a way of life. I'm a professional, you might say."

"I could learn a lot from you," she said loftily, "unless I flunk the training and start planning a future with Mr. Forever, right?"

Peter wasn't sure she was the one in danger of losing focus on the simpler life, but he was afraid confessing that would send her into hiding.

"I'm having a good time as *friends*." Peter made sure to hit the last word and pause for effect. "There's no reason we have to go further."

This time she lifted their hands. "I don't hold hands with my other friends like this."

"We can be trailblazers." He didn't resist when she pulled away. "Or not."

"Let's concentrate on winning Davey's case," Lauren said, "for your adorable family, whom I love and want to adopt me at their earliest convenience. I used to think I missed being a part of a wall of old photos like yours, but I wasn't aware of the downside. Lucky for you, your awkward phase only makes me like you more."

Peter crossed his arms over his chest. "That is the first time I've heard that. I am grateful. I'd like to find a time machine to travel back to high school so you can tell Eliza Garcia that so she will go to prom with me instead of laughing in my face."

Lauren wrinkled her nose. "Stop. I already like you."

"You like me," Peter sang under his breath.

Lauren groaned. "Less when you do that."

Peter grinned, the urge to bring up the kiss right there, but he didn't want to send her running away. He wanted to stand here in front of his parents' house as long as she would be there with him.

"Charming Peter Kim," she said softly.

He waited. She was working her way up to something important, he could sense it.

"Do you ever think about how different we are? Our backgrounds couldn't be farther apart. Our goals." She studied his face. "And you're quickly becoming a friend, the lifeline who is keeping me afloat."

A relieved smile was his only available response. He never saw the *but* coming.

"But you're dangerous, too. I can't relax or float along *professionally*, Peter." She inhaled slowly. "I jump in. I did that with my career, and I wouldn't be surprised if I do it again, if I ever figure out what my next career will be." Her lips were a tight line as she exhaled. "You could break my heart so easily."

Peter realized there was more to what she was saying. On the surface, she was making a case for friendship. He got that. Underneath? She was asking him not to hurt her.

She'd been hurt by the people who should have protected her and so she'd learned to protect herself.

Something about him, about them, was a threat to that protection.

"Okay. Davey's case. Let's get that settled. And your career." Peter smiled. "That should keep us busy for a while, giving me an opportunity to untangle the chaos you've put in my brain."

Her jaw dropped. "Chaos? In your brain? I don't know whether I'm flattered or offended."

Peter pretended to think. "Hold off deciding." Then he squeezed her hand. "All I know is that I don't want this to be goodbye, so, see you soon."

"Okay. I get that." She moved to get into her car.

"Text me if you need me," Peter said softly. "For anything, help with the case, to talk or a dip in the pool."

Lauren hesitated but she smiled as she got into the driver's seat. If there hadn't been a car between them, he would have kissed her again. The concern, the fragile trust, the humor on her face... He wouldn't have been able to resist.

As Peter walked back inside the house, he realized it was time for more advice from the midnight pool support group. He knew who was the one for him. He just had to convince her to take a risk on charming Peter Kim.

CHAPTER TWELVE

LAUREN DECIDED TO ease her way back into public defending by starting her investigation into David Kim's arrest at the police station, instead of the prosecutor's office. There were logical reasons to do it that way, but her biggest motivation was to avoid the nosy stares from former opponents who would have heard the gossip about her unplanned job exit. So she put on her second-best suit, a pair of comfortable heels and a half-genuine smile before entering the police station.

If she were still buried under casework, a phone call would have been all she could manage, but every request was stronger when made in person.

Lauren's faith in her ability to step back into the ring with her head up was rewarded when she saw Officer Estevez at the front desk. Another officer would have been a challenge. She and Estevez had that friendly "we're sort of coworkers so we can exchange news about our weekends" kind of relationship.

"Well, now, I didn't expect to see you again, or not so soon, at least," the police officer said. "Figured you'd take a minute to choose from all the fancy offers that would come rolling in."

Lauren set her briefcase down. "I've taken a minute, spent some time relaxing, and it was wonderful. I'm only back in the suit and here today to help a friend."

Officer Estevez nodded happily. "Handsome friend. About this tall?" She held her hand up above her head. "I thought his face lit up when I mentioned your name. He was looking for a good lawyer."

"That's him," Lauren said. It didn't surprise her that Peter had made an impression on the woman.

"I was hoping to get some help with an information request. Here's the formal request letter." Lauren bent closer to say under her breath, "But I need it faster than the usual time frame. Do you know anyone who can assist me with these records?" Lauren waited as she watched the other woman scan her request.

"Traffic stops made in the past six months," Officer Estevez read slowly. Her eyes met Lauren's. "Are you digging up dirt on someone in particular?"

Lauren smiled as she asked herself if she should have sent Peter with this request. As a rule, officers weren't too happy to contribute to efforts that might overturn their arrests. Estevez had always been friendly, but she might choose her fellow officers over Lauren. It would be easy enough. If the police pushed the maximum turnaround time under their information request policy, David's pretrial hearing would be over by the time they complied.

Since she'd still need it for the trial, if it came to that, Lauren would take what she could get.

"I'm interested in the timing and location of similar traffic stops that preceded my client's arrest," Lauren said in the same low voice. Simple enough. If everything was legitimate, no one was going to face any trouble. There would be enough to show a pattern one way or the other, random traffic stop that netted drugs or a focused search that targeted kids from Davey's apartment complex. That alone wouldn't be enough for any judge to toss the case, but if Lauren could convince the judge that there had been no reasonable suspicion of drugs in the first place and the officers had failed to gain Davey's permission for a warrantless search…

Convincing this judge to dismiss a drug case at the pretrial hearing was almost impossible. That drugs were found in Davey's car was indisputable.

Long shots were all she had at this point, including this special quick-turnaround request.

Officer Estevez looked up from the letter. "The communications office will handle the response." She entered something on her computer. "But I'll go ahead and pull the report. All this information is available, so I can't see them fighting the request." She looked back at the letter. "You want it via email. Easy enough."

Relieved, Lauren relaxed.

Then Estevez leaned forward. "Give me a hint. Who are you going to work for? I love to have the hottest gossip first."

"If I had the answer, I would tell you, but…" Lauren shrugged. It was one of those questions that took too many words to answer properly.

"Okay, okay," Estevez said with a grin. "If your friend mentions me, make sure to tell him I'm single, and we'll call this even."

Lauren laughed. She definitely should have asked Peter to handle this info request. He'd have had printouts and Estevez's phone number before he walked out of the station.

"I'll do it. Thanks." Lauren nodded and picked up her briefcase. As she trotted back down the steps to the sidewalk, she realized her shoulders were straighter. She had more energy, and while she wasn't looking forward to entering the prosecutor's office, she knew it was the next step. She had a handle on this job. Why would she quit when she was so good at it?

By the time she made it up to the prosecutor's office after a walk in Miami's heat, Lauren was thankful all over again for John Gorrie and his invention of blessed air-conditioning that made life possible. When the receptionist noticed her, Lauren stopped fanning herself with her hand and said,

"Could you see if the state attorney has time to speak with me about the David Kim case?" Lauren gripped her briefcase. "Or the prosecuting attorney, if you have that information."

"Have a seat," the receptionist said, "and I'll check."

Lauren wandered over to the cushy couch under a long line of windows that looked out on the sidewalk leading to the courthouse. She'd been in the same spot so many times, but it hadn't felt like this, like it was out of the ordinary, not just another part of the job. Was a week away from the routine long enough for the familiar to become unfamiliar?

"Ms. Duncan, you can go back." The receptionist pointed to the double doors beside her desk. "The prosecuting attorney will meet you in the first conference room."

Lauren smiled at her and followed her direction. She'd never introduced herself. At some point, she'd made an impression on the state attorney's office well enough that the receptionist must have recognized her. That boosted her confidence again. Lauren opened the door to the first small room set aside for client or attorney meetings and realized she might be facing another hurdle.

"Hey, Lauren," Monica Holt said as she held out her hand. "It's been a minute. How are things?"

Lauren shook her hand and tried to gauge whether Monica was asking a small-talk type of question or if she was interested in information like Officer Estevez. "Good. Things are good. I'm glad to see you today." That wasn't exactly true. Lauren would have preferred to face off with someone with less experience than Monica Holt, but she wasn't going to show fear. "We should be able to work this out easily."

Monica slid a folder across the conference table. "Sure. We'll offer the minimum, as we do for all first-timers, in exchange for a guilty plea. Time served. Probation." She brushed her hands off as if it was all taken care of.

Lauren grimaced. "Yeah, the only thing is, my client is innocent, so that won't work for us. Dropping the case would be better."

Monica huffed out a breath. "How many times have we danced this same dance, either with each other or new partners, Lauren?" She shook her head. "You know 'innocent' is one of those things that is easy to claim but hard to prove in cases like this. Are you pushing for a jury trial here? Judge Kincaid will not be a fan."

She was right about that. Judge Kincaid took a narrow reading of the law and didn't extend much grace to anyone, not even first-timers. He'd see the plea as fair and reasonable and rejecting it as gumming up the system.

"I know. I know, but it's the right thing to do." Lauren ran her hand over the smooth table. "Is there any evidence you plan to submit in addition to the officers' report of the traffic stop?"

Monica raised her eyebrows. "Do I need any other evidence?"

So that was a no then.

"And you don't have any interest in dropping the charges because you don't have any additional evidence to convince the judge," Lauren said.

"Do I need any other evidence?" Monica repeated. "This is one of those cases that we take care of quickly, Lauren, so we can move on to the bigger questions. David Kim is cut-and-dried."

If Lauren had been standing across the desk from Blake, he would have said exactly the same thing. Her old boss might even have used the same words and the same bored tone.

A touch of the old frustration simmered under her skin. It was time to go.

"Okay, I'll see you in court. Thank you for your time today. It's been a big help." Not quite the truth but a nice exit line.

"Not enough to keep you busy? You want to sweat the small stuff, huh?" Monica asked as she came around the table and followed Lauren back to the lobby.

"It's not small stuff to the innocent kid who has plans for his life," Lauren said slowly. She was going to be calm about this. Losing her temper over the same issue that had caused her to quit her job? Yeah, further proof that she was not under control would sweep the courthouse quickly. She didn't need the judge to be watching for emotional outbursts when Monica Holt pushed her buttons.

There would definitely be button-pushing. That was part of the grand legal tradition.

"I guess even a little time off is enough to make you forget how your clients are *always* innocent," Monica drawled, "even when they're not."

"Innocent until proven guilty. Exactly.

Isn't that the whole premise of our profession? My client is innocent. That's the work I do. You have to prove he isn't. That's the job you signed up for. Why don't we both do our best." It sounded so simple when she said it like that. Why wasn't it that simple in the real world?

Monica shrugged. "Okay, I'll see you in court, but if you decide you want to switch over to the winning side, I'll be happy to put in a good word for you with the state attorney. She's always looking for top lawyers."

Lauren smiled, even though there was one thing she knew deep down and that was she'd never switch sides. She might need a break from fighting a losing battle, but she couldn't put people like her father away.

The justice system worked when the two sides were in check. Lauren had faith in that.

"Thanks, Monica." Lauren made her way back to the street, where she shook out her hands and waited for them to stop trembling. She'd learned valuable information in the exchange and she'd managed to keep her cool, so both visits had been successful. These nerves were a problem, but she understood better now what they meant.

Lauren had believed the responsibility of the position was what was grinding her down. That was only part of it. Spending time with people who treated the process like a job was the real trigger, because to her, it was personal. There was a piece of her father in every defendant and of herself in the family members who showed up in the courtroom. The system wasn't perfect, but she was beginning to see that she wasn't perfect for the job, either. Caring too much could cloud her judgment and wear her down.

She'd made the right call to leave, and this would be her last case.

Eventually she'd learn to be okay with walking away from the one thing she was best at. Today wasn't that day, but she had to believe something else could fill that place in her life.

PETER USED HIS discarded T-shirt to wipe the sweat off his forehead as he sat on the curb in front of the Concord Court office. Brisa had texted their running group an SOS after a hard day, so he, Mira and Jason Ward had shown up to go running with her after sunset. Their normal routine was early in the morning before the sun baked Miami, but it was hard to decide if the heat was any less miserable than now.

Jason stretched out beside Peter and rubbed his knee where it met his prosthetic. Peter never asked but he was pretty sure it was habit more than pain because the guy never lagged in their runs, not even when Mira pushed them twice as far as usual. Sean? He would complain loudly, but that was true of any distance. It had been nice to run without all the whining.

"You feeling any better?" Jason asked, and everyone turned to Brisa.

She closed her eyes. "A little. Thank you for joining me. I could have run by myself but Wade would have lectured me and…" She smiled. "I've had enough of navigating upset people today."

"Tell us," Mira said before she tightened her drooping ponytail. "That's what you really need. Vent to your friends."

Brisa nodded. "Yep. You're right. First there was a call from my father. He's negotiated the final fee for using Sunshine Park for the outreach to the veterans here in southern Florida who might be looking for Concord

Court's programs. Good. Hmm. The popular professional ball players I had lined up for publicity dropped out. Bad. Cheeky, the Hollywood Beach Chickens' mascot, can be used for all posters and advertisements. Good. Up and down, you know? And through all of it, the only real candidate I've been excited about to take over the business lab called to say he'd accepted another position and I..." Brisa flopped back on the sidewalk to stare up at the sky. It was a picture that contained a thousand words of overwhelming frustration.

The buzz of Peter's phone caught his attention, so he pulled it out of the strap on his arm.

Do you have a minute? I'd like to talk to you about how you can help with the case.

Lauren's text filled him with energy. Before? He'd been thinking of a shower, a beer and falling asleep to the TV. Now? He could work all night long if that's what she wanted to do.

Sure. Can I call you in thirty minutes? He hit Send and then stared at his phone as Mira said, "Brisa, that is too much to handle on your own. You deserve to feel every bit of frustration. How can we help?"

Brisa's groan made him smile as Lauren answered, Can I come over and show you what I have? Tonight or tomorrow if it's too late.

That energy boost turned into excitement. Yes, come over.

She answered immediately. See you in fifteen.

Peter would never leave Brisa hopeless on the sidewalk, so if Lauren showed up before they'd solved the problem, he'd tell Lauren how to find his place.

"I keep telling myself this is temporary and it's all good. I'm having this trouble because we're growing, which is what everyone wants." Brisa sat up gracefully. "I can do this."

"I can do more with the lab, but I need direction," Jason said. "Maybe your father could help, free up some of your time there? We work together pretty well."

The fact that Brisa appeared to be considering the situation was clear illustration that she was struggling. She and her sister, Reyna, had fought to get their father out of Concord

Court business, and it hadn't been an easy battle. Pulling him back in would be a setback.

"Thanks, Jason. I'll think about it." Brisa sighed. "Reyna's going to take over all the publicity for the baseball game. That will help. I'm going to call a recruiter my dad suggested to assist with filling the job. None of you are going to tell Wade about this. Peter, you wanted to run. That's why we all showed up."

"Aha," Wade said from where he was walking to meet them. "Busted."

Brisa groaned again, but before she could start her defense, a car turned into the driveway.

Lauren spotted him and parked in front of them. "Hey," she said, her eyes on his, and then added "Hi" for the rest of the group.

Peter wasn't watching Brisa's reaction, but he could feel the change in the atmosphere. If Brisa had been gasping and wheezing before, she was reenergized at the latest arrival. As Peter stood up, he understood that feeling.

He also realized there was no way to make it through this without introducing Lauren.

That would make their work on solving his "being single" problem easier.

"Lauren, this is Brisa Montero, Mira Peters, Jason Ward and Wade McNally." Peter pointed at each person in turn. "Brisa runs Concord Court. Wade keeps an eye on Brisa. Mira makes us run. Jason works here with anyone who needs career guidance." As the words left his mouth, the light bulb came on over his head. "I should have introduced you two sooner."

Then he faced his friends. "This is Lauren Duncan, the old college friend who is defending my nephew in his drug case."

"Friend," Lauren said slowly. "I like that. What he means is we were once locked in a battle for the number one spot of every class, but we've mellowed now." She stepped up to shake their hands. "And career guidance I could use, Jason. What have you got for a lawyer who needs to make a difference but not at something that will suck the joy out of every day?"

"Suck the joy out of every day," Jason repeated before he whistled. "Let's make an appointment. We can talk about it, but your situation is a little out of my wheelhouse.

Have you ever thought about going into business for yourself?" He clapped Peter on the back. "Set your own rates and hours, be your own boss. That's Peter's plan for career success after law school, and I'd say it's a good one for him. Could work for you, too."

Peter was grateful for his support group all over again. Not a one of them had told him he should be pushing harder or reaching for more because he could. They believed he knew what he wanted. Sometimes he wondered if he was right, but they didn't.

Lauren frowned. "That might be my only option, but I don't want to be a boss?" How her voice rose at the end was proof of her uncertainty. "I looked into office rent prices. That made me think of insurance and repairs and employees and payroll and…" Lauren shook her head. "The amount of stuff I don't know is overwhelming."

Peter was reminded again of one of the big differences between them. He knew he could figure all that when the time came, but Lauren was buried in the research before she'd even made up her mind to go for it.

"Eventually, Concord Court will have resources for that, too," Jason said, and cut a look at Brisa. When Peter checked on her reaction, he frowned. Whatever frustration that had her stretched out on the ground had evaporated. If light bulbs over heads for clever ideas were a real thing, hers would be glowing.

"I'm not a veteran, but that's an amazing resource. The odds of success for small business owners with good ideas would be improved with someone with experience with the details to support them," Lauren said.

Brisa's smile beamed as she stepped forward and took Lauren's hand. "Have you ever considered a career change, one that would help provide that support? Because I am hunting for the right person to lead our business lab."

Lauren looked confused. "Me? I don't know anything about that."

"Neither do I. Neither does Marcus Bryant, but he waded through all the steps to establish his own business and he's doing so well. People without experience do those things you listed, every day, but can you imagine how nice it would be to have someone who understood the legal language behind leases and payment plans and licensing as backup?"

Brisa leaned forward. "It would be huge, Lauren. You could change lives here at Concord Court for forty hours a week and then go home and have a life. You could. Your boss would insist on it." Brisa brushed her hair over her shoulder. "I would be your boss."

Peter watched Lauren struggle for a moment in the face of Brisa's persuasion before he waved his hand between their faces to break the hold Brisa had. It was like watching a hypnotist dangle a watch in front of Lauren's eyes and tell her she was getting very sleepy. If he didn't break the spell, Lauren would have a job and no memory of accepting it.

"Thank you for the offer, Brisa. Lauren will take some time to think it over and get back to you," Peter said loudly, and urged Lauren back to her car. "Drive around this side and look for my car. I'll meet you there."

Lauren nodded and followed his directions. When he turned around, Brisa was right there, having stepped up close behind him. Very close, and she had her mean face on. "I want to hire her. Do not mess this up for me."

Peter held up his hands as a shield and stepped back. "Consider her my client. I'll handle all negotiations and she won't come cheap."

Mira slung an arm over Brisa's shoulders. "Ask her to think about it when she's not caught under Brisa's tractor-beam stare. The rest of us will see how we can help Brisa out in the meantime."

Peter saluted and jogged between the buildings to meet Lauren in front of his door.

"She's intense. I've seen her on TV, in the paper, that kind of thing, but in person, she's magnetic." Lauren smiled at him. "You saved me. I might have signed a contract right there."

"I only got you a temporary reprieve. The thing about Monteros is that they don't give up, so you might think about it and start building a case if the answer's no." Peter unlocked his door and pointed at the seats around his kitchen bar. "Grab some water. I'll be right back."

He hurried to shower and change clothes before meeting her in the kitchen. "How are you? How can I help?"

Lauren pointed at the long canvas hanging on the wall opposite the door. "Tell me about this first. Is this one of Nicole's paintings? It's amazing."

Peter watched her and wondered how often he walked past the canvas without seeing it. Lauren was right, though. "That's Nic's work. She gave it to me when I moved in here. I don't know much about art, but I know that is in the style of Korean folk art. The pine tree and crane are symbols of longevity." He moved closer to point out details. "She hides the Korean words for the elements somewhere on the painting. See? That's water." The small stream running along the side of the canvas was easy to miss.

"Are the clouds embroidered on the canvas?" Lauren asked. He could see her urge to touch the artwork, but she didn't.

"Yeah," Peter said, pleased that Lauren appreciated Nic's talent. His sister had struggled to find her place, but it was impossible to ignore the effect her art had on many people, including Lauren. "If you're interested, you should visit her studio in Wynwood. She teaches classes and demonstrates her technique."

Lauren frowned. "I do not belong in an

art class. No experience, and I'm guessing no talent."

"It's folk art, it's meant to be for everyone. No real training needed. That's what Nic says," Peter said.

"Think she'd give me a private lesson? I can handle humiliation without an audience," Lauren asked as she moved back to the bar.

"My sister would love that, but you should be prepared for her to pry every secret you've ever had out of you in the process. She's relentless."

"Sounds like she got a touch of the Kim law gene, too!" Lauren smiled. She pointed at the laptop she'd set up. "I've gotten more information. I don't know whether this will help or not, but I was hoping you'd have time to handle plotting these traffic stops for me. I want to know if there's a pattern of days and times where stops are being made around Davey's apartment complex. Let's say a five-mile radius of streets around it. If it's random, okay. We can still pursue their warrantless search. If there's a pattern, it might be something to bring up in front of the judge to suggest that the officers set up in that spot with the intention of performing drug searches. Not any proof that Davey is innocent, of course, but it might call into question whether they followed correct procedure." She shrugged. "That's all I've got for now. The prosecuting attorney has no interest in doing anything other than the usual here, so they'll offer a plea. They and the judge will expect us to take it, but we don't have to. It wouldn't be right. So we'll have to gamble that if we take this case to trial and lose, the sentence will be as light. I'll talk this all out with Davey and your sister, too, but if you've studied winning trial cases, you understand what I'm saying."

Peter braced his elbows on the counter. "That it's a big gamble. I get it."

Lauren nodded. "Like the job offer I just received, we don't have to decide now. We can take time to weigh Davey's options."

He met her stare. "Yeah. Okay. I'll be happy to sort through the data. Anything else I can help with?"

"I'm going to stop by and talk to Davey about his options. I'm sure your family will want your opinion. I'll outline the dangers of going to trial, so please do the same." She tilted her head back to study the ceiling. "For the pretrial hearing, wear a nice suit, sit beside me in court and be prepared to lay on the charm if it looks like we're losing. If we go to a jury trial, I'm sure you can win them over." When she looked at him again, she added, "Officer Estevez would like for you to know that she is very single. You, specifically."

Peter propped his chin on his hands. "You're about to call me 'charming Peter Kim' again, aren't you?"

Lauren winced. "If the shoe fits…"

"Why does it feel like you're pushing me away when you say it?" he asked. He'd finally realized that was part of her pattern.

"I am," Lauren said, "because I forget how far apart we are, but then something reminds me. A memory from school or acquaintances hinting for information about you."

When she remembered their differences, she also remembered that she suspected him of pretending interest in her or playing to win.

"I've spent a lot of time learning to hide the image of the math hero hanging on my parents' wall for all to see, Lauren. What if you could drop your guard and look at the whole me? Your dad says a leopard can't change his spots, but I'm proof that it can happen, if you want it to. I did. I decided who I was and who I wanted the world to see, and I made changes." Peter sighed. "But I guess, down deep, I am still the geeky math hero faced with a pretty girl."

Lauren frowned. "Am I the pretty girl in this metaphor?"

He rolled his eyes. "Okay, maybe it's not so much how you see me as how you see *you*, then. You gotta trust yourself first. The rest of us are on board. I don't have any strategies. I'm not trying to win anything here. I just…like you and want to spend time with you. That kiss? That was a geeky math hero move, not charming Peter Kim, for sure."

Her slow grin gave him a bit of hope that his words were untangling the knots between them. There was still a mess to straighten out, but he could see the path through it.

If she was willing to walk beside him.

But he'd also learned snap decisions were not Lauren Duncan's thing. She researched and made choices.

"I'll analyze the data and let you know what I find, okay?" He pointed at the laptop. "Email me the info."

She nodded. "Davey's pretrial hearing is set for next week. That's sooner than I expected, probably because the judge expects us to take the plea and he can move right along to the next case. When I talk to Davey, I'll explain what kind of look and attitude we're going for in front of the judge."

"I can take care of that. Wrangling my family is kind of my thing," Peter said immediately.

Lauren folded up her laptop and put it away before she met his stare. "While we're handing out truths, Peter, here's one for you." She inhaled and exhaled. "You don't have to wrangle them anymore, but I think you like to."

Peter straightened slowly and crossed his arms over his chest. He'd wanted to help her. Taking charge of his family was easy because it was second nature. That was his role, or it had been for a long time. Stepping right back into that spot when he came back home made sense. Did he get something from it, too? Maybe.

When he could face her again, he tipped his chin up. "You think so, huh?"

"I like you so much, Peter Kim, but the two of us together are a mess, just charging in to save the day and then wondering why we're so tired all the time." Lauren was happy to have him on her side. It didn't happen often. "We both need to figure out what to do about that before we do anything else."

She left him knowing that Lauren was always right. If that held true again, he had a lot of thinking to do.

CHAPTER THIRTEEN

ON THE DATE of David Kim's pretrial hearing, Lauren brushed a nonexistent wrinkle from the dress she'd chosen carefully that morning. The deep pink sheath wasn't one of her usual power suits, but it had never let her down. This was an important day. She'd done everything she could to prepare herself and the Kims, but she'd been awake most of the night running scenarios in her mind and replaying the facts to make sure she wasn't missing any angle that might help Davey.

The data she'd asked Peter to go through showed that traffic stops around the Royale Apartments had begun after the spring semester started. Peter had confirmed all the stops made were students at the college, not neighborhood residents. There had been no other drug busts, so either the cops had gotten lucky the night Davey ran the stop sign or they were targeting the kids who lived there and coming up empty. Casting doubt on their methods was the only extra shot she had, and she still wasn't sure whether it would help or hurt in Kincaid's courtroom.

"If anyone can pull this off, you can, Lauren," she muttered to herself as she picked up her briefcase on the other side of the courthouse's metal detector.

Then she saw Peter and the small Kim delegation behind him. He was wearing a nice suit, the kind she'd pictured him in when she imagined him commanding a courtroom. There was also his handsome smile that Lauren couldn't seem to get enough of. He had a drink holder in one hand that held four coffees.

"Today's the big day, and everyone is ready." Peter pointed over his shoulder with his thumb. Lauren smiled at his parents, who were waving. Nicole was doing her best to straighten David's tie and his hair and his shirt cuffs in the manner of all nervous mothers throughout time. She'd also gone for a stiff suit that was definitely not her usual style; the smudge of yellow paint Lauren could see on the underside of her elbow fit her better.

Before Lauren could answer, Nicole spun

on one heel and wrapped her arms around Lauren's neck. "I didn't sleep at all last night. I hope you did." She cut her eyes to indicate her son, who was pale and quiet. "Don't tell him I said that."

It was impossible to resist the family. They were watching her as if she was a rock star and an angel combined, and that felt good. Where else could she find that?

That admiration would last only as long as she managed to win. The sudden clench of her stomach reminded her of the downside of all that faith.

Then she saw her old boss peek around the corner from the courtroom. His wave was much less welcome.

"Why don't you go in and find seats near the front," Lauren said to Nicole. She escorted her parents inside. David followed them but not before he sent a longing glance in Peter's direction. Peter nodded to encourage him and watched them go. He held the drinks in front of his chest like a shield.

Lauren gripped the handles of her brief-case to steady her hands. "How bad is your habit, Peter?"

He frowned so she motioned to the drinks he was holding.

"Oh," he said, and shook his head, "I couldn't sleep last night. Thought you might have the same problem, but I wasn't sure how you'd take your coffee so I have black—" he turned the drinks "—with cream, with cream and sugar, and with only sugar. Which do you prefer?"

"You bought four? Hoping one of them would be right for me?" Lauren reached to take the cup with cream only from the holder. "That's...nice of you."

"I wanted to do something, and buying coffee was the best idea I had this morning." Peter shrugged. "Air force life means you learn to drink coffee however you can get it, so any of these work for me. Nicole needed a relaxing herbal tea because she was nearly vibrating with tension when I picked everyone up."

When Blake Bennings's head popped out around the door again, Peter noticed. He raised his arm to check the time. "Still fifteen minutes. We aren't late."

"That's my old boss. Apparently he'd like to talk to me," she murmured. "Since I've blocked every phone number he uses, a personal appearance here is his only choice."

Peter raised his eyebrows. "Interesting. He's made a special trip to the courthouse to wait patiently for you. He must want you back badly."

"Hmm." The knot in her stomach tightened, but there was no reason to pass that tension on to Peter.

He squeezed her arm. "Nothing has changed. He's not your boss anymore."

Lauren clutched the coffee and nodded before he opened the door to the courtroom. Peter waited for her to step through ahead of him, and Lauren remembered how she'd always hated the way lanky Peter Kim had loomed over her when they faced off. This Peter was older, more mature, and something about his expression made it easy to walk beside him. Her nerves disappeared.

Blake Bennings was waiting for her at the defense table. "No coffee for me, Duncan?"

Peter stopped next to Lauren. Before he could do something nice, like offer one of his spare coffees to Bennings, Lauren shook her head. "You're in my seat, Blake." She forced herself to smile as he slowly stood. "Why are you here?"

When Lauren moved past him, he said, "Since you aren't answering my calls anymore, I wanted to make one last plea for you to come back to work with us. There are so many other people who need you."

Lauren glanced at Peter, who was obviously eavesdropping. She said, "Those offers you were sure I was going to get? You haven't done anything to prevent them, have you?" Her two weeks of forced relaxation was up, and none of the private criminal defense firms had been in touch. Taking one of those jobs would be a terrible idea, but refusing an offer would have propped up her confidence.

Blake put one hand over his heart. "I'm hurt. Do you honestly believe I'd use my connections to keep you from moving on?"

A grim smile was the best answer she could come up with. She hadn't thought about it before this conversation, but now it was easier to see how political ties might be leveraged to call in a favor like that.

"You've blocked my number, too, Ms. Duncan," said someone from behind her left shoulder. "If you want to talk new job offers, you'll have to answer when we call."

Lauren turned to see Derek Rainey.

"Officer Estevez mentioned you were representing the defendant in this case, taking the matter on for a friend. So here I am." He held out his hands. "Shall we set an appointment where I can show you what Miller and Rainey can offer you?"

Lauren did her best to anticipate everything that could happen when she stepped into a courtroom.

This? Yeah, it had never occurred to her to prepare for an impromptu job conversation here. The right words wouldn't come.

"Is this a party?" Monica Holt asked as she stepped into the mix. "Everyone asking Lauren to dance? Better wait and see how this decision goes."

"Good suggestion," Peter said defensively.

Lauren motioned David to take the seat next to hers and tried to still her racing heart.

"I'll take your business cards. Lauren will get back with you on her own time." Peter gave a curt nod.

Cold. She'd never heard Peter's voice so

cold before, but it worked. Blake and Derek Rainey filed into the general seating area.

Monica Holt walked up to Peter. "Nice presence. Who are you?"

Peter didn't have a chance to answer. Before the bailiff could complete announcing the judge's arrival, Judge Kincaid was flapping both arms and telling everyone to keep their seats. His hair was wet. His black robe was undone. There was a dark thundercloud in his expression.

"I'm late, apologies. I'm never late. We're going to catch up. We do not run late in my courtroom, not even when the judge has a flat tire and a flat spare." He brushed back his hair, took a calming breath and picked up his paperwork. "David Kim. What are the charges?"

Lauren watched Monica Holt stand and read the charges.

Sipping her coffee hid the tremble of her lips. Everyone was counting on her. She had to get herself together fast.

"Your Honor, in a routine traffic stop, officers searched David Kim's sedan and found enough cocaine hidden under the rear seat to justify a felony charge. We would like to move forward with charges of possession with intent to distribute."

Kincaid grunted.

It was hard to tell if that was an agreement or something else.

"And you have entered a 'not guilty' plea, is that correct, Mr. Kim?" Kincaid asked as he glared down over his glasses.

Lauren put one hand on David's arm and then stood. "Your Honor, I'd like to request an examination of the facts of this case to determine whether or not it should move forward." Lauren stepped out from behind the table, determined to convince everyone in the room that she was the most trustworthy authority there. "David Kim is a twenty-year-old college student with no prior arrests or indication of drug use. He's an excellent student on an academic scholarship who pays his bills by working janitorial night shifts and sharing an apartment with two other students. He was returning home from work when officers pulled him over for a routine traffic stop that somehow turned into search and seizure of drugs Mr. Kim had no way of knowing were in his car. The officers had no warrant, and Mr. Kim did not give permission for the search."

Kincaid raised his eyebrows. "No way of knowing? How many times have I heard that? How many times does that turn out to be true, Ms. Duncan? None."

Lauren had expected something like that. "Mark this down, Your Honor. David Kim lives at the Royale Apartments, a middle-of-the-road complex favored by college students who can afford it by having lots of room-mates. At least two of David's neighbors at the Royale have been stopped by the same officers at the same spot. I can present data showing a clear pattern of police targeting this location as well as timing that indicates the students at the Royale were their main, if not only, interest."

Kincaid's lips thinned but he didn't ask any questions. Surely he was following her implication.

"Many of those kids at the Royale are in the same boat as David Kim, but he's luckier to have his own car, supplied by his grand-parents," Lauren said, and gestured grace-fully at the Kim family lining the front row. "So David generously loans out his car when friends need to drive to the store or to class when they're late."

"Your Honor, none of this is proof against the charges," Monica said. "We have a generous plea offer on the basis of Mr. Kim's history."

"Then why are we here today? Do you know how busy this court is, Ms. Duncan? Have you forgotten the caseload already?" The judge peered at her over his glasses. "We don't all have unlimited time."

"Yes, sir, I have only one point left. I'll make it brief." Lauren tapped her hand on the file David's mother had handed her. "I have evidence to demonstrate that this illegal search and seizure was a pattern by the arresting officers. I don't know who they are hoping to catch, but I would suggest a closer look at David's roommates." Lauren tipped her head to the side. "Ex-roommates. Now that David understands the dangers of life at the Royale, he is finishing this summer semester from his grandparents' home."

Kincaid flipped through the thin file on David Kim. He stared over his glasses at the family sitting patiently. David's lips were white and his hands were tight knots, but he was doing his best to remain calm. Lauren was afraid he'd stopped breathing, but she saw Peter reach under the table to squeeze his nephew's hand, and some of the color returned to Davey's face.

Kincaid cleared his throat. "All well and good, but you know how this goes."

His decision was written all over his face. "If you won't accept the plea deal, we'll go to trial. Put this in front of a jury and see what they think." He picked up his gavel and Lauren was disappointed but not surprised. It wasn't the answer they wanted, but they were still in the fight.

"Your Honor, may I speak?" Peter asked and stood. Lauren was almost certain a cold frost had descended on the courtroom. Judge Kincaid would not appreciate anyone derailing his decision.

But she hadn't counted on charming Peter Kim stepping up. He commanded the room.

"Your decision is fair and impartial, of course, Your Honor," Peter said slowly. Lauren wondered if he was making this up as he went along. If so, none of the strain she would experience in the same situation showed on his face. "I'm David's uncle, an air force veteran who is working on his law degree at Sawgrass University, and an old friend who dragged Lauren Duncan out of a well-earned vacation because someone told me she was the very best defense lawyer in town." He stopped in front of Monica Holt. "I believed it, of course. She was an infuriating thorn in my side when we were in undergrad classes together. I'm certain it's the same for anyone she faces off against in a courtroom. Ms. Holt, is that true?"

Monica rolled her eyes but nodded reluctantly.

The judge's beleaguered sigh almost convinced Lauren to stand up and drag Peter back to his seat. They were going to be before Kincaid for the trial. There was no benefit to irritating him now.

"And I've been witness to two fine job offers from people who have gone out of their way to get Lauren's attention." Peter glanced at the back of the courtroom. "Make that three." Lauren turned to see whom he was referring to and saw Brisa and a man wearing a Concord Court polo seated behind the Kims.

They were here to support Peter, of course. That was real friendship.

"As happy as I am to know that Ms. Duncan will be gainfully employed soon," Judge Kincaid drawled, "how does that pertain to the case at hand?"

It was a valid question. Lauren couldn't see the connection, either.

"Fifteen years as a public defender. Lauren Duncan understands very well how often defendants who say they are innocent actually are. Yet, here, her career is no longer on the line. Doesn't it beg the question, why would she make this more difficult for herself? Taking the fair deal offered by the prosecutor makes the most sense if her client is guilty. Why would she do anything else here?" Peter paced in front of the bench before slipping his hands in his pockets and shrugging. As if the answer was obvious and true. It was a touch of television law drama but it looked good on him. "I would suggest it's because she knows her client is *innocent*."

Silence followed his statement until the judge said, "So I'm supposed to base a decision not even on the defendant's character but his lawyer's?" Kincaid chuckled. "I've never heard anything like that. Ms. Holt, have you? Is that what they're teaching at Sawgrass's law school these days?"

Both Monica and the judge laughed and Peter smiled. "You might be right. Naive, I guess, to think the system is made of good people who want justice and not quick decisions so they can go home on time."

Before Kincaid could register the slight, Lauren stood. "Thank you, Mr. Kim. I've got this." When Peter sat back down, Lauren said, "My client is innocent. I said that to Monica when we met and her response was 'aren't they all.'" She decided to try some drama of her own and stepped out to the center of the courtroom. "But isn't that what we all agree to uphold, Your Honor? Innocent until proven guilty. I have evidence to suggest that the police did not follow the correct procedure at David Kim's traffic stop. I have the word of a straight-A student that he had no idea the drugs were there and a plausible theory on how that might be true. I have character witnesses who will swear under oath the truth of David Kim's character and assertions that he does not use or sell drugs." Lauren crossed her arms over her chest. "I would suggest that the State has not carried through with their part, the proving piece of this justice equation. You want efficiency. So does David

Kim. I'm asking you to dismiss these charges. At the same age, I had a lot in common with David Kim. He's planning his future, one that includes law school and perhaps even a career as a criminal defense attorney someday. He can't surrender that future here with a guilty plea, not as an innocent person."

The courtroom was quiet as Lauren walked back to her seat. Her stomach was in a full revolt at that minute. Coffee wouldn't help. The silence was making everything worse, and she was worried she was sweating through her dress as she waited. This was something about the job she would not miss, not ever again.

"Ms. Duncan, I don't know how the kid got lucky enough to find a defender like you, but I'm convinced the State's case against David Kim is too weak to move forward. And Ms. Holt, based on these assertions, a word to the police chief regarding the proper procedure for traffic stops is in order. I don't need to explain how a pattern of questionable searches could impact the community, as well as your office and the state attorney's office." He waited for Monica Holt to nod her understanding.

"I'm dismissing these charges, but Mr. Kim…" Kincaid gave David an evil glare. "I better not ever find you in my courtroom again, not as a defendant anyway. I don't give second chances." He smacked the gavel. "I'm taking ten minutes to soak up the air-conditioning. Bailiff, clear the court for the next case."

Everyone in the courtroom stood as the judge stomped away.

CHAPTER FOURTEEN

PETER STOOD ASIDE as his family swamped Lauren. Davey was the first one to throw his arms around her. It was impossible to understand everything his nephew said, but Peter did hear, "Thank you. Thank you. Thank you for not giving up. Thank you for everything." The tremor in his nephew's voice convinced Peter that tears were coming. Like most, Davey would hate the public display, but this kid had been through so much.

Lauren hugged Davey and then stepped back. "You understand what it means to have an attorney that believes in you. If you ever want to ask questions about law school or criminal defense, please call me. The world needs more lawyers who understand this the way that you and I do." Nicole was next to grab Lauren and squeeze, followed by both of his parents. Lauren's eyes met his over his father's shoulder, and if he was reading her correctly, she was begging for an escape from the hot, happy, sweet pile of emotion.

"Let her breathe, please," Peter said as he urged his family to let go of their lifeline. "This is not part of the usual court sequence."

"I'm going to ask you all to leave the court now," the bailiff said. "Next case'll be coming in."

Lauren nodded and turned to gather up the neat stack of evidence she'd been prepared to submit. Meanwhile, Peter ushered his family out into the lobby. They managed to maintain their cool until they'd cleared the doors. Then his sister whooped for joy and his mother started replaying events in an excited commentary-extras style.

Something about Lauren's startled expression convinced Peter to rein it in. "Got it. We're excited. Can you head on out to the car? Lauren needs a minute."

None of the Kims were happy with that request. The urge to carry Lauren on their shoulders like a victorious gladiator was easy to see, but his nephew stepped in. "Yes, sir, we'll wait outside." Then he wrapped his

arms around his grandparents and led them
to the door.

Peter was ready to explain to his sister why
she needed to follow the others, but watching her wipe away tears stopped him in his
tracks. Luckily, he was wearing his best suit,
the one that had a spot for a handkerchief, so
he pulled the bit of cloth out and offered it to
her. Her frown as she examined the handkerchief was cute. "What year is it? You can't do
tissue like normal people?" Then she wiped
under her eyes. "Sorry. I meant to swear my
eternal gratitude for all your help, but old hab-
its die hard." Then she collapsed against his
chest with her arms clutching his shoulders.
"Thank you. You have it. My eternal gratitude. Remind me when I forget."

Relief washed over him.

The fact that his sister was being nice to
him was confirmation. The world had turned
upside down.

Peter patted her shoulders for a minute
until they both recovered. "I only did what a
big brother is supposed to do, Nic. I hate to
turn away eternal gratitude, but I don't think
it fits us well, anyway."

She sniffed loudly and then pressed his handkerchief to her nose. "You and I both know that if there were a competition for world's best big brother, you'd win. I hate to further contribute to your enormous ego, but I don't know what we would have done without you this time. And not *only* this time." The warning that she was about to launch herself at him again was in her eyes, but she straightened. "And Lauren..." The tears started flowing as the words dried up. All Nicole could do was hug Lauren and sniff back tears.

Lauren patted her back until Nicole had her emotions in check. "I'm sorry," Nic said. "I was so worried."

"I get it, but you all did everything you needed to do, including charming Peter Kim," Lauren said with a smile.

Nicole's face was twisted in misery. "I know. I'm going to be forced to be nice to him from now on."

Peter smiled back and enjoyed how the tension of the past few weeks rolled away. It had been tough, but Lauren had done the impossible, and now he knew he couldn't let her go back to…the past. She had to keep moving forward.

"Davey's uncle promised to buy him all the lobster he could eat if we won this case," Nicole said, beaming ear to ear. "That will be where we're headed next, if I know my son. Please, Lauren, come to lunch with us to celebrate. Peter will buy you the biggest lobster in the place."

Peter knew it was the least he could do for his friend.

"This is the time for your family to celebrate together. I appreciate the offer," Lauren said as she cut her eyes toward Peter, "but this win has put me in the mood for family time of my own. Please tell Davey congratulations again for me."

Nicole frowned, then she shook her head at Peter. "What did you do?"

Before he could defend himself, Nicole slipped her hand into Lauren's. "Okay, but we're going to plan a family feast where you will be the guest of honor. We'll do it soon. I want you to come to my studio in Wynwood, too." Nicole stepped away. "And martinis. I still want to do that." She was sniffling tears again, but smiling as she stepped from the courthouse onto the sidewalk.

Lauren's shoulders immediately slumped, as if she'd been using the last of her strength... Why?

"You okay?" Peter asked as he guided her over to a bench in an alcove.

Lauren nodded and kicked off her shoes to wiggle her toes on the cool floor. "Tell your family no feast is needed. I was doing my job. I do want to see Nic's studio, though. Let her know that I'll try to come in next week. This week..." She sighed.

"I hate that we're floating on air, celebrating, and you're on the very last bit of your willpower," Peter murmured as he knelt in front of her. "I had no idea what this would do to you when I tracked you down. I can't tell you how much it means to me that you took on all this added pressure because I asked you to."

"You forget. I also believed Davey was innocent," Lauren murmured, "but it was mainly because you asked."

Peter wanted to give her energy or strength or...something.

"You better go. Your family will be roasting in the heat." Lauren smiled at him. "But give me those business cards before you go."

He pulled them out of his coat pocket. "I can toss them in the trash can and save you the trouble." There was one right next to the door. Easy reach.

There was no way he wanted to see Lauren in any job that would have this effect on her. The Lauren he'd known had been serious but filled with joy in the little things around her. This Lauren was barely holding herself together. This was the Lauren who had quit without notice.

"I don't want to do anything I might later regret." She held her hand out and took the cards.

"Why would you even consider those offers an option?" Peter asked. "No one should work at a job that makes them feel like this." It was easy for him to say that.

She pursed her lips. "But I'm good at it and there are other people like Davey who deserve a defense from someone who is good at it."

"Right, okay," Peter said as he ran his hand through his hair, "but there are other competent lawyers."

She raised her eyebrows. "Oh, I know. Some of them command a courtroom while they're monologuing to buy time, but they only want to write wills and mediate arguments over Grandma's china. They aren't going to step up and take the demanding cases. If we're trading career advice, when is it my turn? Because you are wasting all your talent that could be helping so many people."

Peter felt that shot to the gut. "I've spent plenty of my life working for other people's benefit. Why shouldn't I do something easier now?"

She snorted. "Because that's not who you are. Peter Kim takes on his family's problems and solves them. He joins the military and dedicates himself to protect countless lives. You will be bored in a heartbeat with wills and estates, and you will be wasting your skill and intellect, which is even worse." She closed her eyes. "I have to decide if I'm willing to do the same and I'm not convinced yet."

Peter slowly stood. Lauren said, "We are the same person, and yet, so different."

"I guess so. I don't waste my energy like you do worrying about things that might never happen or looking back at what did. I can handle whatever comes from my decisions, Lauren." Peter shook his head. "You can, too. Do what's right for you. For the record, even I can see that going back isn't right for you. I know that."

She nodded. "Your family is waiting."

He shifted toward the courthouse doors. "I don't like leaving things this way between us. Come to lunch. We can go somewhere after and talk." He wasn't sure he wanted to hear her opinions about his future career plans, but he'd take that chance to keep her close.

"I'm going to go talk to my mother, and then I'm taking a nap." Lauren leaned her head back against the wall. "Tomorrow I will figure this out."

Peter knew he had to go, but he hated it. He pressed his hand to her cheek and watched her eyes flutter open. "I want to kiss you. I don't know why, but it's what I want more than anything."

"More than anything?" Lauren said as her lips curled. "Kiss me, then. No thinking required, just…"

Peter had his lips pressed to hers before she finished whatever it was she meant to say.

The first time he'd stolen a kiss, it had been too quick to commit to memory. This would be their first real kiss. The quiet halls of the courthouse, her gasp that faded as her lips met his and the certainty that they weren't done yet, not with this discussion and not with each other.

This was the kiss that they would both re-member.

When he drew back, she was staring at him, her expression serious. "We can fight about jobs whenever you like. Doesn't change the fact that there's something between us that works. We owe it to ourselves to dis-cover what that is, Duncan." He brushed hair away from her face and pressed another kiss against her lips before he walked away. "If you feel up to it, I'd like to know how your talk with your mother goes." He waited for her nod and went to find his family. The Kims would celebrate this win.

And soon, Peter would turn all of his at-tention to solving the question of what to do about Lauren Duncan.

CHAPTER FIFTEEN

AFTER LAUREN TEXTED her mother to see if she could meet at their usual coffee place, she rested her head against the wall and soaked in the quiet. Adding a conversation with her mother to this jumble of emotions was probably a mistake, but she couldn't put it off any longer.

A stirring of air was the only warning Lauren had that someone had sat down next to her on the bench. How many other benches were there in this hallway? The irritation welled up, but it was as good a reason to leave as any.

Then she saw Brisa Montero beside her. "You were about to tell me exactly what you thought of my crowding you, weren't you?" Brisa asked with a sparkling smile. "Sorry, not sorry."

Lauren chuckled. Brisa was absolutely unrepentant and it was still cute.

"Good job in there." Brisa crossed her legs.

"Sean and I wanted to support Peter. The guy never asks for anything, so it's unusual to have a chance to step up for him the way he does for everyone else. Having another shot to convince you to talk to me about this job I have? That was a sweet bonus."

Lauren didn't have any trouble believing that Peter was the kind of friend who showed up. He'd bargained with her for more time to convince her to help Davey, but then he'd worked to entertain her.

"I'm still thinking about the business lab, Brisa." Lauren clenched the handle of her briefcase. "Today confirmed that I can't do this anymore, not without becoming numb or building a callus that makes it harder to care about winning and losing and the people sitting next to me in court." If she could stop feeling, she could do the job forever, but days at the beach or on the ocean had reminded her the world was full of fun and joy. Who wanted to stop feeling that?

Brisa nodded. "Do you know how I got involved at Concord Court?" She waved a hand. "I mean, other than being born into a rich family with a father who pulls strings whenever it suits his plans? I am not a veteran, either. I figured that might be one of your concerns about the job. What do we know, right? We didn't serve."

Lauren sighed. "That's one of the obstacles. The other is that I have no business experience. All I have are questions about setting one up…" She held out her hands to show how empty they were. "What would I bring to the table other than a need for a paycheck?"

"Okay, so what I brought to Concord Court was curiosity and enthusiasm and a deep love for one particular veteran, my sister, Reyna." Brisa raised a brow. "I know you don't know Reyna, but when you meet her, you will understand that she is an incredible person, smart, tough, determined to do right in all things, and for a long time, I measured myself against her and allowed that to make me feel small. She was my father's favorite. Mine, too! And Concord Court was supposed to be her project, the thing that kept her safe at home."

Lauren had read news stories about the development of Concord Court, and the Monteros had been in the press on and off for as long as she could remember, but it was hard to pull up an image of Reyna Montero. Listening to Brisa talk about her? That reminded Lauren of Nicole's tour of the Kim family photo gallery and her absolute glee at pointing out Peter in his Math Hero T-shirt.

At one point in her life, Lauren had wished for a younger sister. Maybe they weren't all they were cracked up to be.

Brisa added, "Reyna had plans of her own that didn't involve Concord Court. Did my father ask? Of course not, so my sister and I teamed up to take on Concord Court together. It gave her a chance to do what she truly wanted to, and it gave me a shot to prove myself. All my mistakes and false starts turned into real advantages, and now, everyone who knows about Concord Court knows I'm behind it and won't let it fail." She wrinkled her nose. "Not being very humble with my bragging, am I? I'm proud of what we're doing and of myself. That's with no military service. I love my sister and now I love Wade and his daughter…and Marcus Bryant and Peter Kim and Mira Peters and so many other veterans who I'm proud to know. See?" She put her hand on Lauren's arm. "We didn't serve in the military but we can support the ones who did. That's what's important. Not everyone is meant for Concord Court, either. You'll need to determine if our business lab is the right place to employ your experience and skills, your curiosity and commitment to doing hard things for the right reasons."

Lauren chuckled. "Concord Court is definitely your calling. I can hear passion in your tone. I love it. I've spent too much time with people who had no emotional connection to the important work they were doing, but it pulses off you in waves."

Brisa narrowed her eyes. "Sort of like a fanatic? Someone who should be feared instead of loved or…"

"Definitely loved," Lauren interrupted. "And slightly feared."

"Excellent. My plan is working." Brisa rubbed her hands together, her grin wicked. "How about this? We've got an outreach program, and our next event is a minor league exhibition baseball game at Sunshine Park in Hollywood. All the local veterans' groups are involved and we're going to tell as many people as we can about Concord Court. I need every volunteer I can find. Please come. You'll meet a ton of people connected to the

Court and be able to see how you can help. I know it."

Lauren glanced at Brisa. "I've never actually been to a baseball game."

"Let's fix that," Brisa said, and squeezed her shoulder. "I'll ask Peter to introduce you to everyone, people who live at the Court and friends who are there to volunteer. When you hear the stories, you will be as hooked as I am."

Hearing Peter's name reminded Lauren of the weird spot they were in. He wanted to tell her how to live her life and she wanted to show him he didn't have it all figured out. That they were at odds wasn't surprising, but the uneasy restlessness it caused was.

It must have shown on her face.

"Ah, Peter," Brisa said as she scooted closer, "let's talk about Peter."

Lauren laughed. "What is there to say?"

Brisa snorted. "So much! Please don't tell me you've fallen for the picture he shows the world. The happy heartbreaker content with his boat and his easy life."

Shocked, Lauren turned toward Brisa. "No?" She wasn't certain how to answer.

"While working with veterans, I've run

into so much of the strong, silent type, you know? These men and women carry all this experience, some good and some unbelievably bad, and the people in their lives may have no understanding of any of it, so most of them are determined to keep it all tightly contained. At least, in the beginning. Peter has always been different, though. He's funny, happily takes center stage and will frankly tell you he has no problems. Life is good. Life is easy. No worries. Move on to someone else." Brisa shrugged. "That's his wall, the thing that keeps all that other stuff at bay. People don't look closely at Peter because he shows them he's all good."

"But he's got things to work through, too," Lauren said as she remembered their conversation about the struggle of work that could mean life or death if he missed the right pattern of data and how he took the lead at home with his family.

Brisa agreed. "You know and I know that his plan to live the simple life after law school is doomed, but I can't get through to him."

Lauren raised her eyebrows. She was impressed with how well Brisa saw Peter.

"He's the one who always steps up. Sean

needs trainers for his service dog program, so Peter volunteers." Brisa ticked points off on her fingers. "Marcus wants to build a website for his new business, so Peter goes out to take photos of completed projects to help out. Last week I needed someone to meet a photographer at the office because I was running late, so Peter camped out in front of the locked door to wait. He's a good guy, someone you can always count on. Writing wills might offer a nice, steady paycheck, but there is something bigger out there for him. He just doesn't know what it is yet."

Brisa had no doubt about it; it was clear on her face as she said it.

And the longer Lauren considered it, she knew Brisa was absolutely correct.

"The other thing I know? Whatever kind of law he practices doesn't mean that's what he'll do for the rest of his life. We can all make decisions and then change direction if they don't work." She waggled her eyebrows at Lauren. "Do you hear what I'm saying? Even accepting the coolest job in the world, the one I am offering you, doesn't mean you have to stay in it forever. If criminal defense is your calling, it will still be there when you're ready to go back."

Lauren had to close her eyes as tears welled up and her nose started to sting. The emotion took her aback, but Brisa had hit the nail on the head; the reason she'd been up nights and turning herself inside out had vanished. She could return to law and the public defender's office if she made the wrong decision.

Brisa said, knowingly, "You smart, dedicated, successful types amaze me. If you'd failed early and often, you wouldn't need anyone to tell you that, but I'm glad I could. Come to the ball game. And this has nothing to do with the rest of it, but if you push Peter Kim away, you'll regret it someday. He's one of a kind." Then she held her hands up in surrender. "Listen, I am no expert in the ways of love. I wanted to be, but it is unpredictable. I don't have to sell you on Peter."

Lauren shook her head. "Charming Peter Kim does that all on his own."

Brisa was laughing when she stood. "That he does. See you at the game."

After Brisa was gone, Lauren walked out to her car and made the drive to the small coffee shop in Hollywood where she usually met her mother. Lauren preferred it to going to the apartment where her mother lived. It was easier to let go of the past and be who she was today in the coffee shop. Going home stirred up memories of being afraid of whatever might come next for her dad, or for them all.

Her mother's blond ponytail was easy to spot in the uncrowded coffee shop. She was up at the cash register, chatting with the owner. Barbara Duncan had never met a stranger in her life, so that was usually how Lauren found her mother when they met, deep in conversation with someone.

When there was a lull, the owner asked, "Hey, Lauren, you want the usual?"

Lauren nodded and wrapped her arm around her mother's shoulder. "Hey, Mama. Sorry I'm late."

"Were you?" her mother asked, and checked her wrist. "I didn't even notice, baby. I'm happy to have this unexpected break, though, so never you mind about that."

Lauren swiped her credit card for the coffees and picked hers up before following her mother through the shop. "Instead of sitting, what do you think about a manicure today?

My treat." She wanted something fun, and her mother would always jump at the chance.

Her mother's eyes brightened. "You don't mean it! I'd love to."

Lauren followed her mother for the short walk to the nail salon. When her mother pushed the door open, she said, "Sheila, honey, I'm here for those sparkles we discussed last time!"

Sheila, their usual nail tech, hopped up from her seat in the waiting area. "I had a premonition it was going to be a good day, and here come my favorite customers. What are we celebrating?"

When her mother turned back to Lauren, she answered, "Friday? That's a good enough reason to celebrate."

Sheila nodded happily. "Yes, ma'am, it is. Y'all take a seat. I'll be right with you."

Lauren sipped her coffee and sat next to her mother, laughing when her mom reached over to hit the switch that turned on the massage feature on her chair. "We gotta have the full experience. You gonna go with that same ol' French manicure?"

Lauren nodded. "Yeah, I like that same ol' French manicure."

Her mother sniffed. "Well, since you don't have to deal with judges and court appearances anymore, seems like you could go wild if you wanted to. I'm getting flowers with little crystals in the centers. Why don't we match?" Her mother patted her hand.

"That's gonna be pretty, Mama, but I'll be happy with my usual."

Her mother sighed with resignation, which sounded familiar to Lauren.

"I guess Daddy told you about me quitting." Lauren picked up a magazine and pretended to study the cover.

"We have a bet on how soon you'll be back at your desk. He said next week, but I said you weren't going back. Ever." Her mother pushed the magazine down. "I want to win that bet, you hear me?"

Lauren hadn't expected her mother to have an opinion one way or the other. Had she expected them to talk about her at all? Not really.

"How did he look?" her mother asked. "He sounded better yesterday when we spoke on the phone, but I'm afraid he's losing weight."

"I left him with enough snacks to share with Larry and put any pounds he's lost back on," Lauren said. "He seemed...good." Like he always did.

"Well, I've already started menu planning for when he gets out. You'll come, right?" Her mother shook her head. "He said something about amberjack, and I cannot for the life of me figure out where that would come from. He doesn't even like seafood."

Lauren knew it was silly, but the pride that bubbled up could not be contained. Her father had remembered her story about the fish. She dug around in her purse and pulled out her phone. "This is what he was talking about." Her mother pushed her glasses up on her nose to peer at the picture.

"Where in the world did you catch a fish, Lauren?" her mother squawked, and then flashed the photo at Sheila.

"A friend invited me out on his boat to take my mind off quitting the job." Lauren dropped her phone into her purse. "I threw it back. You won't need any amberjack recipes."

"Hmm, a friend," her mother repeated. "His *boat*. Now I'm even more determined that you are not going backward, baby. You've done enough. Let someone else take a turn and step up. I'll be sure to include an extra place setting for your friend."

Relief settled over Lauren when her mother lifted her hand to blow on the first coat of paint. She didn't want to answer questions about Peter.

But the fact that Lauren was certain she would enjoy any dinner at her mother's house more with Peter by her side was another point in favor of working things out with him.

Lauren dropped the magazine as Sheila waved her over. Once her hands were soaking and softening, she said, "I have a job offer, Mama, for something different. I'm thinking of taking it."

Her mother glanced over. "You should. If you think for a minute you might like it, give it a shot."

Getting any advice from either of her parents was rare enough that Lauren paused as she considered it. "Whatever happens, I can keep up the rent on your place, Mama. Don't worry about that." She straightened as Sheila plucked one of her hands from the dish it was soaking in and got started. Lauren and her mom had talked about all kinds of things in front of Sheila, so if either of them ever reached any position where extortion might be lucrative, Sheila would have a new retirement plan, but Lauren didn't talk about money with her mother. Ever.

This time, her mother sniffed. "I do not fret over finances. You know that."

Years of moving from one place to the next as her father's situation changed had made that clear to Lauren. Her mother never was big on planning and looking to the future. It was all about the here and now.

"I was planning to talk your daddy into a vacation when he gets out. We'll load up the car and head out to visit the Grand Canyon. I've never seen it. Neither has he." Her mother studied her face. "Do I need to put a hold on that notion? Stay close in case you need us?"

The snort that welled up was squashed before it escaped; still, Lauren coughed into her coffee cup. When had her parents ever been the help she needed? "Taking a vacation sounds like a good idea. Do you have enough time off work?" Her mother had been a cashier at a family restaurant for almost ten years, and it suited her perfectly.

"I'll worry about that if your daddy agrees," her mother answered.

Because his arrival would upend her mother's life.

Because her mother would upend her life to make her father happy. That used to upset Lauren. Today, she realized it was a decision her mother chose to make. It had no effect on Lauren anymore.

"We need to be thinking about some work for him," her mother murmured as she watched Sheila paint a second coat of hot pink on her nails. "That color is nice."

Sheila nodded, but she didn't interrupt.

Immediately, the pressure of finding something that would keep her father busy, without being too physical, and would pay enough to keep him out of trouble but not offer serious temptation settled on Lauren's shoulders.

The Concord Court business lab and the connections to all those new companies who might need part-time help sprang immediately to mind. Recommending her father would help him overcome his prison record, but what would happen if he turned the job into his next jail sentence? How would she continue to work with the unlucky soul who had trusted her and her father? The burn in her stomach was too much to keep her coffee down.

Then she remembered what she'd said to Peter outside the courtroom.

She didn't have to take this problem on.

Her father was an adult. So was her mother. Viewing them as less than that protected her from some of the hurt, but it didn't do much to lend a hand here.

As she watched Sheila drop tiny white dots on her mother's brilliant pink nails, everything became clearer.

All she had to do was come to terms with where she could help and where she had to let go. Making sure her mother had a roof over her head? That made it possible for Lauren to sleep at night.

Trying to change the tides of her father's past and whatever that meant for his future? That was beyond her duty as a good daughter.

Interfering to protect her mother from more disappointment when her mother wouldn't protect herself?

That was more than Lauren could or should take on.

She was as guilty of stepping in and picking up responsibility that wasn't hers as Peter was.

He was going to gloat when she admitted that to him.

"Mama, this trip is a good idea. Have you ever wondered if moving out of Hollywood would help? A fresh start could be what he's missing." Lauren nodded as Sheila held out the nude polish to begin her French manicure.

"We couldn't leave you, baby. We gotta keep an eye on you, make sure you're okay," her mother whispered.

Lauren smiled at Sheila's raised eyebrows, but the nail tech didn't make a peep.

"Don't you fret about me, Mama. If you can take care of Daddy, you'll have your hands full. I'll keep an eye on your place for as long as you need." Lauren met her mother's stare and nodded reassuringly. This was a promise she could make and keep and rest easy. What her parents did would be up to them.

And the next time she saw Peter, she was going to tell him all about it, show him that learning was always possible. She would offer to teach him how and laugh at his response, no doubt.

For the first time since she'd snapped under

the strain of her job, Lauren knew she was on the right track. Davey's case had confirmed the toll of the job was too much for her as it was. The conversation with Brisa had shown her what she wanted most: work that mattered with people who were passionate about it.

And talking to her mother set her free from the anchor that had tied her down ever since her father's first arrest. He'd made his own decisions, and Lauren had given enough of herself to pay for them. It was time to live for herself. Luckily, she knew the guy to show her the way.

CHAPTER SIXTEEN

On Saturday, Marcus, Peter and his nephew were standing clear of the milling group of Concord Court volunteers. They were waiting for their final instructions inside the gates of Sunshine Park, home of the Class AA Hollywood Beach Chickens baseball team.

The giant Beach Chicken mascot, namely a seagull, kept wandering too close to Rocket, making the therapy dog Peter was responsible for nervous. Peter didn't blame Raymond Washington, the ex-marine with PTSD and Rocket's owner, for skipping this event. Under normal circumstances, Peter didn't have too much trouble with noise or crowds, but this was pushing his limits.

"Good job, Rocket," Peter said as he pressed his hand on the dog's back and glared at the mascot. He'd been lucky enough to train Rocket for Sean's Shelter to Service program. He was thrilled to have the chance to catch up with her. Glossy hair, wagging tail and about ten extra pounds suggested Rocket was living the good life as a therapy dog. He'd had some worries in the early days, mainly because she'd liked to chew up carpet, but she was proof that the right kind of love could change lives.

Rocket didn't trust the large Beach Chicken, so he didn't, either. There was absolutely no reason for it to be hanging around yet. The gates wouldn't open for fifteen more minutes. The urge to shoo it away like a real seagull was strong.

"Don't see your girl yet, Pete," Marcus said. He smoothed a hand down the T-shirt all Concord Court volunteers were wearing. Cheeky the Beach Chicken's grinning face was front and center. Peter had already decided his was going to be donated to some worthy cause ASAP. "Did you call her last night like I told you to?" his friend asked.

Peter shot a glance at his nephew, who was listening intently but pretending not to, before shaking his head. He'd wanted to, but he wasn't sure what to say.

"I guess you didn't know how to tell her you thought about what she said, she was right, you were wrong and would she love you forever on one call." Marcus rubbed his chin. "Isn't that what you told us last night at the pool?"

Mira stepped up to close their circle. "That seagull is giving me the creeps. Peter didn't call her, did he?"

Marcus shook his head, his expression set on "of course not."

Peter pulled out his wallet and handed Davey a twenty. "Could you grab us some water before the game starts?"

Davey reluctantly took the cash and headed for the concessions.

"Anything you say in front of the kid will go directly back to my sister, who will crow about it to my parents, so...be cool. I wanted to introduce Davey around, maybe convince him to get involved, not get their hopes up any further regarding Lauren," Peter said slowly, determined not to lose his temper with his friends. "Besides, that's not something you tell someone over the phone."

"It is if you want them to show up to see you the next day." Mira patted his shoulder. "It's okay. We'll reconvene tonight and come up with a no-fail grand gesture for you to execute flawlessly."

Peter blinked. "I wish I'd realized how much easier it is to give advice than to receive it."

"Because you might have been less annoying?" Marcus asked.

Peter had to laugh. "Yeah, that, and I didn't have any idea how the right person can turn somebody's world upside down. The movies don't capture the experience of falling in love accurately, in my opinion. I blame Hollywood."

"Stick with us, kid. We'll get you through this," Mira said. "I'm happy Lauren set you straight. Saved me a lot of time and energy this go-round."

Peter and Marcus exchanged a glance that asked, "Why is she like this?" and "What would we do without her?" at the same time.

Before Peter could return any of the teasing he absolutely deserved, Brisa pointed at Sean, who blew a whistle someone had made the terrible mistake of giving to him.

Davey offered him a bottle of water and murmured, "What did I miss? Is Lauren coming?" His eyes lit up and Peter wondered if he was the only Kim with a crush on Lauren Duncan.

He held one finger to his lips to save himself from coming up with an answer.

"All right. Gates open in ten. Before the game starts, all Monteros will be down on the field where we will welcome everyone, thank our partners who have made this game free for veterans and their families, and I will sing the national anthem." Brisa waved her clipboard. "During the game, we will answer questions here at the booths and move through the crowds down in the concourse, handing out these pamphlets about services available at Concord Court, and through our partners at the hospital, Sawgrass University and local groups. Everyone grab a stack of the pamphlets from this box under the table and come back for more. I want the box to be empty by the seventh-inning stretch. David Kim, I am putting you in charge of that. No one leaves this stadium without one."

Peter watched his nephew nod firmly in response to his assigned duty. He and Brisa had only been introduced briefly, but the kid was smart. He read people well and caught on fast.

"If David brings pamphlets, you hand them out. Hand all of them out." Brisa shot a warning stare to the group to make sure everyone understood how serious she was. It was a sign of how much everyone supported Concord Court and appreciated everything Brisa had done to build it into what it was that no one seemed to mind.

Peter included.

"Reyna is in charge of the volunteer sign-up table," Brisa muttered because there was no need for any further explanation there. Reyna Montero completed every mission faithfully and well, and her sister trusted her. "Marcus and Jason, you both need to be over at the booth for the business lab. Please talk up the employment services, too. I'll be here with Wade, talking about Concord Court itself and how to refer any vets who need us. There are forms and clipboards at each table. If a person requests more information, fill out the form. Make sure to get a phone number."

Rocket stepped on Peter's foot, so he knelt down to make sure she was okay.

"Peter, are you paying attention?" Brisa asked from the front of the crowd. "We don't have much time."

He was trying to come up with a polite answer when Brisa's face suddenly brightened.

"Lauren! I'm so glad you decided to come! You're exactly the person I need." Brisa held her hand out and made the universal "come here" motion. "I want you to work the business lab booth because it will be the best way to convince you of how much we need you."

Lauren shot him a glance before weaving through the crowd. Davey grinned and waved like they were long-lost friends. Marcus squeezed Peter's shoulder. No words were necessary. Peter knew his best friend was happy and wishing him luck and telling him not to screw up this opportunity.

"That leaves Sean and Peter. Take the Shelter to Service volunteers over there. Divide up who will go where and when. I want someone at the welcome table at all times." Brisa pointed toward a corner of the park concourse. When Sean peeled away with the dog he was training for the newest class of service animals, Peter followed.

"It's like General Patton has replaced Brisa," Sean muttered as they reassembled the group in the quieter corner. "If she'd joined the air force along with Reyna, they'd have to add a sixth star because five stars wouldn't be enough for this general."

"Yes, or she might have been court-martialed for crimes against her own," Peter added. "With pure talent like that, you never know."

Sean nodded. "What does it mean that your Lauren showed up?"

"My Lauren?" Peter asked. "She'd be the first one to tell you that isn't true." He scratched Rocket's ears and relaxed as the dog leaned against his leg. "My guess is she's seriously considering Brisa's offer."

Sean pushed up his imaginary glasses and pretended to make a note. "And how does that make you feel?"

Peter scoffed, but it was hard to ignore the flutter that had taken root in his stomach after her eyes met his. "I want her to take it. The job will be good for her, and she will make a difference here. I know it. She's the kind of person who can do anything, but I'm not sure she knows that."

"Lucky she's got you on her side, then." He felt Sean clap a hand on his shoulder. "Does it help our case or hurt it with Lauren to have you stationed up here, buddy? If you're going to make her mad or sad, then you'll be walking up and down the aisles with Rocket instead," Sean warned as he bent down to add, "who is a very pretty girl."

Rocket's tail whacked against Peter's leg as she returned Sean's love.

"Flip a coin. I don't know the answer," Peter said finally. He wanted to be next to Lauren. Maybe he wouldn't be able to change her mind about them or even about Concord Court, but being able to see her was worth something. Then he realized he owed it to himself to make the decision, to take the chance, or not. He was the kind of person who made decisions, not just let them happen.

"Scratch that. I want to be up here close to Lauren's booth. If it looks like we're arguing or she'd like to stuff some of those pamphlets in my mouth, switch me out. I'll regroup and try again later." Peter shook his head. Never in his life had he been nervous to go after what he wanted. Never. But Lauren made him jittery and scared, as if a no from her would ruin his life. Peter had never expected to find anyone who had that much power over him.

But now that he had, there was no doubt in his mind what that meant.

Lauren Duncan was important to him. Regardless of what happened today or tomorrow, she would matter forever. Peter patted Rocket's head and stared into her brown eyes as he listened to Sean divide the volunteers and explain the goals of introducing vets to his program that took shelter dogs and trained them to provide support. Sean, who was a teasing, laughing laid-back guy most of the time, became all business when he spoke about the program he loved.

When the group dispersed, Peter realized Rocket had worked some of her magic. Instead of annoyed and on edge, thanks to the noise and milling crowd, Peter was calm. He understood his assignment for Concord Court, and he knew what he owed himself regarding Lauren.

He could do both. Taking a chance with her might mean more commitments, more responsibility, making serious plans for his future that would come with people depending on him. There was no way the people he cared about deserved anything less. That would never change.

She'd also been right about him. He did take on more than anyone asked him to. He'd spent the last two days coming to terms with what that meant. At this point, it was who he was. Having someone else around who understood him and would help him find the right balance between too much responsibility and none at all would be huge. Lauren could do that. She saw him.

Lauren would take all that and turn it into a life that he, that they, could be proud of.

When the gates opened, every one of the volunteers hurried to their assignments. He and Sean moved closer to the streams of people who were heading for their seats or the concessions on the concourse and introduced the dogs to anyone who stopped for a closer look. Peter could see the volunteers flow through the crowd, handing out pamphlets and welcoming people to the game. David was watching from one side, his hands full of pamphlets and a managerial expression on his face.

Even the large mascot, Cheeky the Beach Chicken, had moved into position. Little kids were flocking to have their photos taken with the seagull.

Peter spotted Lauren's crown of shining hair now and then. As game time drew closer, the crowd thinned. Lauren's eyes met his and her tentative smile was sweet enough to fill him with hope. Whatever she had to say about the job or them, at least she was here. This thing between them was still here, too, and he was grateful for that.

"Hey, we're all going to meet behind the home team's dugout before the game to watch the Monteros' presentation," Mira said as she bumped his shoulder. "Make sure to tell Lauren, okay? I'll grab Davey." Then she exaggerated batting her eyelashes at him.

"Does Brisa know about this change of plan?" Peter asked, his mind on the sharp orders she'd issued and her mean glare.

Mira shook her head slowly and her eyes lit up. "She most definitely does not. This is it, the moment Wade and Sean have been waiting for to pop the question." She frowned. "Plural? Two questions?" Then she checked her clipboard and the time. "Anyway, unless they chicken out, there will be marriage proposals. Today. Here. Now. Then, depending on the answers…" Mira stretched her arms out to imply the whole world might be included in the likely celebration and he totally understood.

"They are brave." Peter wondered when he'd missed the finalization of this part of the plan and what he would have advised if he'd had a chance to make any changes to it.

Mira patted his shoulder. "I had the same reaction. Reyna has been scared this day was coming, and Brisa? It's hard to say how she'll take someone stepping on Concord Court's night. Wade and Sean are hoping for safety in numbers and the public venue to protect them from any potential backlash. This is either brilliant or doomed for failure and ignominy. Sean's ideas are always like that. I have my fingers crossed. You know what a wise philosopher once said?" She grinned. "No guts, no glory. No matter the answers, this will be epic."

Peter laughed. "Yeah. They definitely opted to go all in. Let's hope it works out the way they and everyone want it to."

"Hurry. Tell Lauren. I'll make sure the rest of the program's volunteers join us." Mira jogged away before Peter agreed, but that was fine. It was great to have a reason to break the ice.

"Rocket, this is important business. I'm going to need your support." He pulled a treat out of his pocket and gave it to her. Bribe? Insurance that the dog would be on his side? Hard to say, but Peter straightened his shoulders and maneuvered between the stragglers in the crowd.

"I wasn't sure you'd come today," he said as he stopped in front of Lauren.

Lauren shrugged. "Brisa's hard to say no to. Besides that," she added as she met his stare, "I wanted to see."

"See what?" Peter asked.

"More." Lauren sighed. "My first baseball game. More of Brisa, her programs, Concord Court, if there was any way I could plug into work that is totally foreign but could also be fun. Satisfying."

He hadn't made her list. The nervous knot in his stomach tightened. It was a setback, but he wasn't going to give up.

Then she reached for his hand. "And there's this amazing guy here, too. I'm having a tough time going back to living my life without him, now that he's shown me his two-step system for success."

Relieved, Peter grinned. "It's good, isn't it?"

Lauren wrinkled her nose. "Good, but I can make it great with the addition of one step.

Possibly two. What I'm saying is that the two of us together need to revise it a little."

"Interesting. Partners instead of rivals. Think the guy'll go for it?" Peter asked.

"He's really smart. I think so. I'm also going to apologize for bluntly telling him the truth outside the courtroom, about how he gets involved in everyone's business."

Peter frowned. They'd talked about his family and his role there. When had she expanded his problem to include "everyone"? Before he could ask, she wrinkled her nose a second time. "You see, I have the same problem. I guess that's how I can recognize it in you, Peter. I'm sorry. My mom, my dad, I've been doing the responsibility-for-everyone thing forever, except I also made it my job. I'm going to be smarter, even though obviously I'll never stop caring about them. I love them. But we are going to work on this problem, our problem, together."

He grinned. "I can see how my system can be improved with the addition of that step."

Lauren pointed at Rocket. "I know he's a service dog. Can I pet him?"

Peter reached into his pocket for another treat. "She is a service dog and she is doing a fantastic job so far. Her name is Rocket. Give her one of these and she will follow you anywhere."

Lauren bent down to give Rocket her treat and then scratched her chest. "I've never had a dog. She's beautiful."

"She belongs to a vet named Raymond, but she came from a shelter for Sean's training program. If you want to try life with a dog, I know the man who can set you up. You have to be ready to eventually send them to their forever home, though, and that nearly killed me with Rocket. I love seeing her when I get the chance." Peter pointed down at the field. "If we don't get there, we're going to miss the most important piece of this show and Sean will never let me forget that." He held out his hand.

Relief and overwhelming satisfaction swamped him when she slipped her hand in his. Whatever his idea had been before he'd tracked down Lauren Duncan, he knew he was on the right track now.

CHAPTER SEVENTEEN

LAUREN WAS HAPPY she'd decided to take a chance on the baseball game and seeing Peter. Everything around her was new and interesting, but nothing topped walking up to a large group of Peter's friends with her hand in his. Being welcomed by his friends was sweet, but the pride she felt standing next to him was new. And it surprised her.

Sure, she'd been proud of all of her accomplishments. Those things made sense. Whereas this satisfaction of being next to Peter Kim? Romantic relationships had never been her priority; however, she'd known there was something different about him even at twenty-two. If she'd had any idea how this fragile connection would change the way she viewed herself, it would have been even scarier.

She had always made her own decisions, her own plans, and she'd taken comfort in that control. Allowing Peter to have a part in that, giving him that much power in her life…

Fear welled up before she understood it was happening.

Lauren had worked hard to build up protective barriers that kept people who could disappoint her or hurt her at a distance.

She was in danger of losing all that protection. Peter could hurt her. He wouldn't mean to disappoint her, but wasn't it inevitable? Was she ready for that?

As she untangled her fingers from Peter's, he shot her a curious glance but slipped his arm around her shoulders instead.

Lauren watched as the Monteros walked out on the field, and ignored the pleasure of his touch. Victor and Marisol Montero had been in enough media and society pages that she'd recognize them in any crowd.

"I hear there's going to be a surprise ending to this presentation," Peter whispered in her ear, sending a shiver across her skin, and reminding her of their too-quick kisses. When he wrapped his hand around her nape, Lauren couldn't pretend the shiver was anything other than a response to him, his voice, his closeness.

"I'm glad I'm here to see it, whatever it is," Lauren said before forcing herself to look down to the field.

Brisa began her speech by introducing the volunteers. Lauren happily waved at them with everyone else. They stood patiently while Brisa described Concord Court and listed the programs available. Her father outlined the new plans to expand the business lab with plenty of training for veterans running their own small businesses. Every second Lauren listened to the Monteros' vision for supporting military veterans convinced her that theirs was a cause she could join. Brisa Montero stepped up onto the pitcher's mound and sang the national anthem beautifully to wrap up their presentation.

"Is there anything she can't do?" Lauren stood on her tiptoes to speak closely to Peter's ear. The way his attention snapped over to her convinced her of her own effect on his nerves. His hand shifted from her nape to urge her closer.

"She's not great at matchmaking. We've asked her to retire." Peter's slow grin was adorable. "I was her last hope, and her friend Candace was open to another date, but I might be taken at this point." He raised his eyebrows.

This was how he'd done it, how he'd slipped past her guard.

The words, the expression, disturbed the butterflies that had almost settled inside her. "Candace? One of Brisa's friends, you say?" She frowned at him, and he winked.

"I'm definitely taken," he said next to her ear.

Before she could ask for more details to torment him with and put more "friend" zone back between them, Victor Montero accepted the microphone from his daughter. Lauren watched as he was handed a baseball. Was the surprise that he was going to throw out the first pitch? Didn't that happen at all games? She had no idea, honestly.

But when one of the men knelt down in front of Reyna, Lauren gasped out loud. That had to be it. A proposal on the pitcher's mound. Wow, talk about grand gestures.

It was impossible to hear what he said, but since Reyna threw herself into his arms while a happy dog danced around their feet, it was easy enough to interpret her answer. Lauren squeezed Peter's hand. "How romantic. Is she a baseball fan?"

He frowned and shook his head. "No. I don't think so. Sean wanted the whole world to see this moment. Reyna's been nervous about the whole idea of getting married. I think he was hoping she'd say yes if an encouraging crowd was watching."

Lauren frowned. Was that romantic or kind of...pushy?

"I get how that may sound, but believe me, Reyna Montero doesn't do anything she doesn't want to do." Peter smiled. "They're absolutely perfect for each other, and the fact that she didn't shove him off the mound for ambushing her like this is testament to how happy she is. I promise."

"Okay." Lauren nodded uncertainly. They might be her friends, sooner or later, but she still had a lot to learn about everyone at Concord Court. "Should we head to our assigned spots? I don't want to get in trouble with Brisa."

Peter pointed back out at the field. "I don't think we're done yet. Wade is in on this, too."

Lauren saw Brisa cross the pitcher's mound to face the other man in the group. When

Brisa crossed her arms over her chest in the pose of "patiently waiting," he shook his head and then knelt in the grass in front of her. Brisa was laughing and nodding, and the whole family was tangled in a group hug and the crowd was going wild.

"Two proposals! That is a surprise!" Lauren cheered. "Was Brisa nervous about getting married, too?" Lauren knew herself, knew that she would be. Marriage was a risk. Her parents, even with all her father's trouble, had managed to make it work somehow. Still, theirs was no one's goal for a great marriage.

The memory of the way Peter's mother had leaned against his father's shoulder for strength outside the courtroom...

Building a marriage like that might be worth all the risk.

"Brisa wasn't as nervous as Wade. He wanted something that she'd remember. He's had a tough time coming up with a gesture that could top any of her high-flying exes, but a double proposal with the sister she loves more than even Concord Court and in front of this crowd that she sacrifices so much for?" Peter said. "It's perfect. I haven't been at the nightly group therapy sessions around the pool lately, dealing with…stuff, so I don't know whose inspiration this was."

After Victor Montero threw out the first pitch, the crowd went wild again. He reminded everyone that Concord Court had set up booths and had volunteers ready to answer questions. Anyone who knew a veteran who might benefit was welcome to come find out more.

"Now we better hustle to our spots. No matter how happy she is, Brisa will rain down fire if we miss any single person who wants to find out more about Concord Court." Peter urged her up the steps.

Lauren was still laughing as she stopped in front of the table for the business lab. "Is she that tough? She's pretty determined to be my boss."

Peter's expression was thoughtful. "Never worked for her, but I can't imagine anyone finding fault with Lauren Duncan. The truth is, Brisa has been desperately searching for someone to take over this business lab because she wants to do more. Brisa will enthusiastically support any idea and she will help you succeed. The Monteros have connections all over Miami. Anything is possible as long as you're doing this for the right reasons, namely the veterans."

Lauren bit her lip as she considered that. "Even politically?"

Peter blinked. "Don't tell me you have political ambitions?"

Did she? "I meant speaking up for better support for veterans who are caught unfairly in the criminal justice system, but…" What if there were no sympathetic legislators or contacts the Monteros could talk to? Did it bother her enough to step up and say she'd be that voice?

Peter shook his head sadly. "Pretty sure your additions to my established system for relaxation and recreation are going to be my downfall. If you want to run for office, where will that leave me?"

He was already jumping into the deep end by imagining a future for the two of them, while Lauren was dipping her toe in the water. Was there any way to slow him down?

"On your boat? Not fishing? Whenever I need to get away from my cell phone or my job or Brisa's master plan? You could be my getaway driver, Captain." Lauren bit her lip. "I have no idea. It never once occurred to me to run for anything, but if I want to change things..."

Peter pressed his lips to hers. "Whatever you want, Duncan. I'm going to love you through it."

"Love?" Lauren closed her eyes. "Love?" Why was it so hard to breathe?

He nodded. "Confused, that's how I felt at first, too. How can it even be true?"

"No kissing on the job," someone said from behind them. Lauren immediately straightened, convinced Brisa had caught them and grateful for a distraction.

"Hey, Cassie, this is Lauren," Peter drawled. "Introduce yourself before you scare her, please."

The petite brunette with a wicked gleam in her eyes said, "Ohhhh, Lauren. Right."

Lauren guessed she'd been thoroughly discussed by...probably everyone.

"That guy making heart eyes at her, is Marcus, your helper at the booth," Peter added.

"I'm this guy's best friend." Marcus grinned. "These two together can be a lot." Marcus glanced down at Cassie, who had sat on the concrete to talk to Rocket.

Lauren realized why Cassie looked so familiar. "Do you write for *Miami Beat*? The column that does out-of-the-box stuff, like the story about the actor who found her role as a mermaid in a local dinner theater? That's yours, right?"

Cassie immediately bounced up and hugged Lauren tightly. "I like you. I'm so happy I like Peter's…whatever you are." She motioned at Lauren.

Lauren wanted to ask so many questions, but a young woman was approaching their booth. Marcus shooed Peter and Cassie away, and said, "Hi, do you have questions about the business lab at Concord Court?"

The young woman frowned. "Maybe. My husband is active duty. He's not with me." She waited for their response, so Marcus nodded. "I run a small cake-decorating business out of my home. Nothing big." Her hesitation convinced Lauren to pick up the clipboard with Brisa's form so she could make notes as her words trickled out. "I'd like to expand, but all I know for sure is that my website isn't bringing in business like I'd hoped it would. There are times when access to a commercial kitchen and part-time help would expand my options." She held her hands out. "But I don't know enough about hiring and paying people, and if my husband gets new orders and we have to move, I want the business to go with me. Is this anything you might be able to work with?"

Marcus answered immediately. "Yes. These are exactly the kinds of things the business lab can do. We know a couple of web designers who can address your site immediately. The rest, we'll have to research, but…" Marcus held his hand out to Lauren.

As if he was handing it over to her.

"Let's do first things first," Lauren said, and motioned to a quieter spot. "Let me get down some information." They covered the top part of the form first. "Payroll. I know there are easy-to-use programs. I'll ask our other business owners for recommendations. Then you could come in and we could review them together. What do you think about that?"

The way the woman gripped her arm convinced Lauren she was on the right track. She immediately felt more assured, stronger.

"Explain to me a bit about commercial kitchens," Lauren said as she flipped the form over to the back.

"They're inspected like restaurants for

health and safety, and you can rent them, usually by the hour. There's one in downtown Miami that I've toured, but it's not easy to book because…" She shrugged. "It's so busy. Caterers and bakers like me can bring in the things they need, use the equipment and carry everything back out, so it saves on the overhead of a full-time kitchen."

"And the demand to book them is constant?" Lauren asked. The potential to set up a kitchen like that and divide it for use was her first thought. They could set a fee and have open slots for anyone in order to pay the overhead while reserving slots for vets or people connected through the lab. Were there other cooks, bakers or caterers involved with Concord Court who could use support like this? Where would they house it? What would the licensing steps be?

When she glanced up and noticed the woman watching the way she scribbled her notes, Lauren realized she was doing it again. Thinking fast and writing hard to make sure she didn't miss anything.

Just like old times.

And the whole exchange had naturally become how Lauren could help in a meaningful way at Concord Court, not just be another unknown cog in the wheel.

"I'd like to give you a call next week. We can set up a time for you to come in and outline the changes we can make now to assist you, versus the steps that aren't in place yet at the lab." Lauren wasn't prepared when the woman hugged her. The responsibility of helping the young woman with her dreams settled on Lauren's shoulders, but it didn't worry her. This was stepping up to support someone, not bearing all the weight alone.

Lauren could do this without any problem.

After the young woman left, Marcus held up his hand for a high five. "Good job. It was easy, right?"

"It felt good." Lauren stared at the form and realized all she felt was excitement.

"What do we do with the forms?" she asked.

"Better check with Brisa. We do not want to get it wrong." Marcus shook his head as if the consequences were too scary to think about.

When the crowd died down at Brisa's table, Lauren went to ask about the forms.

Brisa frowned at the form, as if it was the

most precious, important document she'd ever seen in her life.

"Are you okay?" Lauren asked, and Brisa shook her head.

"I keep catching sight of this ring on my finger." She held her hand out. "I would hurt him for derailing my brain like this on this night of all nights, but look at how beautiful it is." The diamond and Brisa's smile both sparkled.

"Congratulations." Lauren pointed at the form. "We have someone interested in help finding commercial kitchen time." The question was in her voice.

Brisa focused on the form. "Of course. Makes sense. I haven't been able to find another restaurant that might be willing to rent time and the one downtown is always booked. I wish we could afford..." Her voice trailed off as she stared at the ground.

Her new fiancé leaned over. "She does that. She's trying to find a way to make something happen."

"If we could find the space, it sounds like we could open it up to other businesses at a fee that would cover the expenses, and reserve times, certain days of the week or something, for our lab businesses." Lauren realized she'd said "our" at the same time Brisa did. The whoop she let out stopped everyone around them. Brisa clasped her hands and did a happy dance.

When Peter grinned at her, Lauren shrugged. "I only came over to ask what to do with the forms."

Brisa pointed at the volunteer table. "I was going to ask my right-hand woman to take care of that, but look what they did to her." Brisa's sister was staring at her own hand as if she'd never seen it, the ring there flashing in the light. "So you're up. Please gather the forms and hold them for safekeeping until we return to earth and business as usual."

David Kim joined the small group to say, "The volunteers are making good headway handing out the pamphlets, Brisa. If it's okay, I'm going to start rotating them through breaks for food and enjoying the game, then we'll all be back in the concourse for the last innings."

"Yes!" The way Brisa squeezed him caught the young man off guard, but Lauren shared an amused glance with Peter.

When Brisa let David go, Peter thumped him on the back. "Good job, kid."

Brisa ran her fingers under her eyes as if she was wiping away tears.

David straightened his shoulders and marched away, a man with a mission.

Brisa patted Lauren on the shoulder and moved toward her sister's table when she turned back. "You're in charge of the forms we're collecting here. Meet me at Concord Court Monday. Nine? I want to show you everything and we can talk salary."

Lauren gave a firm nod and pulled all the forms together. Over the weekend, she could look through them to see what kinds of requests had come in and where she might help.

"Already on the job?" Peter asked from over her shoulder.

"Maybe?" Lauren turned to smile at him. "This could be fun." She was growing more convinced about the job.

But she'd have to weigh the danger to her heart presented by continued close quarters with Peter Kim.

CHAPTER EIGHTEEN

ON SUNDAY, LAUREN OUTLINED where to begin with each of the veterans who'd filled out a form at the game and created a longer list of questions that needed input or development before she had enough information to decide how best to assist. The forms were color coded and arranged from easiest to most complex.

If and when she decided being in such close quarters with Peter at Concord Court was safe for her heart.

That left a long afternoon to consider all the ways in which Peter could upend her life…some good, others scary.

Desperate for a distraction, Lauren picked up her phone. "Hey, Mom, did you go visit Dad yesterday?"

"I did. He makes me so mad sometimes, sweetie," her mother said, her voice raspy as if she'd been crying.

"What happened?" Lauren asked as she stared at her car keys. Should she leave for her mother's condo now?

"He said he'd been *resting for months* now and was bored. That he was ready to get working again." Her mother's huff of a laugh was resigned, not amused. "*Resting.* That's what he called it."

Lauren slowly stretched her neck and shoulders, and remembered other similar conversations she and her mother had in the past. This surprised her mother every single time, but her father never changed.

The urge to order her mother to look out for herself first trembled on the tip of Lauren's tongue, but she'd said it so many different ways already. None of them ever worked.

"All the worry he puts me through and to him it's a vacation." Her mother sighed. "Why do I expect any different?"

The urge to jump in with suggestions was strong, but Lauren forced herself to swallow them all. What to do next was her mother's decision. Nothing would change until she made that choice.

Then Lauren realized what she could change was how she responded to her mother's outlook.

"What if you and I planned a trip to see the Grand Canyon, Mama?" Lauren asked before squeezing her eyes shut. She wasn't going to get involved, but... This was different, wasn't it? "I haven't seen it, either. We'll take a girls' trip. That will be fun."

This was the moment her mother would tell her how much she missed Mike Duncan while he was in prison and couldn't bear to be separated from him any longer. Lauren expected the reply and would not be disappointed when it came.

"Baby, I believe I will take you up on that. A woman should not be wasting all her years because a man cannot get with the program." Some of her mother's bright energy had returned.

Lauren laughed. "No, ma'am, she should not. When you go to work, talk to your manager about when you can take a week off and we'll go." Whatever happened with her job, Lauren was making time for this adventure. She wanted to make up for lost time, too, with this road trip with her mother to see sites she'd missed out on thanks to her old way of thinking when it came to her career.

"All right, I'm gonna do that. Now, what are

you up to on this hot Sunday? Why haven't you talked your 'friend' into taking you out on the water?" her mother asked.

"I…" Lauren wasn't sure how to answer. She was working at a job she didn't have yet? She was doing her best to avoid thinking about what to do about that man, but everything kept turning back to him?

"Oh, boy, I know that tone. You're trying to come up with a good cover story, aren't you?" Her mother tsked. "Gets you into more trouble, all that thinking too hard, even if you are the smartest person I know, Lauren Duncan."

Lauren rubbed her forehead. "How did you know you were ready to take a chance with Daddy? I know marrying him had to change your own life plans. If you knew then how it would all turn out, would you still do it?"

"Of course I would," her mother immediately said. "I got you out of the whole deal. Now, him? Him, I might change." Her mother sighed. "But the thing about love is… Well, loving them changes you, and you hope it does the same on the other side, but there's not much I can do to make your daddy a different man."

"And that's okay with you?" Lauren asked. This was the part she'd never understood. Walking away might have hurt, but how much better would her mother have been in the long run, divorced, but independent of her father's mistakes?

Her mother said, "Thing is, I have to make that decision every day, not just when things get better or worse. Am I going to love him today? Then the next day, I do it again. It's so easy to say yes that it doesn't even register as a question, you know? Not even so much 'will I love him' but 'am I in love with him' and it's always still yes."

"Even when the stuff he does hurts you?" Lauren asked softly.

"Even then. In spite of his mistakes and bad choices, my life is still better because he's in it," her mother answered.

"That's pretty brave, Mama." Lauren had spent so many years frustrated because her mother wouldn't protect herself.

"Pretty sure falling for someone is the scariest thing on the planet," her mother drawled in response.

Lauren laughed, relief settling within her as she realized that her mother would never change, either, and that was okay. Her mother was strong enough to deal with her father, partly because she'd chosen to do that over and over, healing and growing each time.

"I'm going to look up places along the way where we might like to stop. This is going to be a great road trip," Lauren told her mom, and pulled out her notebook to make a note to have the tires on her car checked. Should she replace them before they left?

"You already got a to-do list and a budget in mind, don't you, Lauren?"

Lauren stared down at her notepad and silently set it aside.

"If the boat's not an option, go to the beach or something. Rest your mind for a minute, girl." Her mother said the same thing the irritated voice in Lauren's head was saying.

"Good advice, Mama. I'm going to do that." Lauren's mood was improved as she hung up the phone, but the problem she'd started with remained.

Lauren stared at her phone, her finger hovering over Peter's contact info. Then, on impulse, she picked the name right above his.

When his sister answered, Lauren said, "Hey, Nic, how are you?" Breezy. She wanted a breezy tone, not an "I'm desperate for a distraction, please be a distraction" tone.

"Bored. Come to Wynwood. I want to show you my studio. The crowd is very light today, and I need the company," Peter's sister said. "I have cheap wine for guests and better wine for friends. There is also a cheese plate that I put out for every tour that no one eats. You can take your chances with that if you're hungry."

"How can I resist an offer like that?" Lauren asked as she scooped up her car keys. "I'm on my way."

LAUREN PARKED IN front of Nicole's studio in Wynwood, still singing along with the radio, her worries blown away by the wind through the open window.

A young couple was leaving Nic's place as Lauren reached the front door. One of the men held a gorgeously wrapped rectangular package that might have been a canvas. He and Lauren exchanged a nod before she went inside.

David was clearing off a counter positioned

next to the door. Brown wrapping paper, heavy twine and delicate tissue paper littered the surface. His face brightened when he noticed her. "Lauren!" He stopped abruptly and asked, "Is it okay to call you Lauren?"

She grinned. "Definitely. Are you working today?" With a wave, she indicated to all the paper and twine. "Do you wrap the canvases you sell like that every time?"

He motioned toward the back of the studio. "My mother insists. It's art, but it's also an experience." The way he stressed the last word convinced Lauren that Nicole said it that way every time, so she smiled.

"My grandparents worried about the hours I worked at the hospital, so I quit. Until I find something everyone agrees is good for me," he said, with a beleaguered face, "I'm working for everyone. All at once. Uncle Peter said volunteering at the game would be good for me. My mother says helping here will give me an understanding of entrepreneurship."

"And we were both correct," his mother added from the open doorway. "Weren't we?"

"Yes, Mother," David said in a patient tone that made Nicole giggle. "But I'm going to be a lawyer."

"Maybe Lauren has some ideas on good internships for undergrads, something that can help with law school admission. Job experience that will boost your résumé, not just your checking account. That will comfort your grandparents and make the move to the dorms in the fall much easier." His mother held up a wineglass. "But first, we're going to tour the gallery."

Lauren nodded to David. The kid was smart and patient. He would make an excellent lawyer. "I will enjoy that. I might also be able to make some calls to see if anyone is hiring a part-time law clerk." She pointed at Nic. "After the tour."

David smiled and returned to clearing the wrapping materials.

"The kid's so serious. I was afraid we'd never get to the wine," Nic murmured as she poured Lauren a glass. "Let's actually tour to make this whole thing legit."

Lauren grinned as she followed Nic. Her hair was a messy bun with one strand pointing straight up that waved Lauren forward. They walked slowly from canvas to canvas as Nicole pointed out the Korean words woven or painted into the artwork.

"I saw the piece you gave your brother. I love this style," Lauren told her as she stepped closer to see how Nicole had embroidered the needles on a tall painted pine tree.

"Folk art. It's something for everyone." Nicole climbed up on a stool and crossed her legs. "Now that I'm successful and saving for retirement, even my parents agree."

Lauren took the stool opposite her and set her wineglass down.

"Okay, spit it out." Nicole made the continue motion with her hand. "Whatever it is that's on your mind. Let Nicole help."

"I needed this today." Lauren bit her lip. Was she going to unload her worries on Nicole? That wasn't like her, not really, but it was tempting.

Nicole calmly sipped her wine, obviously waiting patiently.

Lauren realized she had nothing to lose. "In my family, I'm the serious one, while my parents… Well, my dad spends time in and out of jail and my mom has accepted that's the way it is. At work, I'm the weird one who believes in the mission, and I burned myself out because of it."

Nicole braced her elbows on her knees and waited.

"Being the different one has protected me so I can't get hurt." Lauren shrugged. "But now, I have an amazing opportunity that is going to mean falling head over heels for this guy, and I have to decide whether to let my guard fall or reinforce it instead."

Nicole picked up the wine bottle and topped off Lauren's glass. "Good job."

"Thank you." Lauren ducked her head in a bow that made Nicole laugh.

"I'm an artist. I'm a Kim. Peter is my older brother." Nicole met Lauren's stare. "I understand not fitting in. I do."

"Do you have advice for me? How do I let go of that fear of being disappointed or hurt by someone I need and want?" Lauren asked. This was it.

"When I was eighteen, I made a bunch of wild choices. None of it made sense but that didn't matter to me. I disappointed my family, and yes, changed the course of my whole life. You would think nothing scares me now, but we both know that isn't true. Davey's trial reminded me of how hard it is to shake fear. It was completely out of my control." Nicole wrinkled her nose. "I'm not sure I would recommend tearing up every safety net to conquer your worries, but no one is asking that of you. Most people, even heroes like Peter Kim, have their walls, feelings, memories they protect. All you have to do is trust a little and then a little more until the trust is stronger than the fear." Nicole pursed her lips. "That almost sounds like I know what I'm talking about!" She raised an arm in triumph.

Lauren cheered because Nicole was absolutely right. It did. "There *is* wisdom in the wine."

Nicole laughed and picked up her glass and clinked it with Lauren's. "Also, my older brother survived our teenage years and put up with a lot, and still answers my phone calls. I trust Peter Kim like no one else on this planet. You can, too."

Lauren stared hard at her wineglass as the realization dawned on her. Logically, emotionally, in every way it made perfect sense to take a chance on Peter Kim.

The only question remaining was whether she was as brave as her mother had been time and again.

No matter what might happen today, could Lauren make the same decision to trust Peter tomorrow?

CHAPTER NINETEEN

PETER WATCHED LAUREN park her car in front of the Concord Court office, where he and Brisa were standing. He was extremely conscious that he was crashing what was essentially a job interview, but Brisa hadn't ordered him away. As long as Lauren didn't eject him like a bouncer in a rowdy bar, his plan was to keep his mouth shut and his ears open. It was hard to explain his need to see how this meeting turned out, but there was more riding on the outcome than an employment opportunity for Lauren.

"Good morning." Lauren held a stack of file folders in front of her like a shield. "I hope you weren't waiting long."

"No worries. You are right on time. I didn't plan on having a committee here to greet you, but I'll allow Peter to tag along with your approval," Brisa said airily as she pointed at her golf cart. "Load up. There's something I want to show you and I can't wait any longer."

"What are you doing here?" Lauren whispered as she stepped in his path to prevent him from getting in the golf cart.

Peter ran a hand through his hair. He'd anticipated this but hadn't been able to come up with a good answer. That was annoying. He always had an answer for Lauren when they squared off.

"I missed you?" he tried.

She rolled her eyes.

He shrugged. "It's weird. Maybe because I'm the one who introduced you, but I feel a connection, a responsibility. Plus, I'm nosy. I'll be quiet. I promise." He hoped he could keep the promise.

Peter urged Lauren into the seat next to Brisa before sliding onto the back, the seat facing away from the driver.

"It's safer next to the driver, Duncan, and you need all the protection you can get with Brisa behind the wheel," Peter said. "Please hold on."

Before he could warn her that he wasn't exaggerating, Brisa hit the gas and the golf cart shot away from the curb with a whir.

Brisa made the turn out into the road in front of Concord Court. Lauren shouted, "Is this legal?"

It was a valid question. Peter would suggest even if it was legal, it probably wasn't safe or a good idea. Brisa replied, "Sean's going to build a path for us to use, but there's a ditch between the properties that will require a bridge first."

As if that answered Lauren's question.

Luckily, it was a short trip around the block to the small shopping complex that backed onto Concord Court. The golf cart bounced along the access road and thumped down into the parking lot. They all caught their breath.

"Welcome to the Concord Court Business Park." Brisa gestured like a game show hostess. Peter swiveled to see what she meant. "The name is subject to change."

"Where?" Peter asked. "That is an automotive store. Parts. Tires. Things like that."

Brisa frowned.

"That *used* to be an automotive store, but today it is six thousand square feet of potential. It's all mine, courtesy of a purchase by Montero Properties and the world's longest lease with my father. Within six months, we have to take over the payments and cover all expenses."

"Okay, but..." Lauren said breathlessly. "Six months seems fast."

"It does," Brisa said as she accelerated. She pointed at the strip of stores that extended from the empty automotive shop. "There are businesses leasing spaces still. We'll honor those leases. In fact, they're going to get us most of what we need to cover our first six months of payments. I have ideas for immediate sponsorships and fundraising requests for the lab. Lauren, when you start, you're going to work with me to organize this attack."

When Lauren didn't respond, Peter was afraid it was because she was second- or third-guessing her decision to sign up for Concord Court, so he interrupted. "This whole business park is the development? Not just the one store back there? Everything?" As Brisa drove around to the front of the property that faced the traffic on the main road, he could see a second level over the shops there that appeared to be office space.

Brisa slammed to a stop. "Yes, isn't it exciting! We have that extra office space to set up operations there, and we have all this space to lease to our small businesses at favorable rates. We'll have a grouping of veteran-owned businesses that will be easily identifiable to anyone in Miami who wants to support them. If companies are based here, then people will know they're helping veterans when they're—" Brisa pointed at the different storefronts "—ordering birthday cakes or hiring an accountant or shopping for bicycles or whatever we end up with."

Silence filled the golf cart until Peter said, "So you've taken this huge idea, the business lab, which will support many small businesses, and you've blown it up to also include real estate and being a landlord and…" He didn't know where the idea would end. Brisa's ideas were like that.

"Exactly," Brisa said with satisfaction.

They did a full circle around the development and ended up back at the front of the empty automotive store. Brisa parked the golf cart and slid out. "Why aren't you all as excited as I am? All this potential fills me with ideas and I can't wait to get started."

Lauren followed her. Peter could see the death grip on the stack of folders she'd been carrying. It was a miracle they'd survived the golf ride.

"Come inside." Brisa unlocked the doors and waved them in before anyone could answer.

Peter tangled his fingers with Lauren's and followed her. Maybe this was going to be more than either one of them had anticipated. Whoever stepped up to take the job was going to be buried under an onslaught of tasks. Was it more than Lauren was prepared for? The memory of her on his boat flashed in his mind.

"The back half of the place was for storage, there's a receiving area for trucks, and a tiny office. We're going to keep that office, but the rest of this space will be divided." Brisa held her arms out to show them what she meant. "Computers. Monitors. Whiteboards. Capability for videoconferencing. This will be training central." Brisa waited for a response. When Lauren nodded, she pivoted. "On this side, we can set up cubicles that will contain the basics for anyone who needs computer access for business or developing marketing plans or applying for grants or even college applications. Jason's career guidance work will move here, too. These cubicles can be booked by the hour, see?" This time Brisa didn't even pretend to care what he thought. She only had eyes for Lauren.

Lauren let go of his hand and stood next to Brisa. Peter relaxed a fraction. If he had to guess, she was hooked, and if he knew Brisa at all, she was going to reel Lauren in and have her hired before they left.

"Two offices, one for Lauren and the other for Jason." Brisa paced as she pointed out the dimensions. "There will be a small conference room in front and two desks on either side." She marched back to meet them near the door. "This is going to be a nice reception area. I want kids' toys and books, comfortable chairs, and we'll have someone to greet every visitor."

"How are you planning to staff that? The front desk, someone to answer the phone and book the cubicles?" Lauren asked.

"Volunteers? Interns who need work experience?" Brisa said hesitantly. "I'm not that far down the road yet."

Lauren nodded. He couldn't read her face.

"You have the forms from the ball game. Did you see anyone who might be good at manning a front desk?" Brisa snapped her fingers. "And we're going to set up a reservation system online. That will help."

"Unless whoever wants to come in doesn't have computer access," Peter murmured.

Brisa frowned. "Good point."

Lauren handed the files to Brisa and began pacing in a slow circle, considering the options. Peter had seen that focus so many times. She was working the problem out in her head.

"What are these notes?" Brisa asked as she opened the first file. A hot-pink note was stuck to the form.

"Hot pink is for volunteers," Lauren murmured before she paused. "Sorry. I went through the forms we gathered. If there's a note stuck to the front, it's something we can act on immediately. That one on top? She wanted to know if we have a list of accredited babysitters that we can recommend if vets and their families ask. She's nineteen and going to Sawgrass, so she babysits to earn spending money." Peter frowned. They were standing in a business center. Were they going to support that small of small businesses? "My thinking was..." Lauren shrugged. "I bet military families who are far away from extended family and new in town would appreciate the referral of a good babysitter. We'll ask for references, of course, and check them before sending out some kind of email blast to let people know the sitter is available. It's not small business, per se, but it is relevant to the mission of improving the lives at Concord Court."

Brisa frowned. "When I set Wade up with Mira, I had a playdate with his daughter for that very reason. He needed a babysitter and wasn't sure who to call."

None of them were prepared when Brisa threw her arms around Lauren, but Lauren recovered first. She was adjusting to the ups and downs of emotion quickly and patted Brisa's back.

"Initiative. Clear planning. Organization. Where have you been all my life?" Brisa wailed.

"Practicing law?" Lauren said softly. "And I'm not sure I can give that up."

When Brisa stepped back, Lauren said, "I can't stop thinking about how I dreamed of doing what I'm doing now and how hard I worked to get there."

Brisa's shoulders slumped. "But we need you."

"I know. I think about my dad, a veteran who's serving time because he never found a way to fit in, to feel accepted, to have the career he was looking for." She sighed. "He also told me about an army buddy who ended up on the streets. Concord Court can make a difference. I believe that."

As Peter stood between his friend and the woman who was going to change his life, he felt the tension. No one spoke for a long while. In the quiet moment, though, it was as if inspiration hit, and he knew he was going to break his promise to be quiet.

"Now that we have seen the scope of this project, it is time we begin negotiations. Peter Kim, Esquire, on behalf of Lauren Duncan. At your service." He bowed and wondered if even TV lawyers went this over-the-top.

Brisa crossed her arms. "Begin negotiations?"

He nodded. "Any agreement we come to today will be in effect for six months." He didn't want Lauren to experience a second of angst about leaving Concord Court if that was what was best for her. When Lauren blinked rapidly, Peter knew she was amazed at the audacity. She had the upper hand here, even if she didn't realize it and wouldn't use it even if she did.

He stopped to wait for Brisa's agreement. Her lip curled but she nodded. "Is that your only condition?"

Peter shook his head slowly. "In addition, there will be two interns provided for office support. Each will be current students, possibly even a law student." He raised a finger. "You may be asking why."

"So theatrical," Lauren whispered to Brisa. "It's adorable."

He cleared his throat. "Lauren Duncan is a world-class attorney." He checked to see the effect. Lauren mouthed "world-class" doubtfully. "She will, if she chooses, represent Concord Court in legal matters and may even decide to take the cases of veterans or their families who need her legal expertise. Interns doing her research and legwork will learn valuable skills that may translate to corporate law, real estate law and other types of law and services. If she should decide to pursue cases, she will have the flexibility to use the office and equipment here for support."

If she wanted to go into business on her own someday, Lauren would have the thorough knowledge to do so.

"Do you have any specific interns in mind?" Brisa asked sweetly.

"David Kim would be an excellent consideration. I can have his lawyer contact you with a personal reference." Peter smiled. "I'd like to nominate myself for the other position."

"Not much estate planning expected around these parts." Lauren stepped into his path to interrupt his show.

"A respected adviser told me I shouldn't waste my talent that way, not when people need me." He held out his hands. "Or my flair for courtroom drama. I'll do more investigating into my career options while I'm working here."

Lauren's slow smile was beautiful and exactly what he was going for. "So much for keeping quiet."

"Neither one of us believed I'd be able to do it anyway." Peter took her hand and turned to face Brisa. He was unprepared for his friend's wicked grin.

"I knew I would get you here one way or

another! How many times did I beg you to take this job?" she asked.

He sniffed. "You didn't offer part-time. I need to bond with my boat on my off days."

Lauren's low laugh filled him with warmth.

"We still haven't talked salary." Brisa moved closer.

"I'm going to leave that particular bit of negotiation to the pro." He gestured to Lauren, who mimicked his earlier bow to perfection.

Brisa sighed. "Okay, is that all of your requirements for now?"

Peter turned to Lauren and raised a brow. She pursed her lips as she thought. "I only have one added condition," she said. "We're going to need a golf cart on this side, too. This place is huge."

With a clear nod of respect, Brisa held out her hand to Lauren. "I will give you driving lessons. A second cart is a reasonable request."

LAUREN NOTICED RIGHT away that Peter had driven them to the same beach that she'd recently visited in her quest to fill her unemployed day. Lauren wondered about the coincidence and asked herself how many other places they had in common. Had they been crossing each other's path without intersecting? There was plenty of time to find out.

"Do you always carry beach blankets in your trunk?" Lauren asked as Peter took her hand and led her to the sand. At this time of day, right before sunset, the beach was less crowded. The families Lauren had enjoyed watching were already gone for the day.

"Not always or not until now. I'll start, though. When we need to get away, we'll escape to the water. If there's not enough time to take out the boat, there's always enough time for the sunset." Peter handed her the bottle of wine they'd picked up along the way and the plastic cups she'd sent him back into the store for. He spread out one blanket and rolled the second one into a pillow before inviting her to sit with a grand swoop of his hand. "Milady, let's enjoy the sunset."

Lauren sat and unscrewed the lid of their fine beverage. Lauren poured and held her cup up in a toast. "To a good day filled with successful negotiations and a long working relationship."

Peter yanked back his glass before hers

touched it. "That's your toast? Not very romantic."

Lauren laughed. "I guess your friend Candace would have done it differently." She tapped her chin. "Oh, and let's not forget Officer Estevez, who was concerned you didn't know she was *single* single."

Peter's sigh was the long-suffering reaction she was hoping for.

"Okay, you can toast." Lauren waited.

"Flirting with them was fun, but then I met you," Peter said. His soulful look kept her from being offended.

"And you gave up on fun?" Lauren schooled her expression into a suspicious stare.

Peter huffed. "Charming Peter Kim... When I need him, that guy is nowhere to be found." He held up his glass again. "Let me give this another try. You are the amazing woman who showed me how much real fun I was missing in my life."

Lauren bit her lip as she weighed his answer. "Better. I like that one better."

Peter scooted closer to her on the blanket. "To years of winning and losing and enjoying every minute with you." Their cups touched as he pressed his lips against hers. Lauren couldn't fight the smile that curved her lips and filled her head to toe when Peter was beside her. Every part of her was more alive than she could remember before.

"As long as you kiss me, at least once, every day like that, I'm not too bothered by the women who want charming Peter Kim," Lauren murmured, and he leaned back.

"Every woman wants a geeky math hero. What can I say?" Their laughter echoed on the deserted beach and was the perfect soundtrack for this moment.

"I'm going to beg your mother to give me that photo." Lauren wedged her cup carefully in the sand and stretched out to stare up at the sky that was turning pink overhead. "In case I need to remember when I realized that you were exactly my type of guy."

He stretched out next to her, his head propped up on an elbow as he stared down at her face.

"You've always been my type." He brushed hair off her cheek and Lauren bit back the argument that sprang to mind immediately. "You have. At sixteen, I would have been unable to speak in your presence and you would have run rings around me. But at twenty-two,

I'd learned to pretend confidence and shot way past the mark into obnoxious too often. I knew I was doing it, but I couldn't stop. You stayed one step ahead of me at all times."

Lauren studied his face. She was ready to argue, but it was clear he believed every word was true. His smile was sweet.

"It took me this long and a lot of air force training and growing as a person to be ready for you, but I'm thankful I've made it."

"Are you sure about this internship?" Lauren asked. "I'll be okay. We both know Brisa will be the kind of boss everyone dreams of having. If I need help, she'll get it for me. There's no reason to change your plans for me."

"I meant what I said. When you warned me against wasting my talent, it struck a chord with me. Commanding a courtroom was exhilarating. I've proven I have the research skills necessary. I want the challenge. The first one I've wanted in a long time, if I'm being honest."

"I'm going to make a note to reserve one of those storefronts we'll be leasing in seven or eight months to Kim and Kim, attorneys-at-law." Lauren held her hands up as if she was picturing the sign on the door.

"A law dynasty begins," Peter said in a movie-announcer voice. "I hope Davey doesn't mind me planning out his whole future without his consent."

Lauren laughed. "It's a good thing you stepped aside when you did and had me talk salary with Brisa, or you and I would be on the outs." When Peter wrapped his arm around her shoulder to urge her closer, her head on his chest, Lauren was happy life took the turns it did.

"Perhaps I'm getting better at learning when to speak and when to keep silent. There's hope for me yet," he murmured.

"Do you want to know when I realized you were exactly right for me, charming Peter Kim?" Lauren asked.

Peter was serious as he focused on her. "Of course."

"My career is important to me. When I saw you standing there, waiting for me this morning, I was shocked. I've done everything on my own, even when I could have used the help." She ran her hand over his chest because he was close and she could. "But I trusted you. Whatever your plan was or is, I trust you. At some point, in the far distant future, you will be wrong. You will make a mistake." She grinned at his frown. "But you will have made that decision, whatever it is, for all the right reasons."

He pulled her closer. "I'm going to do my best to live up to that, even if I am someday mistaken. But never wrong."

Lauren laughed and rested her head against his shoulder. She'd missed so many beach days in the past, but watching the stars appear with Peter Kim's arms around her was a dream come true.

EPILOGUE

PETER RELAXED IN his seat in the cockpit of the *Hardly Working* and brushed his hand over Lauren's bare shoulder. The sun was setting on another beautiful day on the water. This time, he'd managed to cram every one of his friends and their significant others onto the boat for a short but special trip out from the Cutler Bay Club's marina.

Marcus, Jason Ward and Mira's husband were on the swim platform, while Mira, Cassie and Angela Simmons were huddled together on the banquette seating middeck. Taking center stage were Sean and Reyna, Brisa and Wade, and the justice of the peace who oversaw the simple, sweet ceremony that was unexpected for such an over-the-top family.

Victor Montero and his wife, Marisol, were standing in the cockpit while everyone listened to the couples recite their vows. Victor tugged out his handkerchief to wipe away the streaks of tears, and Peter and Lauren exchanged a knowing smile.

The Monteros weren't laid-back individuals, any of them, but it was easy to see how much they meant to each other. Victor had given his daughters fits in the early days of the Court, but now the whole family worked together well. Any squabbles were usual family friction, as proved by this crammed ad-hoc wedding on a boat that did nothing to satisfy Victor's quest to show off his daughters to Miami society any chance he got. There had been a tense discussion, moderated by Peter and Davey, not-quite-attorneys-at-law, where the brides-to-be agreed to have a huge reception open to anyone their father wanted to invite as long as this wedding was only theirs.

Peter was happy to offer up the *Hardly Working* for the occasion.

Reyna and Brisa were beautiful and beaming. Sean and Wade were ecstatic and relieved to have finally managed the end goal after months of drawing up and discarding plans to wow the Monteros.

"And now, Sean and Reyna," the justice said, "and Brisa and Wade, it is my great honor to pronounce you husbands and wives. If it pleases you, you may seal these unions with a kiss."

When the couples kissed, everyone on the deck yelled their congratulations and cheered. Lauren leaned back against Peter's chest. "You did a good job, Captain."

"I can't understand why they wouldn't let me marry them. I am the captain of this ship," Peter murmured close to her ear. "I bet they were afraid of all the secrets I might spill. Little do they know, I have excellent reception toasts already written."

"You're going to be too busy dancing with me to torment your friends." Lauren tangled her fingers with his and rested their hands on her waist.

"Fine. I guess I'll have to embarrass you instead. You never asked me whether I can dance." Peter pressed a kiss to her cheek. "I have shocking news. That is not part of charming Peter Kim's arsenal."

"We could stay here instead. Camp out under the stars." Lauren turned her head to stare up at his face.

"Okay, lovebirds, take us back to the dock before we sink this ship with too many passengers or too much emotion," Sean called out from the deck. "We've got a party to get to!"

Peter saluted and went back to the steering wheel. "What if we dance badly first and then camp out under the stars? We've got plenty of time for both."

Lauren rested her chin on his shoulder. "I like the way you think, Captain."

Peter started the engines, enjoying the rumble of the motors and the buzz of his friends' happy conversation in the background. "Have you ever thought about what kind of wedding you'll have someday?"

Lauren wrinkled her nose. "No, have you?"

As Peter navigated the marina and slipped the boat back into its spot at the dock, he considered the question. He and Lauren waited for everyone to head up to the Cutler Bay Club's clubhouse, which had been booked for the double wedding reception. They wandered slowly after the crowd, hand in hand.

"I haven't done much planning for my wedding," he said as he looked at Lauren, "but it might be time to start."

She raised her eyebrows. "Yeah? Got a bride in mind?"

"I do." Peter laughed. "I had planned to drink champagne with her tonight, spin her around the dance floor when everyone else is too tipsy to notice my moves, and then later on when we were stretched out on the deck of the famous *Hardly Working*, I was going to ask her to marry me. But I'm nervous. About what she'll say."

Lauren's skeptical "Hmm" was adorable. "Peter Kim is nervous. Right."

"She's pretty special. She deserves a grand gesture. As my first mate, I should consult with you. What do you suggest?" Peter asked.

Lauren stopped and waited for him to face her. "She already knows she wants to spend the rest of her life with you, dreaming of the stars. As head of toiletries and second-in-command, I give you my stamp of approval."

He leaned in and pressed his lips against hers, the moment memorable and perfect there in the shadows next to the cool water with his friends nearby. These were the people who made it all worthwhile, the planning, the responsibility, the sacrifices and the hope. How amazing was it that his search for the best lawyer in Miami had brought him exactly where he needed to be?

"Let me take over the planning. That's where I shine. You want the best planner in Miami, don't you?" she asked. "Or at least the best one on your boat?"

"The best one on our boat has yet to be determined. We need an impartial contest in order to decide it." Peter stroked her cheek.

"*Our* boat?" Lauren said with a hoot. "Oh, man, you've got it bad for me. Peter Kim is totally in love with Lauren Duncan."

He grinned. "Yep. Can't argue my way out of that judgment."

Lauren patted his shoulder. "It's okay. I love you more than molten chocolate lava cake in the shape of a parrot, which is definitely what we are having at our wedding reception."

"Wow." Peter winced. "You're coming strong right out of the gate. I can't even challenge a genius plan like that."

She slipped her arm through his to squeeze his waist. "Don't worry. This is a challenge we'll both win."

* * * * *

*For more titles in the
Veterans' Road miniseries from
USA TODAY bestselling author
Cheryl Harper, visit
www.Harlequin.com today!*

Get 4 FREE REWARDS!

We'll send you 2 FREE Books plus 2 FREE Mystery Gifts.

FREE
Value Over
$20

Both the **Love Inspired®** and **Love Inspired® Suspense** series feature compelling novels filled with inspirational romance, faith, forgiveness, and hope.

Get 4 FREE REWARDS!

We'll send you 2 FREE Books plus 2 FREE Mystery Gifts.

FREE Value Over **$20**

Both the **Harlequin® Special Edition** and **Harlequin® Heartwarming™** series feature compelling novels filled with stories of love and strength where the bonds of friendship, family and community unite.

YES! Please send me 2 FREE novels from the Harlequin Special Edition or Harlequin Heartwarming series and my 2 FREE gifts (gifts are worth about $10 retail). After receiving them, if I don't wish to receive any more books, I can return the shipping statement marked "cancel." If I don't cancel, I will receive 6 brand-new Harlequin Special Edition books every month and be billed just $4.99 each in the U.S or $5.74 each in Canada, a savings of at least 17% off the cover price or 4 brand-new Harlequin Heartwarming Larger-Print books every month and be billed just $5.74 each in the U.S. or $6.24 each in Canada, a savings of at least 21% off the cover price. It's quite a bargain! Shipping and handling is just 50¢ per book in the U.S. and $1.25 per book in Canada.* I understand that accepting the 2 free books and gifts places me under no obligation to buy anything. I can always return a shipment and cancel at any time. The free books and gifts are mine to keep no matter what I decide.

Choose one: ☐ **Harlequin Special Edition** ☐ **Harlequin Heartwarming**
(235/335 HDN GNMP)   **Larger-Print**
                                                (161/361 HDN GNPZ)

Name (please print)

Address   Apt. #

City   State/Province   Zip/Postal Code

Email: Please check this box ☐ if you would like to receive newsletters and promotional emails from Harlequin Enterprises ULC and its affiliates. You can unsubscribe anytime.

Mail to the Harlequin Reader Service:
IN U.S.A.: P.O. Box 1341, Buffalo, NY 14240-8531
IN CANADA: P.O. Box 603, Fort Erie, Ontario L2A 5X3

Want to try 2 free books from another series? Call 1-800-873-8635 or visit www.ReaderService.com.

*Terms and prices subject to change without notice. Prices do not include sales taxes, which will be charged (if applicable) based on your state or country of residence. Canadian residents will be charged applicable taxes. Offer not valid in Quebec. This offer is limited to one order per household. Books received may not be as shown. Not valid for current subscribers to the Harlequin Special Edition or Harlequin Heartwarming series. All orders subject to approval. Credit or debit balances in a customer's account(s) may be offset by any other outstanding balance owed by or to the customer. Please allow 4 to 6 weeks for delivery. Offer available while quantities last.

Your Privacy—Your information is being collected by Harlequin Enterprises ULC, operating as Harlequin Reader Service. For a complete summary of the information we collect, how we use this information and to whom it is disclosed, please visit our privacy notice located at corporate.harlequin.com/privacy-notice. From time to time we may also exchange your personal information with reputable third parties. If you wish to opt out of this sharing of your personal information, please visit readerservice.com/consumerschoice or call 1-800-873-8635. **Notice to California Residents**—Under California law, you have specific rights to control and access your data. For more information on these rights and how to exercise them, visit corporate.harlequin.com/california-privacy.

HSEHW22

COUNTRY LEGACY COLLECTION

19 FREE BOOKS IN ALL!

Cowboys, adventure and romance await you in this new collection! Enjoy superb reading all year long with books by bestselling authors like Diana Palmer, Sasha Summers and Marie Ferrarella!

#435 A WYOMING SECRET PROPOSAL
The Blackwells of Eagle Springs • by Amy Vastine

After an accidental Vegas wedding, Wyatt Blackwell and Harper Hayes end up in Eagle Springs. He's trying to save his family's ranch. She's trying to save her online image by playing happy family. Will they end up saving each other?

#436 A COWBOY THANKSGIVING
The Mountain Monroes • by Melinda Curtis

Orphan Maxine Holloway and her daughter are spending Thanksgiving with the Monroes—who seem entirely too warm and boisterous. And there's something about Bo Monroe. He is Max's complete opposite, but could he be her perfect match?

#437 HIS SMALL TOWN DREAM
The Golden Matchmakers Club • by Tara Randel

Businessman Adam Wright went from Wall Street to wilderness expeditions after his broken engagement. Marketing exec Carrie Mitchell is just passing through, chasing the corporate dreams Adam left behind. Will an unexpected connection make her want to stay?

#438 HER MARINE HERO
Polk Island • by Jacquelin Thomas

Fashion designer Renee Rothchild has one rule—don't date military men. Too bad she's falling for Marine Greg Bowman. With his discharge coming, she's ready to give love a second chance after a broken engagement. Until unexpected news changes everything.

Visit
ReaderService.com
Today!

As a valued member of the Harlequin Reader Service, you'll find these benefits and more at ReaderService.com:

- Try 2 free books from any series
- Access risk-free special offers
- View your account history & manage payments
- Browse the latest Bonus Bucks catalog

Don't miss out!

If you want to stay up-to-date on the latest at the Harlequin Reader Service and enjoy more content, make sure you've signed up for our monthly News & Notes email newsletter. Sign up online at ReaderService.com or by calling Customer Service at 1-800-873-8635.

RS20